To Tim, Lianna, and Nicholas

Murder
Takes the Cake

CHAPTER

one

"M RS. WATSON?" I called, banging on the door. I glanced up at the ever-blackening clouds. Although I had Mrs. Watson's cake in a box, it would be just my luck to get caught in a downpour with it. This was my third attempt to please her, and I couldn't afford another mistake with the amount she was paying me. Whoever said "the customer is always right" had obviously never dealt with Yodel Watson. I should've listened to all those people who'd told me Yodel was the meanest old lady in town. But she was my first customer. How could I turn away her business?

I heard something inside the house and pressed my ear against the door. A vision of me falling and dropping the cake when Mrs. Watson flung the door open made me rethink it, though, and I pulled my head away from the door.

"Mrs. Watson?" I called again.

"Come in! It's open! Come in!"

I tried the knob and the door was indeed unlocked. I stepped inside but didn't see Mrs. Watson. "It's me—Daphne Martin. I'm here with your cake."

"Come in! It's open!"

"I am in, Mrs. Watson. Where are you?"

"It's open!"

"I know! I—" Gritting my teeth, I walked through the foyer to the kitchen and placed the cake on the table. A quick glance around the room told me Mrs. Watson wasn't in there, either.

"It's open!"

Man, could this lady get on your nerves. The voice sounded like it came from the left, so I moved slowly down the hallway.

"Mrs. Watson?" I poked my head inside a den on the right.

"Come in!"

I turned toward the voice. A gray parrot was sitting on a perch inside its cage.

"It's open!" the bird squawked.

"I noticed." I'd heard about parrots that could mimic their owners' voices to perfection, but this was the first time I'd experienced it. Great. She's probably not home, and I'll get arrested for breaking and entering . . . though, technically, I didn't break.

It was then that I saw Mrs. Watson lying on the sofa in a faded, navy blue robe. A plaid blanket covered her legs. She appeared to be sleeping, but I'd heard the parrot calling when I was outside. There's no way Mrs. Watson could have been in the same room and slept through that racket.

I stepped closer. "Are you okay?" Her pallor already answered my question. Then the foul odor hit me.

I backed away and took my cell phone out of my purse. "I'm calling 9-1-1, Mrs. Watson. Everything's gonna be all right." I don't know if I was trying to reassure her or myself.

Everything's gonna be all right. I'd been telling myself that for the past month.

AFTER CALLING 9-1-1, I lingered in the doorway in case Mrs. Watson woke up and needed something before the EMTs arrived. Mrs. Watson was old enough that she could be my mother lying there.

I turned forty this year. Forty seems to be a sobering age for every woman, but it hit me especially hard. When most women get to be my age, they at least have some bragging rights: successful career, happy marriage, beautiful children, nice home. I had none of the above. My so-called accomplishments included a failed marriage, a dingy apartment, and twenty years' service in a dead-end job. Cue the violins.

So when my sister Violet called and told me about a "charming little house" for sale near her neighborhood, I jumped at the chance to leave all the dead ends of central Tennessee and come home to southwest Virginia. Surely something better awaited me here.

I'd already moved into my house—which seems to have come with a one-eyed stray cat—and started my own cake decorating business. It took a while to come up with a name and a logo, have business cards made, set up a website, and do other "fun" administrative duties, but now I was settled. The cake and cupcakes I'd made for my niece and nephew to take to school on Halloween had been a hit, leading to some nice word-of-mouth advertising and a couple orders. Leslie's puppy dog cake and Lucas's black cat cupcakes were the first additions to my website's gallery.

But my first real customer was Yodel Watson. She'd considered herself a world-class baker in her heyday but no longer had the time or desire to engage in "such foolishness."

"I want you to make me a cake for my Thanksgiving dinner," she'd said. "Nothing too gaudy. I want my family to think I made it myself."

My first two attempts had been refused: the first cake was too fancy, and the second was too plain. I'd been hoping—*praying*—the third time would be the charm. I laboriously prepared a spice cake with cream cheese frosting and decorated it with orange and red satin ribbons for a bottom border and a red apple, arranged in a flower petal pattern, on top. And now it was on Mrs. Watson's kitchen table while Mrs. Watson herself was slumped on her sofa as deflated as a December jack-o'-lantern. Oh, yeah, things were looking up.

I was startled out of my reverie by a sharp rap.

"EMT!"

"Come in! It's open!" the bird called.

I hurried to the living room to open the door, and two men with a stretcher brushed past me.

"Where's the patient?" one asked.

"Back here." I showed them the way to the den, and then got out of the way.

"Come in!"

I moved next to the birdcage. "Don't you ever shut up? This is serious."

"I'll say," agreed one of the EMTs. "Are you the next of kin?"

"Excuse me?" My hand flew to my heart. "She's dead?"

"Yes, ma'am. Are you related to her?"

While one EMT questioned me, the other was on his radio asking dispatch to send the police and the coroner.

"I barely know her," I told the man. "I just brought the cake."

AFTER CALLING IN the reinforcements, the EMTs sent me to the formal living room. They didn't get any argument from me. I sat down on the edge of a burgundy wingback chair and studied the room.

There was an elaborate Oriental rug over beige carpet, a pale blue sofa, and a curio cabinet with all sorts of expensive-looking knickknacks. Unlike the messier den, this room was spotless. Except for a small yellow stain I noticed near my right foot. Parrot pee, I supposed.

"Ms. Martin?"

I looked up at one of the deputies. "Yes?"

"I'm Officer Hayden. I need to ask you some questions."

"Um . . . sure." This guy looked young enough to be my son—scratch that, *nephew*—but he still made me nervous.

"Tell me about your arrival, ma'am."

Ma'am. Like I was seventy. Of course, when you're twelve, everybody looks old.

I cleared my throat. "I, uh, knocked on the door, and someone told me to come in. I thought it was Mrs. Watson, so I opened the door and came inside." I pointed toward the kitchen table. "I'm Daphne of Daphne's Delectable Cakes." I patted my pockets for my business card holder but realized I must have left it in the car. "I brought the cake."

Officer Hayden took out a notepad. "Let me get this straight. Someone else was here when you arrived?"

"No . . . no, it was the bird. The bird hollered and told me to come in."

He closed his eyes and pinched the bridge of his nose.

"I thought it was her, though," I added quickly. *Please, God, don't let me get arrested.* "It told me the door was open, and it *was.*"

Officer Hayden opened his eyes.

Never being one to know when to shut up, I reiterated, "I just brought the cake."

ABOUT AN HOUR later, I pulled into my own driveway. I didn't make it to the front door before I heard my next-door neighbor calling to me.

"Hello, Daphne! I see you're bringing home another cake."

"Afraid so."

She beat me to the porch. For a woman in her sixties, Myra Jenkins was pretty quick. "What was wrong with this one?"

I handed Myra the cake and unlocked the door. "Um . . . she didn't say."

"She didn't say?" Myra wiped her feet on the mat and followed me inside.

I dropped my purse onto the table by the door. I'd let Myra hang on to the cake. She'd kept the other two rejects; I figured she'd want this one, too.

I went into the kitchen and took two diet sodas from the fridge. I handed Myra one can, popped the top on the other, and took a long drink before dropping into a chair.

"This is beautiful," Myra said, after opening the cake box and peering inside. "What kind of cake is it?"

"Spice. With a cream cheese icing."

Myra ran her finger through the frosting on the side of the cake and licked her finger. "Mmm, this is out of this world. You know the Save-A-Buck sometimes takes baked goods on commission, don't you?"

"No, I didn't know that."

She nodded. "They don't keep a bakery staff, so they sometimes buy cakes, cookies, doughnuts—stuff like that—from the locals and sell them in their store."

"I'll definitely look into that. Thanks."

"You should." She put the lid down on the box. "Are you going to take in this one?"

"No," I said. Her poking the side had already nullified that possibility. "Why don't you take it home?"

"Thank you. I believe I'll serve this and the white one with the raspberry filling for Thanksgiving and save the chocolate cake for Christmas." She smiled. "Do I owe you anything?"

"Yes. Good publicity. Sing my praises to the church group, the quilting circle, the library group, and anyone else you can."

"Will do, honey. Will do."

"Um . . . how well do you know Yodel Watson?" I asked cautiously, unsure of how much information I should spill.

Myra pulled out a chair and sat down. "About as well as anybody in this town, I reckon. Why?"

"She—" I said quietly. "She's dead."

She gasped. "What happened? Car wreck? You know, she drives the most awful car I've ever seen. All the tires are bald, the—"

"It wasn't a car wreck," I interrupted. "When I went to her house, I thought she told me to come in, so—"

"Banjo."

"I beg your pardon?"

"It was probably Yodel's bird Banjo tellin' you to come in."

"Right. It was. So, uh, I went in and . . . and found Mrs. Watson in the den."

"And she was dead?"

I nodded.

"Was she naked?"

"No! She had on a robe and was covered with a blanket. Why would you think she was naked?"

Myra shrugged. "When people find dead bodies in the movies, the bodies are usually naked." She opened her soda. "So what happened?"

"I don't know. Since there was no obvious cause of death, she's being sent for an autopsy."

"Were there any opened envelopes lying around? Maybe somebody sent Yodel some of that amtrax stuff."

"I don't think it was *anthrax*," I said. "I figure she had a heart attack or an aneurysm or something."

"Don't be too sure."

"Why do you say that?"

"Because Yodel was *mean*." Myra took a drink of her soda. "Heck, you know that."

I shook my head and tried to steer the conversation away from murder. "Who'd name their daughter Yodel?"

"Oh, honey."

In the short time I've lived here, I've already learned that when Myra Jenkins says *Oh, honey,* you're in for a story.

"The Watsons yearned to follow in the Carter family's footsteps," she said. "Yodel's sisters were Melody and Harmony, and her brother was Guitar. Guitar Refrain Watson—Tar, for short."

I nearly spit diet soda across the table. "You're kidding."

"No, honey, I'm not. Trouble was, nary a one of the Watsons had any talent. When my daughter was little, she'd clap her hands over her ears and make the most terrible faces if we sat behind them in church. Just about anybody can sing that 'praise God from Whom all blessings flow' song they sing while takin' the offering plates back up to the alter, but the Watsons couldn't. And the worst part was that every one of them sang loud and proud. Loud, proud, *and* off-key." She smiled. "I have to admit, though, the congregation as a whole said a lot more silent prayers in church before Mr. and Mrs. Watson died and before their young-uns—all but Yodel—scattered here and there. 'Lord, please don't let the Watsons sit near us.' 'Lord, please stop up my ears just long enough to deliver me from sufferin' through another hymn.' 'Lord, please give Tar laryngitis for forty-five minutes.'"

We both laughed.

"That was ugly of me to tell," Myra said. "But it's true! Still, I'll have to ask forgiveness for that. I always did wonder if God hadn't blessed any of them Watsons with musical ability because they'd tried to write their own ticket with those musical names. You know what I mean?"

"I guess so."

"Now, back to Yodel. Yodel was always jealous of China York because China could sing. The choir director was always getting China to sing solos. China didn't care for Yodel because Yodel was spiteful and mean to her most of the time. It seemed Yodel couldn't feel good about herself unless she was puttin' somebody else down."

"She must've felt great about herself every time I brought a cake over," I muttered.

Myra frowned. "I don't know why she would. Those cakes were beautiful, and I know they'll be delicious."

"Thanks, Myra. I didn't mean to interrupt your story. Please, go on."

"Well, a few years ago, our old preacher retired and we got a new one. Of course, we threw him a potluck howdy-get-to-know-you party at the church. It was summer, and I took a strawberry pie. I make the best strawberry pies. I'd thought about making one for Thanksgiving, but I don't have to now that you've given me all these cakes. I do appreciate it."

I waved away her gratitude. "Don't mention it."

"Anyhow, China brought a chocolate and coconut cake. She'd got the recipe out of *McCall's* magazine and was just bustin' to have us all try it out. Then wouldn't you know it? In waltzed Yodel with the very same cake."

"If she loved to bake so much, I wonder why she gave it up. She told me she didn't have time to bake these days. Was she active in a lot of groups? I mean, what took up so much of her time?"

"Keeping tabs on the rest of the town took up her time. When Arlo was alive—he was a Watson, too, of course, though no relation . . . except maybe really distant cousins once or twice removed or something. . . . There's more Watsons in these parts than there are chins at a fat farm. Is that how that saying goes?"

"I think it's more Chins than a Chinese phone book."

"Huh. I don't get it. Anyhow, Arlo expected his wife to be more than the town gossip. That's when Yodel prided herself on her cooking, her volunteer work, and all the rest. When he died—oh, I guess it was ten years ago—she gave it all up." Myra shook her head. "Shame, too. But back to the story. Yodel told the new preacher, 'Wait until you try this cake. It's my very own recipe.'

"'It is not,' China said. 'You saw me copy that recipe out of *McCall's* when we were both at the beauty shop waitin' to get our hair done!'

"'So what if I did?' Yodel asked. 'I subscribe to *McCall's*. How was I supposed to know you'd be making a similar cake?'

"China got right up in Yodel's face and hollered, 'It's the same cake!'

"Yodel said it wasn't. She said, 'I put almonds and a splash of vanilla in mine. Otherwise that cake would be boring and bland.'

"At this point, the preacher tried to intervene. 'They both look delicious,' he told them, 'and I'm sure there are enough of us here to eat them both.'

"Yodel and China were like two snarling dogs, and I don't believe either of them heard a word he said. China had already set her cake on the table, but Yodel was still holding hers. China calmly placed her hand on the bottom of Yodel's cake plate and upended that cake right on Yodel's chest."

I giggled. "Really?"

"Really. And then China walked to the door and said, 'I've had it with her. I won't be back here until one of us is dead.' And she ain't been back to church since."

"Wow," I said. "That's some story."

"Makes you wonder if China finally got tired of sitting home by herself on Sunday mornings."

Seeing how serious Myra looked, I stifled my laughter. "Do you honestly think this woman has been nursing a grudge all these years and killed Mrs. Watson rather than simply finding herself another church?"

"There's not another Baptist church within ten miles of here." She finished off her soda. "People have killed for crazier reasons than that, haven't they?"

"I suppose, but—"

"And if it wasn't China York, I can think of a few other folks who had it in for Yodel."

"Come on. I'll admit she's been a pain to work with on these cakes, but I have a hard time casting Mrs. Watson in the role of Cruella de Vil."

Myra got up and put her empty soda can in the garbage. "I

didn't say she made puppy coats. I said there were a lot of people who'd just as soon not have Yodel Watson around."

I WAS RELIEVED when Myra left. She seemed to be a good person, and I liked her, but she could be a bit much. Everything was so dramatic with her. She even had me wondering whether or not poor Mrs. Watson died of natural causes.

I got up and walked down the hall to my office. It had a sofa bed so it could double as a guest room if need be. It also held a desk, a file cabinet, and a bookcase full of cookbooks, cake decorating books, small-business books, marketing books, and one photograph of me with Lucas and Leslie. The photo had been taken last year when I was at Violet's house for Christmas.

I booted up my computer. As always, I checked my e-mail first. E-mail is a procrastinator's dream come true. There was a message from my friend Bonnie, still holding down the fort at the company I'd worked for in Tennessee:

> Hey, girl! Are you up to your eyebrows in cake batter? I can think of worse predicaments. We get off half a day Wednesday. I can hardly wait. Do you have tons of orders to fill before Thursday? I hope so. I mean, I hope business is off to a good start but that you have time to enjoy the holiday, too. I really miss you, Daph. Write when you can and fill me in on everything, especially whether or not any of your neighbors are HAGs!

I smiled. HAG was our acronym for Hot Available Guy. It wasn't a flattering acronym, but it worked.

I marked the e-mail as unread and decided to reply when I had better news to report. As I deleted my junk messages, I thought about Bonnie. We had met while I was taking culinary classes at a local college. She was taking business courses and was desperate to get into the field I wanted out of so badly. One evening, we were two of the oldest people in the student lounge. That night even the faculty members present were in their twenties! Bonnie and I were both in our early thirties, and after that initial meeting we had fun people-watching over coffee before all our evening classes.

When a job opened up at the company I worked for, Bonnie applied and got the job. It wasn't long after that my college days came to an abrupt end. Not believing that I could actually be good—make that, great—at something, dear hubby Todd came by the school one evening and saw Chef Pierre. Admittedly, Chef Pierre was impressive in every way, but Bonnie and I had already dubbed him a HUG—Hot Unavailable Guy. Chef Pierre was married, had three young children, and was devoted to his lovely wife. Todd couldn't get past the chef's stellar looks, though. I was the chef's star student, so Todd thought I *had* to be sleeping with the man and made me drop out.

But I'd already been bitten by the baking bug. I watched TV chefs, bought cake decorating books, rented how-to videos, and practiced decorating every chance I got. I'd practice on vinyl place mats. And I'd tell myself "Someday."

Now it seemed my "someday" had come. I was an excellent cake decorator, I'd finally taken a chance, and I was finally tuning out Todd's taunting voice in my head. I was believing in myself for the first time in years. I knew I could make this business work.

I started when the phone rang.

"Hey, I heard about Mrs. Watson. You must've freaked out when you found her," my sister said as soon as I picked up.

"How'd you know?"

"I saw Bill Hayden's wife at the school when I picked up Leslie and Lucas this afternoon."

Bill Hayden. *Officer* Bill Hayden. Married . . . and with children. He must be older than he looked.

"Why didn't you call me?" Violet asked.

"I don't know." Because you're perfect, and in three years when you turn forty, all you'll have to be concerned about is laugh lines? Because I didn't come back home to have a baby-sitter? Because I promised myself I wouldn't be the one thorn in your bouquet of roses? "Myra came over as soon as I got home, so I really didn't have a chance to call."

"No, I don't suppose you did. Did you tell her about Yodel?"

"Yeah. Should I not have?"

"Eh. I guess it'll be in the paper tomorrow anyway."

"Plus, it's a really small town, Vi. There were probably a dozen messages on Myra's answering machine when she got back home. I mean, you heard it at the school, right?"

"I didn't mean anything by it," Violet said. "I'm merely cautioning you to be careful of what you say to Myra."

"With Myra I find myself mostly listening."

"I know that's true." Violet laughed. "Just be careful. As a witness in a homicide investigation, you have to watch what you say to the general public."

"A homicide investigation? The coroner didn't send the woman's body to Roanoke for autopsy until this afternoon. The results couldn't possibly be in."

"No, of course not, but Joanne told me Bill said there were indications of foul play. They believe Yodel was poisoned."

"Is that ethical?"

"He only told his wife, Daphne."

"And she told you and who knows who else. What is it with small-town drama?"

"Excuse me, Ms. Big City. I forgot how boring we must be to you now."

"Sarcasm doesn't suit you, Vi. I just think Officer Hayden should learn a bit about confidentiality, that's all."

"Please don't get him in trouble."

"I won't. I—"

"Let's just talk about Thursday. What time will you be here?" Violet asked.

"I was thinking eleven, but I can come earlier if you'd like."

"No. Eleven's good. Mom's spending the night, so I'll have plenty of help in the kitchen."

"Then eleven it is."

After hanging up with Violet, I went out the kitchen door to sit on the side porch. It was cool outside, but I was feeling a little sorry for myself and I always felt better in the big wide open than I did in an empty house.

Violet had a lot to be proud of. She'd been married for the past fifteen years to a dreamboat of a guy. She had gorgeous eleven-year-old twins. She was a successful Realtor. She had a lovely home. She had curly, blond hair, blue eyes, and a bubbly personality—as opposed to my straight, dark brown hair, brown eyes, and more serious demeanor. *And* she had a great relationship with our mom.

I, however, had been married for ten years to an abusive manipulator who is currently serving a seven-year prison term for assault with a deadly weapon after trying to shoot me. Fortunately, he'd missed, and, in my opinion, he was sentenced to far too little time simply because his aim was off. He'd called it a "mistake." Whether he meant shooting at me or missing, I have no idea. Mom called the whole ordeal a mistake, too. Neither of them could understand why I filed for divorce.

"He said he was sorry," Mom had scolded me over the phone. "You made the man angry, Daphne. You know how you can be. A person can only take so much."

I'd hung up on her. A person *could* only take so much. That was nearly five years ago. Of course, Mom and I had talked since then, but our conversations were more strained than baby food.

I heard a plaintive meow and looked up to see the fluffy gray and white, one-eyed stray sitting a short distance away.

"Me too, baby," I told the cat softly. "Me too."

CHAPTER

two

I AWOKE THE next morning with my head throbbing. Still, headache or not, it was the Tuesday before Thanksgiving and I had a lot to do. I wanted to make a cake that Mom would ooh and aah over, but that was impossible. I had to settle for pleasing myself and Violet's family. Mom thought I was "silly" for leaving a "perfectly good job in order to stay home and make cakes." Being a secretary/receptionist for a government agency regulating housing was a good job, but it had certainly not been my dream. In fact, some days hearing the desperation in people's voices when they were about to lose their homes or were seeking an affordable place to raise their children was downright heartbreaking.

I pressed my fingertips to my temples and tried not to

stress about Mom. Instead I focused on my agenda for the day. First up, ibuprofen and coffee.

I'd planned for the day to be fairly peaceful: shopping, baking, decorating. Little did I know the ghost of Yodel Watson would follow me around all day.

My first errand was going to Dobbs's Pet Store. Being the only pet store in town, Dobbs's had everything from hamsters to poisonous snakes and supplies to care for whatever critter struck your fancy.

Speaking of having something stricken, when I walked through the door of the pet shop, I came face-to-face with a rattlesnake. Fortunately, Kellen Dobbs was holding the snake, but I wasn't entirely sure I trusted his grip.

"Be right with you," Mr. Dobbs said. He squeezed the snake's head, and a stream of thick venom flowed from the snake's fangs into a small glass jar on the counter. "We're not supposed to be open yet. I must've forgotten to lock the door."

I stood dumbly, transfixed by the gray-haired, bearded man milking the snake. I'd never seen anything like it.

A woman came out from the back of the store. She looked younger than Mr. Dobbs with bright red hair and too much makeup. I prayed she wouldn't spook the snake . . . or Mr. Dobbs.

"He does that a lot," the woman said. "Forgets to lock the door, I mean."

"I didn't realize the store was closed," I said. "I can come back—"

"Nonsense," Mr. Dobbs said, placing the snake into an aquarium. "Since you're here, you might as well get what you came for."

"I'm looking for some sort of vitamin-enriched cat food," I said. "I moved to town about a month ago and seem to have inherited a stray cat. I've been giving her—"

"Hey," the red-haired woman interrupted, "ain't you the one who found Yodel Watson yesterday?"

"Yes. How'd you know?"

"Joanne Hayden told me. Her husband's on the police force."

I rolled my eyes.

"They think Mrs. Watson might've been *murdered.*"

"Candy," Mr. Dobbs said, "go grab one of those purple bags of cat food in aisle four." He looked at me. "How much do you think you'll need?"

"A five-pound bag should be enough for now."

"Five-pound bag, Candy!" he called. "What'd they do with the parrot?"

"Excuse me?"

"Mrs. Watson's parrot," he said. "What'd they do with it?"

"Oh. They sent it to animal control, I believe. They'd hoped to turn it over to a family member, but her daughter lives out of town. I guess she can pick Banjo up from animal control when she gets here."

"Did you know Mrs. Watson well?"

"Hardly at all. I'm a cake decorator, and—"

"Ooh, how neat!" Candy exclaimed, returning with the cat food. "Do you have a business card? You never know when you're gonna need a pretty birthday cake or . . . I don't know . . . a wedding cake." She giggled.

Mr. Dobbs rang up my purchase. "This should have that cat fattened up in no time."

"Thank you." I paid for the cat food and handed Candy a business card.

"Thanks," Candy said with a glance at Mr. Dobbs. "I plan on callin' you real soon."

As I left, I heard one of them lock the door behind me.

* * *

THE NEXT STOP on my list was the Save-A-Buck. I needed shortening and confectioners' sugar, as always, along with a few odds and ends. When I got up to the register, Juanita, the usual morning cashier, was at her post. Sure, I'd only been back in town for a month, but bakers tend to get to know the people who work at their grocery stores real fast.

"Good morning, Juanita. Do you have big plans for Thanksgiving?"

"Oh, yes. My family will have a turkey, but we will also enjoy some of our Mexican favorites, like chimichangas!"

I smiled. "Sounds good."

"It is." She beamed. "And what of you? What are your big plans?"

My smile faltered. "Dinner with the family."

Fred, the produce manager, came to the register and began bagging my groceries. He nodded to me in greeting.

"I'm surprised the produce department can spare you this close to Thanksgiving," I said.

"They can spare me, all right." He dropped my shortening sticks into a plastic bag. "I'm a bagger now."

I looked at Juanita, and she confirmed his announcement with downcast eyes and a slight tilt of her head.

"I'm sorry," I told Fred.

He shrugged. "Not your fault. You're not the one who complained about the stupid potatoes." He shook a strand of his long, dark hair out of his eyes. "That was Yodel Watson. It was her third complaint about the produce department in a week, and the manager demoted me to keep her happy."

"Surely it's only temporary," I said.

"That's right," Juanita agreed. "Maybe things will go back to normal now."

"Now that the old bag is dead?" Fred grinned. "Couldn't have happened to a better person."

"Um . . . is the manager in? I've heard the store sometimes buys baked goods on commission, and I'd like to talk to him about it."

"Of course," Juanita said. She called the store manager over the loudspeaker as Fred stalked away from the register.

Within a couple minutes, a short, balding man came hurrying up from the back of the store. He looked wary as he shot his hand out toward me. "Steve Franklin," he said. "What can I do for you?"

"I'm Daphne Martin of Daphne's Delectable Cakes." I shook his hand and then gave him a business card. "I understand the store sometimes buys baked goods on commission?"

"That's right. We take whatever you bring in, and if it sells, we get a twenty-five percent commission. Can you provide references?"

"I just opened my business, but my sister Violet Armstrong and my neighbor Myra Jenkins will vouch for me. Oh, and the Brea Ridge Middle School. I took some baked goods for a Halloween event."

"Great," Mr. Franklin said. "We'll give your products a try."

"May I put my logo and phone number on the boxes?" I asked.

"Of course." He inclined his head. "Tomorrow is one of our busiest days. How many cakes can you bring me before the store opens tomorrow morning?"

"Any special requests?"

He shook his head.

I mentally took stock of my freezer. "Then I can bring ten."

"Fantastic. I'll set up a display table right here at the front of the store."

"Thank you, Mr. Franklin. I'll see you in the morning."

I WAS HAPPY to get back home and get to work. Raging rattlers and bitter baggers did not make for a pleasant morning. Nor had they helped my headache one bit. The ten-cake order, on the other hand, had done wonders for my mood.

I'd finished putting my groceries away and removed the ten cakes from the freezer when Myra knocked on the door.

In the spirit of Banjo, I called, "Come on in!"

Myra entered and deposited her penny loafers by the door. I told her she looked pretty in her peach-colored pantsuit.

"Thanks, honey," she said, sitting down at the table. "What's with all those cakes?"

"I stopped by Save-A-Buck, and the manager is letting me bring ten cakes tomorrow morning." I grinned. "Thank you for the heads-up."

"You're welcome. Glad I could help." She cocked her head. "I didn't know you could freeze cakes."

"Oh, sure. Baked cakes will be fine for up to six months, but be sure to let them thaw to room temperature before you ice them or else they'll crack. Of course, people traditionally freeze the top tier of their wedding cake to eat on their first anniversary, but that takes some special procedures." I smiled. "What have you been up to this morning?"

"I went to prayer meeting. And guess who joined us?"

"Queen Elizabeth?"

"China! China York!"

As if there could be another China. "Did she say, 'Now that Yodel's dead, I'm back'?"

"Not in so many words, honey, but that was obvious." Myra gave a nod of satisfaction. "Of course, she didn't mention Yodel directly, but we all talked with China like nothin' had ever happened. Not that none of us had seen China since the blowup, mind you. We just hadn't seen her at church."

"Did it all seem to come back to her? Like riding a bike?"

"Why, yeah, she—" Myra scoffed. "Now you're pokin' fun at me."

"I'm not," I said with a smile. "I'm only kidding. It's just so insane that this woman would get mad at Yodel Watson and not come back to church until the day after Yodel died."

"It's strange, all right."

"Actually, I had a strange thing happen this morning myself." As I got out my mixer and made up a batch of icing, I told Myra about Fred and about Kellen Dobbs milking the rattlesnake at the pet store.

"Maybe I'll get some business from the pet store visit, though," I said. "A girl who works there took a business card and said she hoped to be calling me soon."

Myra nodded. "That Candy?"

"Uh-huh."

"I'll tell you one thing, Janey Dobbs sure ain't liking that strawberry tart workin' for Kel."

"Strawberry tart? That's a good one."

"Janey's words, not mine," Myra said. "I've seen her, though—Candy, I mean—and I don't blame Janey for not wantin' Kel working shoulder-to-shoulder with that all day."

"Then why doesn't she take Candy from her baby?" I chuckled at my own joke, but Myra didn't seem to think it was amusing.

"I don't know," she said. "She could, you know. Janey owns the shop." She chewed on her bottom lip. "In fact, she holds the purse strings, period. Her family used to own a snack cake factory down next to Greeneville."

"A snack cake heiress, huh? I could deal with that."

"Me too." Myra stood and smoothed out her slacks. "I'd better get home, honey." She walked over to the door and slipped on her loafers. "*Y & R* will be on in a few minutes, and it might be about that sweetie Paul today. I met him one time when he came to Kingsport for a store opening. He's the nicest thing." With that she was gone.

I smiled. Myra and her soaps. *The Young and the Restless* had stood the test of time, though. My sister had watched it nearly all her life. She'd even named my nephew and niece Lucas and Leslie after some long-forgotten characters. Clearly, Vi hadn't forgotten them. She must've watched the couple during her formative years or something. I suppose it could've been worse. She could've named the twins Jack and Jill.

I guess she got her naming talents from Mom. I was named after Daphne du Maurier, and Violet was named after Mom's other favorite author, Violet Winspear. You might say Mom has eclectic tastes in literature.

When I was a little girl, I'd tell the other kids I was named after the Daphne in the *Scooby-Doo* cartoons. I thought she was cool. Plus, Violet and I would play *Scooby-Doo* with two boys in our neighborhood—Joe Fenally was Freddie and Ben Jacobs was Shaggy. Naturally, I'd be Daphne, and Violet would be Velma. Vi hated being Velma.

Ben and I had been best friends growing up. We eventually graduated to being sweethearts. It was an easy, comfortable relationship, and people got to the point where they simply assumed we were together. In fact, for every year of high school, I had half a dozen photos of Ben and me—at the Sadie Hawkins dance, at the St. Valentine's Day dance, the annual sock hop.

But everything fell apart when we parted ways for college. We'd intended to keep in touch, write every day, get together for each other's dances and sporting events. But I suppose we'd been together for so long we'd grown complacent. And then I met Todd.

Todd was tall and handsome, and he played football for my college—the University of Tennessee, where I majored in business administration. In southwest Virginia and east Tennessee, UT football ruled. You couldn't blame a freshman girl from Brea Ridge for getting her head turned by a junior UT running back. Plus, Todd was something of a bad boy. He ran with a tough crowd, often drank too much, and all the girls were crazy about him. I'd been thrilled when he'd asked me out.

At the time, I had no insight into his abusive behavior. Looking back, I see it so clearly. Even "suggestions" like, "You should keep your hair short. I love it that length" were simply the beginning of my relinquishing control of my life to Todd.

Compared to Todd, Ben had seemed too safe, too predictable. I know he was hurt when I told him about Todd. And then I didn't hear from Ben again until he sent me a graduation card. Todd had snatched it away from me and had thrown it in the trash.

Ben had e-mailed me after Todd was arrested. I'd written back and thanked him for his concern, but I'd kept the message brief. I'd been so ashamed of how my life with Todd had turned out, and I imagined how different it might have been had I stayed with Ben.

I knew Ben worked for the *Brea Ridge Chronicle*. A wave of sentimentality hit, and I decided to give him a call.

By the time I'd looked up the number and had spoken to the receptionist, the wave of sentimentality had broken against the shore of common sense. However, also by that time, I was already on hold for Ben. As I thought about hanging up, he came on the line.

"Ben, hi," I said. "It's Daphne Martin."

"Hi, Daphne. What can I do for you?"

My mind raced. *Ask for a subscription. Say I have the wrong number. Ask if he wrote the obituary for Yodel Watson.* "Nothing really. I'm feeling a tad sentimental with the holiday so close, and I decided to give you a call and say Happy Thanksgiving . . . Shaggy."

He laughed. "You too, Daph. I . . . I heard about your finding Yodel Watson."

"Let me guess—Joanne Hayden?"

"No, I heard it at the police station. Are you all right? I mean, I remember you used to hyperventilate when we came across roadkill. . . . Uh, n-not that Mrs. Watson was . . . that . . . I mean . . . but . . . well, you know what I mean."

"I do know what you mean," I said with a chuckle. "And thank you. You're the first person I've talked with yet who's been concerned for me because I found a dead body."

I remembered how Ben used to try to shield me from the sight of a dead animal lying by the road while trying to keep his leashed dog, Mutt—alias Scooby—under control.

"Hey," Ben said, "have you had lunch yet? I was getting ready to go grab a bite, and—"

"Of course," I said. "I didn't consider what time it was when I called. I'll let you go."

"Well, if you haven't eaten, I'd like to buy you lunch and catch up."

"No," I said. "I couldn't possibly. I have ten cakes to decorate today."

"Whoa. Maybe another time, then."

"That'd be nice."

We hung up, and I took another ibuprofen and checked the consistency of my buttercream icing. The last thing I needed today was a pity lunch. I transferred the first batch of icing into a bowl and began preparing batch number two. I was going to need at least seven to complete the cake request for the Save-A-Buck and one cake for Thanksgiving dinner.

After I'd whipped up all the icing and set it into the refrigerator, I took out my favorite mixing bowl. It's blue. No corny reasons. It's just blue and deep enough that I don't slop cake batter all over the kitchen when I'm mixing. I love it. Almost as much as I love my kitchen. It's the main reason I bought my house. The walls are beige, and the cabinets are white. There's a light-colored wood floor and a huge island with a butcher-block top—perfect for decorating cakes.

I was taking three yellow, three spice, and four white cakes to the grocery store in the morning. I was making a chocolate cake for Thursday because it was Lucas's and Leslie's favorite. I thought about adding a white chocolate ganache filling to try to impress Mom, but she probably wouldn't notice and the tweens might not like it.

I measured out the butter and sugar and beat them together with my hand mixer. I added the vanilla and eggs, and then took out my second-favorite mixing bowl—yellow—for the dry ingredients.

The phone rang. I decided not to answer it, but then realized it might be someone wanting a cake for Thursday, and I desperately needed to build up my clientele.

"Hello," a soft female voice said when I answered the phone. "Is this Daphne Martin?"

"It sure is. How can I help you?"

"I'm Annabelle Fontaine, Yodel Watson's daughter."

"Oh, my." I caught my breath. "I'm so very sorry for your loss." I gripped the phone tightly.

"Thank you." She sniffled. "The police told me you found her."

"That's right."

"D-did she say anything to you before she . . . before she—"

I interrupted to try and ease her discomfort. "No, Annabelle. She was . . . um . . . unresponsive when I got there. I'd knocked on the door and thought she'd invited me in, but it turned out to be the parrot."

"Goofy bird." She made a sound that was somewhere between a laugh and a sob. "So the door was unlocked?"

"Yes."

"And Mother was in her pajamas?"

"Yes, her pajamas and robe."

She was quiet for a few moments before saying, "Mother never left her door unlocked."

Annabelle's voice was more pensive than accusatory, but I still didn't know how to respond so I kept my mouth shut.

"Did anything seem to be . . . out of place?" she asked.

"I couldn't say. I'd only been as far as your mom's front door the other two times I'd been there. Yesterday was the first time I'd been inside."

"Would you do something for me?"

"If I can."

"I need for you to go to Mother's house and get her diary for me."

"Excuse me?" I asked.

"Mother kept a diary—a virtual tell-all of the happenings in the community. If someone killed her, the reason why is in that book."

"Wouldn't it be best if you retrieved the diary yourself?"

"It would be," Annabelle agreed, "but I'm in Florida and can't get a flight out until tomorrow."

"And you don't think you could get it tomorrow?"

"I'm afraid to chance it. If someone did—God forbid—kill my mother, and that person knows or finds out about her diary, he or she might go back for it . . . if it isn't gone already. I know where Mother kept it. You'd only have to look in one place. If it isn't there, you could leave." She sounded desperate now.

"But won't the police—"

"I've already spoken with them. They know you have my permission to go inside the house."

"Annabelle, what makes you think your mother was killed?"

"I don't know. I pray she wasn't, but if the wrong person should get their hands on that diary . . . Oh, Daphne, it could be horrible."

"But why me?"

"You've only been in town a month. You couldn't possibly have done anything in that amount of time to warrant more than a casual mention."

"Well . . . I would hope not."

"So you'll do this for me?" she asked.

"Sure." Did I really just say that? Terrific. What had I gotten myself into now?

CHAPTER

three

I FINISHED MIXING the cake batter for the chocolate cake I'd planned for Thanksgiving on Thursday. I poured the batter into a square pan and put it in the oven. I had to get the cake done quickly; I had so much to do. Though, I was mainly putting off going to Yodel Watson's house. I would've liked to take someone with me—and I knew Myra would've jumped at the chance—but Annabelle had made it clear she didn't want anyone else seeing that book. I must admit, I was intrigued about the diary's contents myself.

As soon as I'd turned off the oven and put the cake on a wire rack to cool, I got into my car and drove to Mrs. Watson's house. I felt odd parking in the driveway, so I parked on the street a short distance from the house. I felt as if I should be doing this deed under cover of darkness. I guess under cover of cloudy sky would have to do.

A drop of rain splattered on my arm as soon as I got out of the car. The rain picked up as I sprinted to Mrs. Watson's back door. I found the fake rock with the hidden key exactly where Annabelle had said it would be. I hoped the diary would be as easy to locate.

I unlocked the back door and stepped inside the kitchen. "Hello?" I called. (No, I didn't expect Mrs. Watson to answer me, but this whole ordeal was giving me the creeps.)

As I closed the door behind me, the furnace kicked on and I nearly peed my pants. I must've been in shock during the entire finding-the-dead-body episode because my senses were on red alert now. I stood breathing heavily, straining to hear footsteps or the rattling of ghostly chains over the roar from the basement.

On leaden legs, I eased through the kitchen. Were the floorboards in this house always this noisy?

As I stepped into the hall, a door creaked open. "Is a-any-body th-there?" I backed up, wanting easy access to the kitchen door if I needed it.

Silence.

My heart pounded in my throat. I stood poised for flight. When I didn't hear anything, I hurried down the hall into the messy den. All I wanted was to find the book and get out.

I went straight to the bookcase on my left. It was overflow-ing with books, magazines, and junk mail. On the third shelf, I saw the large black Bible Annabelle had told me to look for. Be-side it was a book encased in a Bible cover—tan with a light-house on the front. This was it.

I shoved the book inside my jacket and zipped it up. Then I left, double-checking to make sure the kitchen door was locked on my way out.

The rain was really coming down now. As I jogged toward the front of the house, I heard a woman's voice call out, "You there!"

I stopped abruptly and peered around at a woman in a neon green rain slicker holding a covered casserole dish. "Who, m-me?"

"Yes." She had to tilt her head back to see me from under the slicker's hood. "Are you a member of Yodel's family?"

"No. They'll be here tomorrow."

"What are you doing here?"

"I was checking on a couple things for Annabelle," I said. "Is there anything I can help you with?" *I'd always heard the best defense is a good offense.*

"I'm Janey Dobbs, and I've brought this casserole for the family. Since you're a friend of Annabelle's, could you please pass this along to her?"

"Of course, Mrs. Dobbs. I'd be happy to."

"I'll try to come by later, but just in case I don't."

"Thank you. I know the family will appreciate it." With my right elbow keeping the diary firmly tucked against my side, I held out my hands for the dish.

Mrs. Dobbs gave it to me and got into her black Mercedes.

I rushed to my car. By the time I got the door unlocked and unloaded the dish and the diary, I was completely drenched. Shivering, I cranked up the heat.

As soon as I got home, I peeled off my clothes. Mrs. Watson's back-door key fell out of my jacket. Oh, well, I'd give it to Annabelle when she picked up the book.

I took a hot shower. It was wonderfully soothing and chased away the chill brought on by both the rain and the hint of death that lingered in Mrs. Watson's house.

It was only 3:00 p.m., but the day was bleak and I had nowhere I needed to go, so I put on my favorite PJs. I padded into the kitchen and made a cup of green tea. While the tea brewed, I took the chocolate cake off the wire rack, put it on a decorative plate, and covered it with plastic wrap. I went to the refrigerator and took out the tub of buttercream frosting I'd made earlier. It needed to warm up a bit before I could use it.

I took my tea and went into the living room. Mrs. Watson's diary lay on the coffee table. I wondered if it would hurt to take a peek. After all, Annabelle didn't ask *me* not to read it. On the other hand, I didn't want to invade Mrs. Watson's privacy. But she was dead. What harm could it do just to see if she'd said anything about my cakes?

I picked up the diary. It wasn't as thick as one would expect of a book containing years' worth of gossip. I flipped it over thinking the most recent entries would be in the back. I bit my lip as I settled into my cozy pink-and-white-checked chair and opened the book. I thumbed through the empty pages until I found an entry. Feeling a weird combination of masochism and apprehension, I decided to put Annabelle's theory to the test.

She was wrong. I *had* been in town long enough to merit more than a casual mention.

Daphne Martin has moved into town and hopes to start up a cake decorating business. I plan on ordering something so I can see how good she is.

Another entry related:

The girl is pretty good, but she doesn't know how to take direction worth beans. I told her exactly what I wanted, and you should've seen what she brought me!

At that I nearly choked on my tea. I wanted to tell someone—anyone—that Yodel Watson had never given me the foggiest idea of what sort of cake she wanted. "Nothing gaudy" is not an exact description.

The book went on to detail my two failed efforts. Mrs. Watson had personally given me the same criticisms, though, so this wasn't anything new to me. I decided to move on and see if there were any other names I recognized.

I was still moving through the book from back to front and the first name I recognized besides my own was Kellen Dobbs.

> I went to Dobbs's Pet Store this morning to get some pellets for Banjo. No one was in sight, so I went looking for Kel. I'd asked him to order some special treats for Banjo, and I wanted to see if they were in yet. When I opened the office door, Kel and that girl Candy were in "fragrant delecto," or whatever they call it.

"Fragrant delecto" made me laugh out loud. She and Myra must've gone to the same school of terminology.

> Kel tried to convince me I wasn't seeing what I was seeing, and I got both the pellets and the special treats for free.

I thought I'd detected a certain spark in the air between Candy and Mr. Dobbs. On the other hand, Mrs. Watson had misquoted her directions to me with regard to the cake she'd ordered. I suppose it was conceivable that she got this wrong, too. After all, Mr. Dobbs seemed too old and, well, unattractive for Candy . . . unless Candy didn't know it was Mrs. Dobbs who actually owned the store.

Then there was an entry detailing what great lengths Ben Jacobs would go to get a story.

He wants to work for one of them fancy city newspapers like Knoxville or Charlotte, and he knows he'll have to come up with some big stories in order to make that happen. Trouble is, I'm not convinced he cares whether those stories are true or not.

I knew that was hogwash. I might not have seen Ben in over twenty years, but I remembered his strong sense of integrity. It was one of the things I had liked most about him.

Like Ben, Fred from the grocery store's produce department didn't fare very well in Mrs. Watson's diary. According to Mrs. Watson, Fred allowed moldy produce to be mixed in with the fresh. The produce didn't look clean enough. Fred didn't keep the produce watered properly. He didn't keep the nuts sorted adequately.

And everyone knows that, especially this time of year when people are starting their holiday baking, you need to be able to quickly separate your walnuts from your pecans. To think Fred was vying for assistant store manager! I'd hate to see what kind of shape that store would be in with Fred running the show.

Boring. I turned back the years, so to speak, and saw that the incident with China that took place at the church potluck was written about in agonizing detail. Naturally, China was the villain who stole Mrs. Watson's recipe because she was desperate for attention. When she failed to wow the crowd with her cake, she drew the spotlight to herself and Mrs. Watson with "a reprehensible catfight that left my new lavender blouse ruined."

I was surprised to see that even Myra merited some ink. Actually, there was an entry about a particular fight Myra had with her late husband, Carl.

There they were at the steakhouse in Abingdon. Annabelle was waitressing that night and saw the whole thing. Now, everybody knows Carl Jenkins is a cheapskate. He pinches his pennies so tight, you can hear Lincoln holler. I think this night was either their anniversary or Myra's birthday, and she was of a mind to splurge.

The waitress—not Annabelle but another girl—came over to take their order.

"We'll have two of your specials," Carl said.

"I don't believe I'm in the mood for that this evening," Myra told the waitress. "I believe I will have me a filet mignon cooked medium well and a baked potato with sour cream and butter."

"I don't believe you will," Carl said to Myra.

His telling her she couldn't have what she wanted flew all over Myra.

My doorbell rang. I looked down at my pajamas and hoped it was Violet at the door.

"Who is it?" I called.

"It's Ben. Ben Jacobs."

"Um, give me just a minute." I raced to the bedroom, put Mrs. Watson's diary on my nightstand, and pulled on jeans and a sweater.

"Did I come at a bad time?" Ben asked when I opened the door. He looked the same, only older: same light brown hair falling into his pale blue eyes, same lanky build, same lopsided smile.

"No, not really. I—"

"I realize I should've called first. May I come in?"

"Of course." I stepped aside.

"Nice place."

"Thank you," I said. "What brings you by?"

"I feel bad about being insensitive this afternoon." He grinned sheepishly.

"Insensitive?"

"Yeah. I should've never compared Mrs. Watson to . . . well, you know . . . a dead animal. How callous can a guy be?" He threw me a lopsided smile, the same one that used to make me weak in the knees.

We moved into the living room. For just a second as I passed in front of him, his hand lingered on my back, guiding me. He drew back immediately but the touch had already recalled thoughts of holding hands, snuggling in the movie theater, and stealing kisses on his mother's front porch swing.

We sat down on the couch, and I offered him some tea. He declined, and when small talk was dispensed with, he returned to the topic of Yodel Watson.

"I suppose it's all these years of journalism," Ben said. "You learn to remove the emotional element from stories, and you become jaded. Sometimes that makes you come across as cold, but I certainly didn't mean any harm by it."

"No, I understand. You remembered how freaked out I used to get by dead animals, and you knew I'd be terribly affected by finding a dead person."

"Exactly. Then, you don't think I'm a jerk?"

"Never. I have a PhD in jerks, and you are definitely not one. Do you enjoy journalism?" I asked.

"Love it. Though sometimes I hanker for the meatier stories of a larger paper." He smiled. "There's only so much a body can say about the Christmas parade and the county fair, you know."

"You long for the bright lights and big city, huh?"

"Sometimes. I mean, small-town life has its advantages, too."

"Yeah," I said with a laugh, "with so many people willing

to gossip, you probably never have to dig very deep for a story."

Ben laughed as well. "That's for sure. I've even heard that Mrs. Watson had written a book that would make our little town seem like a veritable Peyton Place."

"I'd love to get my hands on that," I said.

"You and me both."

"If you're interested in covering more hard-hitting stories, then why don't you send out some résumés? Surely, with your experience—"

"Ah, it's a little late in the game to switch teams." Ben shrugged.

"I wouldn't be too quick to say that. Look at me."

"Yes, but you have more courage than most of us," he said, his eyes locked on mine, making those old familiar butterflies flap about. "Besides, I freelance some. That gives me the opportunity to focus on some bigger stories."

"That's good."

"How's the cake decorating business working out?"

I sighed. "My first client died, which is a lousy testimonial. I guess I'd have to say it isn't going well at this point."

"Look on the bright side," Ben said with a laugh, "it has to get better. Anyway, Mrs. Watson died before eating the cake. No reflection on you whatsoever."

"You always did try to see the bright side."

"And you always did try to talk me out of it."

I chuckled. "You were a dreamer. I was a realist."

"It seems we've switched places."

"Oh, I don't know about that."

He stood. "It's been great seeing you. You haven't changed a bit."

"There's a lie you could've kept from telling." I got to my feet and walked Ben to the door.

"I'd like to call you sometime," he said with a smile. "But for now, I'd better get home. Sally will be getting antsy."

I nodded. I wanted to ask who Sally was, but it was none of my business.

Ben hugged me gently. "It *really* was good seeing you."

"It was good seeing you, too." He let me go and turned to leave. Suddenly all I wanted to do was ask him to stay a little longer.

"Maybe we can get together after Thanksgiving," he shouted over his shoulder.

"Maybe," I said. "And you could bring Sally. I'd love to meet her."

He winked, got in his car, and drove away.

After he left, I wondered if he was still the Ben I used to know. It was strange for him to mention "Sally" without a qualifier—wife, daughter, girlfriend, roommate, girl Friday, parakeet—and then say he'd like to get together after Thanksgiving. On the other hand, he didn't seem opposed to bringing Sally if we scheduled another meeting. Perhaps my date-deprived mind had merely jumped to conclusions. Still, a girl had to wonder if Ben was a HUG or a HAG. Fingers crossed for the latter.

THE BUTTERCREAM WAS still softening in the kitchen so I put a bowl of soup in the microwave. Making dinner is easy when you live alone. Soup and cold cereal are my favorite staples.

After eating my bounteous dinner, I put on an apron and got to work on the cakes. The store cakes were easy. I used a sixteen-inch featherweight bag and a cake icer tip to quickly ice all ten round cakes. I smoothed the icing with an angled spatula, and then piped an orange shell border around the top and bottom of each cake. I had twenty premade white buttercream roses in the fridge, so I put two in the center of each cake. I tinted a small amount of frosting green and rolled a parchment triangle into a disposable bag. I cut the bottom from the bag and placed the leaf tip and green icing into the bag. After I added leaves to the store cakes' roses, the cakes were ready to go into boxes.

They had been fairly simple to do, but the work had tired me out. Still, I was determined to get my family's cake done and make it look terrific.

I covered a cake square with gold foil, sat the cake on it, and then put the cake on my turntable. Since I'd used a three-inch-deep square pan and had decided not to use a filling, I set to work on the single-layer cake. I iced the cake, and then smoothed the icing using an old trick I learned from a cake decorator while I was still in high school. I dipped my twelve-inch angled spatula into hot water and then smoothed the sides and top of the cake.

I placed a tip coupler into a disposable cake decorator bag and put two large spoonfuls of white icing into the bag. I was going for an elegant look, so I decided on Swiss dots.

I put a number 5 tip onto the coupler and piped medium-sized dots for the top and bottom borders of the cake. Afterward, I changed to a smaller tip and piped small dots on the sides and top. I always get peaks on my dots, so I dipped my fingertip in cornstarch and patted them down.

I took a strand of tiny pearls, cut them to the dimensions of the cake, and placed them above and below the top and bottom borders. I figured that after Thanksgiving dinner Leslie and I could use the pearls to make necklaces for her dolls or stuffed animals.

I piped a large mound of frosting in the center of the cake and inserted artificial flowers into the mound. Then I put the cake in a box and sat it in the refrigerator.

There. My family's cake was finished, and my Wednesday was free in case anybody had any last-minute cake requests.

After cleaning up the kitchen, I was ready to change from my jeans and sweater back into my pajamas. I went into the bedroom, changed my clothes, and then propped myself up against the headboard. I was anxious to see how Myra's fight with Carl turned out. From what I knew of Myra, I'm betting she wound up with that filet mignon somehow.

I picked up the book. This time, however, I opened the book from the front. The book was sketchy. The entries were a lot more scant in the earlier years. As I was leafing through the book to find the story about Myra and Carl, another familiar name jumped out at me.

Gloria Carter.

Mom.

Gloria Carter is at it again. Every time poor Jim goes out of town, Gloria is seen somewhere with Vern March. Vern has even been seen at Gloria's house! What gall!

Vern March. I remembered Vern. Uncle Vern. He was Dad's best friend. Mrs. Watson was just a spiteful old busybody. Mom and Vern weren't having an affair.

I feel sorry for Jim. He's devoted to those girls, and he's been a good husband to Gloria. He deserves better.

Lindy, who works at Attorney Platt's office, says Gloria came in yesterday and had a long talk with the attorney. Lindy says Gloria is thinking of divorcing Jim so she can marry Vern.

What nonsense. Vern was like a part of the family. He did spend a lot of time at the house whether Dad was there or not . . . and he was affectionate to Mom . . . and to Violet and me. But why would this Lindy tell Mrs. Watson that Mom had been to see the attorney if Mom hadn't been there? Could it be true?

Attorney Platt told Gloria that if she did divorce Jim, she was in the wrong unless she could get Jim to agree to the divorce and make some sort of equitable settlement. He said Jim wouldn't have to pay spousal support if Gloria leaves him for another man.

Poor Jim was in Boston on business the week that Gloria went to see Attorney Platt.

I remember that trip. Dad brought Violet and me little Red Sox bears. I still have mine.

I closed my eyes and tried to think back to that week. There had been a night when Mom had sent us into the den to watch TV while she and Vern had sat in the dining room at the table. I remember them speaking in hushed voices, and Violet and I had wondered what they were talking about. Vern wasn't married, and Violet and I thought maybe he'd found a girl he was interested in and was talking to Mom about her. Maybe we were right. We'd never guessed, though, that the girl was Mom.

When Jim's brother Hal found out what was going on, he paid Vern a visit. I didn't see Vern myself, but Ellie who works at the hospital said he was in awful shape. Both his eyes were black, his nose was broken, and he even had a couple broken ribs. When he got to the emergency room, Vern said he'd fallen down a flight of stairs at his house, but everybody knew that was a lie. Anybody who'd even driven by Vern March's house knew there wasn't a flight of stairs in the place. All he had were three steps leading up to the porch, and even if he fell down drunk, he couldn't have done that kind of damage on three steps. Plus, Ellie said they did blood work and Vern hadn't had a drop to drink that night.

Vern never drank, at least, as far as I knew. And we'd been to Vern's house. Mrs. Watson was right—no stairs.

Uncle Hal was also the type who would do anything to protect his family. He was a big bear of a man who always made me feel safe. When I was a little girl, I'd thought he was a giant. I thought he could protect me from anything.

I'd seen his temper flare up a time or two, so much so that it was frightening. But would Uncle Hal beat up a man who was rumored to be having an affair with Mom? Yes. He wouldn't hesitate.

Vern left town about a month after that. He put his house on the market and, as far as I knew, he never came back.

I put the book down and wiped my sweaty palms on the bedspread. I didn't remember Vern being in any sort of accident, didn't ever see him all beat up. But after thinking about it for a few minutes, I didn't remember seeing him after Dad's trip to Boston, either.

Blinking back tears, I picked up the phone and dialed Violet.

"What are you doing?" I asked when she answered.

"Watching television with Jason and the kids. You sound weird. Is everything okay?"

"I-I don't know. I just . . . heard something that blew me away."

"What is it?"

"Do you remember Vern March?"

She was silent a fraction of a second too long.

"Violet?"

"Yes, of course I remember him. Why?"

"You know, don't you?"

"Know what?"

"That he and Mom were having an affair."

"Don't be silly. Who told you that?"

"Violet, this is *me* you're talking to."

"Oh, all right, let me switch phones."

I heard a series of muffled thuds and clicks while she switched over to the cordless and presumably moved to her bedroom where she could talk more privately.

"Look, Daphne, whatever happened between Mom and Vern March was a long time ago."

"So?"

"So it doesn't matter anymore."

"It does to me."

She blew out a heavy breath. "Please, can you just simply let this go?"

"No, I can't. Tell me what you know."

"Mom told me about it a few years ago. She said she fell in love with Vern."

I thought I would explode. "What does she know about love?"

"Hello. You're talking about our *mother*. She made a mistake, okay? She fell in love with somebody. It happens."

"It happens? That's your take on this? It happens?"

"Yes, Daphne. Why in the world are you bringing up this mess now?"

"I *just* found out about it. Unlike you, who has apparently known for years. Why didn't you tell me?"

"Because I knew you'd react like this. And Mom didn't tell you because she knew it, too. It's over and done with. Why are you making such a big deal about it now?"

"Because she cheated on our father! And, not only that, but when Todd tried to blow my brains out, she called *that* a mistake! A mistake, Vi! She thought I should forgive the man and make nice!"

"Please calm down. Is this about Mom or about Todd?" Violet asked.

"It's about Mom! She was gonna leave Dad for a guy she *fell in love with* but wanted me to stay with a man who had tried to kill me?"

"Mom doesn't think Todd was trying to kill you. She thinks he was only trying to get your attention," Violet said. "She believes that if he'd meant to kill you, he would have."

"Oh, so I should've stayed and let him finish the job? That makes me feel so much better."

"No, you shouldn't have stayed!"

"That's not what Mom thinks," I said. "She told me marriage is *sacred* and that I should give Todd another chance."

"She said that because she gave Dad another chance."

"That's rich." I laughed harshly. "*She* gave *Dad* another chance? To what? Bring another friend home?"

"No. Another chance to make her happy. And it worked out."

"Are you telling me Dad knows about Mom and Vern March?"

Violet groaned. "No. He doesn't know. Promise me you won't tell him."

"What about Uncle Hal? Didn't Uncle Hal tell him?"

"Mom begged him not to, and I don't think he ever did. It's in the past, Daph. Can you please let it go?"

"No. I'm not sure I can."

CHAPTER
four

WEDNESDAY MORNING I was at the Save-A-Buck even before Steve Franklin. I had cakes stacked in the trunk and in the backseat. After he unlocked the doors, Mr. Franklin helped me carry in the boxes. I nearly dropped mine when Fred came barreling past, shoving me aside.

"Hey, Franklin," he said. "I saw on the schedule that I'm supposed to work tomorrow."

"I'm with someone right now, Fred," Mr. Franklin said. "We'll discuss this later."

"I'm supposed to be off tomorrow," Fred continued. "You said I could be off."

"Everyone is working four hours tomorrow. If you're not happy with that, you can tender your resignation." He put the two cake boxes he was holding on to a table near the front windows. "Right here, Ms. Martin."

"You'd like that," Fred said, swiping his hand beneath his nose. "You'd like for me to quit."

Mr. Franklin took a deep breath and—impressively, I thought—kept his cool. "You need to punch in and get to work."

As Mr. Franklin went back outside to get more cakes, Fred ambled toward the stockroom, muttering under his breath. I put my cakes down, checked to make sure they weren't damaged, and then followed Mr. Franklin back outside.

"I brought a covered glass cake plate," I told him. "I thought we could display one cake on it in the center of the table."

"Good idea," Mr. Franklin said as we returned inside. "What do we have?"

"We have three yellow, four white, and three spice cakes."

"Great. I'll get Juanita to make a sign for—"

"I've got one." I reached into my tote bag and retrieved an eight-and-a-half-by-eleven-inch sign. It had my logo at the top and a list of cake flavors at the bottom. "I also labeled the cake boxes so there won't be any confusion."

Mr. Franklin smiled and glanced toward the stockroom. "I wish everyone were as competent as you."

I bit my lip. "You handled that outburst much better than I would have."

"I'm used to it. Fred's right—I do wish he'd quit." He shook his head. "Don't get me wrong, before the accident you couldn't have asked for a harder worker or nicer guy than Fred."

"Accident?"

"A car wreck about a year ago. There was some damage to his brain—the frontal lobe. He hasn't been the same since."

"Isn't there something the doctors can do?" I asked. "Some sort of medication?"

"He's on medication. Trust me, you wouldn't want to run across him when he's not."

"If he's that disruptive . . ." I let my sentence trail off.

"I can't afford a lawsuit, Ms. Martin. Besides, Fred needs this job." He nodded toward the door. "Let's go get the rest of those cakes."

Fortunately, I didn't see Fred again until I'd put the finishing touches on the display and was getting ready to leave. He came and stood in front of the table, looking at the cakes.

"They look good," he said. "Smell good, too."

"Thanks." I smiled. "Happy Thanksgiving."

He didn't respond.

I waved good-bye to Juanita and Mr. Franklin, and walked out.

MY NEXT STOP was the newspaper office. I wanted to know what happened to Vern March. If I could get a lead on where he went, then maybe I could find an address or phone number. I had questions I needed answered.

The receptionist looked like everybody's favorite grandma. She had tight gray curls, twinkling blue eyes, and a ready smile. And she greeted me with "Good mornin', darlin'. What can I do for you?"

I smiled and wiped my palms on my jeans. Why was I so nervous? "I'm here to see Ben Jacobs," I said with resolve. "Is he available?"

"You know, I'm not sure whether he's available or not. But if he is, I'm sure a pretty little thing like you stands a real good chance."

My smile faded, and I could feel the color flooding my face.

She picked up the phone. "Ben, honey, there's somebody

here to see you." She replaced the receiver and winked at me. "He'll be right out."

"Thank you. Um . . . could I get a list of your advertising rates?"

"Sure, darlin'. Personal ad?"

"No." I was thinking she might not be such a swell granny after all. "I have a business, and I'd—"

"Oh! What kind of business?"

"I bake and decorate cakes."

She stared at me.

"You know, for special occasions."

"Right." She tsked. "Making all those wedding cakes, no wonder it's got you thinking about the personals. There's no shame in that, mind you. Just be careful. You never—"

"Daphne!" Ben's voice rang out in the reception area, and I felt a relief that was nearly tangible.

"Hi," I said, watching him wave me back, that lopsided grin on his face again.

"Come on back to my office."

I followed him down the narrow hallway.

"Here we go."

His door had a gold nameplate that read BENJAMIN JACOBS, EDITOR-IN-CHIEF. His desk wasn't as cluttered as I'd thought it might be, and I glanced around for photographs—maybe of Sally—but there were none.

"How are you doing this morning?" Ben asked as I took a seat in one of the industrial blue chairs in front of his desk.

"I'm fine. I'd . . . I'd like to see your archives."

He perched on the corner of his desk and crossed his arms over his noticeably muscled chest. "Any year in particular?"

"Around 1975 . . . '76." I looked down at my hands.

"That was a long time ago. We were . . . what . . . eight?"

I nodded.

"You want me to help you look or just take you to the archive room and get you started?"

"I can take care of it," I said. "You've got work to do."

"Okay." He reached over and put his hand on my shoulder. "But if you decide you want to talk about it, I'm here."

Ben always was infuriatingly perceptive. I guess that's what made him a good reporter. And a good boyfriend, I remembered.

Minutes later, he had me ensconced in the archive room with instructions to ask someone named Wanda if I needed any help.

I'd expected the archives to be on microfiche or some sort of digital system, so imagine my surprise when I realized the archive room contained only books of actual newspapers.

A woman with frizzy brown hair wearing a brown jumper over a white sweater and white tights came into the room. "Hi, I'm Wanda. Ben said you were here."

"Yes. I'm looking for some newspapers from quite a while back."

"They date back to the early sixties. The earliest ones are in the back, and the latest are in the front. My office is right next door. Give me a shout if you need anything."

"Thank you." I took a deep breath and got to work.

I started at the back of the room.

1962.

I moved about four feet toward the front.

1970.

A few more steps.

1974.

I was close. I sat down on the floor and began to rifle through the books.

1975 . . . February, March, April.

Daddy had gone to Boston in April. I remember because I got the worst poison ivy rash I'd ever had while he was gone and kept crying, "I want my daddy!"

I pored over every page of every day's newspaper for April. Of course, there was nothing in them pertaining to Vern March. What had I expected? My mother's affair to take precedence over the Vietnam War?

The front page of April 30, 1975, was all about the surrender of the city of Saigon. "Remaining Americans are evacuated, ending the Vietnam War."

There was also a world refugee crisis in April 1975 as millions of Vietnamese fled their country.

The more I read through the papers, the dumber I felt. With everything that had gone on in the world in 1975, why would I expect Vern March's accident—or assault—to make the news? Yet I personally could remember Vern, Daddy's trip to Boston, and even Ben's old dog . . . but I couldn't recall a single thing about the Vietnam War. When I was a little girl, I'd thought it had something to do with Jane Fonda, Anita Bryant, and Florida orange juice. Clearly, I'd been mistaken.

Foolish or not, I decided to continue looking at least through the summer of 1975. I'm glad I did, too. It was on Wednesday, May 7, that I found Vern March—or his obituary rather. So now I knew where Vern was. He was buried in a cemetery in Scott County, Virginia.

BEN WASN'T IN his office when I left. I wrote *thank you* on a sticky note and put it on his phone. In a way, I was glad he wasn't there. I knew he'd ask all the right questions, and I'd end up telling him about Mom, Vern March, *and* Uncle Hal.

I wasn't ready to do that yet . . . at least not with Ben. I didn't want to drag all the scary skeletons out of my closet until I knew why I kept feeling like a schoolgirl around him. Even if we were destined to be "just friends," I didn't want to screw that up with a sob story at this point. Besides, there wasn't a wedding ring on Ben's hand.

Not that I'm interested . . . really . . . very much. I mean, there is Sally to consider.

I gave myself a mental shake, got into my car, and drove a bit over the speed limit getting home. Hey, I had stuff to do: a freezer to replenish with cakes; a diary and a set of keys to return; a call to Uncle Hal to make . . .

When I saw a van in my driveway, I suddenly wasn't in such a hurry. The van had VIRGINIA DEPARTMENT OF AGRICULTURE AND CONSUMER SERVICES emblazoned on the side in large blue letters.

I got out of my car and walked up to the driver's side of the van. A man with an official-looking clipboard put down the window.

"Hello. Are you Daphne Martin?"

"Yes, sir."

The driver jerked his head toward his partner. "We're here to inspect your home."

"Excuse me?"

"We're with the Department of Agriculture."

"And?"

"And under the Virginia Food Laws, you're subject to an inspection."

I glanced from the driver to his chubby partner. They looked like Stan Laurel and Oliver Hardy in drab olive coveralls. Maybe I was being punked. "Is this a joke?"

Hardy smirked. "No joke, ma'am."

"Someone came out and inspected my home a month ago when I first set up my business. There must be a mistake."

"We received information that your products might present a risk," Laurel said, "so we're here to do a repeat inspection."

"What do you mean my *products might present a risk?*"

Laurel consulted his clipboard. "Did you deliver a cake to a Yodel Watson on Monday morning?"

"Yes, but—"

"Mrs. Watson died," Hardy said.

"I know that, but she never even *saw* the cake."

"We still have orders to inspect the residence," Laurel said, waving his identification badge in front of my face. "Do we have your permission to do so or should we suspend your operations?"

I put my hand up to my forehead. "Fine. Come on in."

"We won't take but a few minutes of your time," Laurel said.

"All right." I unlocked the door as Laurel and Hardy got out of the van.

When they came inside, Hardy was carrying what looked like a cross between a toolbox and a doctor's kit.

I pointed at the box. "What's that for? The previous inspectors didn't have anything like that."

"This contains our tools and sample bags," Hardy said. "We'll need to take food samples back to our lab." He sat the box on the island and opened it.

Laurel went directly to the sink, turned on the faucet, and placed his hand in the stream of water. After a few seconds, he announced that the water temperature met regulations. He shut off the water, took a flashlight from the box, and opened the cabinet under the sink.

As he moved my cleaning supplies onto the kitchen floor, I asked, "What exactly are you looking for?"

Laurel didn't look up from his task. "Pest infestation, inadequate refrigeration, and contaminated food."

"That's why we need samples," Hardy said, "of your cakes, icing, flour, sugar, et cetera. And we may need to come back once Mrs. Watson's cause of death has been determined."

"Like I told you, the cake I delivered to Mrs. Watson was never even cut! Mrs. Watson didn't *see* the cake. She didn't *touch* the cake. She didn't *smell* the cake. And she darn sure didn't *eat* the cake!" I flailed my arms. "The police *know* the cake wasn't cut! If they'd thought something was wrong with it, they'd have confiscated it."

"We're not the police," Laurel said. He shut off the flashlight and began putting my things back in the cabinet. "This one's clear." He looked up at me. "I'm sorry this is so upsetting, but we'll be through in a few minutes. You might want to wait in the living room or—"

"I'll wait right here." I crossed my arms in front of me.

"Fine," Hardy said, holding up a sample bag. "Can you give us some sugar?" He gave me a leering grin that nearly brought my breakfast back to the surface.

"Confectioners' or pure cane?"

His grin faded. "Both."

After giving Hardy samples of all my baking supplies, I sat down at the table and watched Laurel go through the rest of my cabinets. He was pretty quick at emptying and refilling them. Where'd he been when I was moving?

Out of the corner of my eye, I saw Hardy going for the cake box with tomorrow's cake inside. I sprang out of my chair. "Don't mess with that! It's for my family's Thanksgiving dinner!"

Hardy looked at Laurel. I refused to take my eyes off Hardy, though, and was willing to do him bodily harm if he touched my cake.

"You have samples of my supplies," I said. "You have some of *every* ingredient in that cake."

Laurel must've given Hardy some sort of signal because he backed away from the cake. He continued to snoop, however.

When they finally left, I cleaned the kitchen from top to bottom. I knew they hadn't gotten anything dirty; they'd worn gloves and had been careful to leave everything as they'd found it. Still, it *felt* dirty somehow. These men had violated my home, my business, my privacy, my life.

After I'd cleaned the kitchen, I poured my mop water outside and sat down on the step. I saw the stray cat staring at me from beneath a tree, and I wished she'd come to me. I'd never felt so alone . . . well, at least not lately.

I heard a vehicle in the driveway and raised my head, afraid the inspectors had returned. I squinted to see the man in the white Jeep as he got out. My stomach flipped. *Ben.* He was carrying a deli bag.

"Hungry?" he asked.

His simple gesture poked a needle into my balloon of self-pity, and I began to sob. Lucy Ricardo would've been proud. Ben rushed forward and sat down next to me, pulling me close as I cried.

Ten minutes later, I was spent and Ben and I were at the kitchen table eating ham and Swiss on rye.

"Why in the world was the Department of Agriculture here?" Ben asked.

"Because in Virginia they oversee bakeries." It was the answer I was given the *first* time the department had shown up to inspect my home.

"But you aren't running a bakery."

"Not exactly, but I do sell baked goods to the public. That puts me in the department's jurisdiction."

"And they just showed up out of the blue?"

I nodded. "They said it was routine, but one of them did mention Mrs. Watson's death."

"How could they think your cake was responsible for that?" Ben tapped his finger against the table in thought.

"I don't know. I tried to tell them the cake wasn't even cut. I said it was in the police report, but they arrogantly informed me that they are not with the police department."

"Even so, I'd expect the agencies to work together, especially if they feel your cake was somehow responsible for someone's death."

"How did they even know I took a cake to Mrs. Watson?"

Ben wiped at his mouth with a paper napkin. "You said it yourself. It's a matter of public record since it's in the police report. But I'll see if I can find out if someone tipped them off."

"Tipped them off? You sound as if somebody has it in for me."

"I don't mean that exactly," Ben said. "I mean, I know these visits are routine, but your kitchen passed muster a month ago. Why did they need to recheck everything because Mrs. Watson received a cake she never even touched?"

I took the Department of Agriculture's invoice out of my jeans pocket and pushed it across the table. "Maybe because the holiday shopping season is upon us and they needed the forty dollars."

"Wait, they actually billed you for this inspection?" Ben shook his head.

"Yep. I believe that's what is commonly known as adding insult to injury."

"That's certainly not the phrase I'd have chosen, Daph. But yours certainly is nicer." I laughed for the first time all day and took another bite of my sandwich.

* * *

BEN LEFT SHORTLY thereafter. I still had to make a batch of stiff buttercream after all. I divided the icing into fourths and tinted one yellow, one pink, one peach, and one red. Thankfully, I'd remembered to put on decorator's gloves before coloring my icing. I didn't want to have multihued fingers at Violet's house tomorrow. My mother would have a field day with that.

As I put couplers in four featherweight bags, I tried to think about something else. *Focus, Daphne.*

I took out a Styrofoam block, my flower nail, and my number 12 and number 104 tips. Deciding to make yellow roses first, I filled a bag one-third of the way with yellow icing. I attached a square of waxed paper to the flower nail with a dot of icing. I put the number 12 round tip into the coupler and made a generous cone base for the rose. After I stuck the flower nail into the Styrofoam, I traded the round tip for my number 104 petal tip and retrieved the flower nail. I made sure the wide end was at the bottom, and I made the center petal. I followed up with the three top petals, five middle petals, and seven lower petals. Voila. One yellow rose. I removed the waxed paper square from the flower nail and placed it and the rose onto a long, flat container. I had several freezer-friendly containers for this very purpose.

I put a new waxed-paper square onto the flower nail and stood the nail on its Styrofoam perch while I switched tips.

The phone rang, and I picked up the headset I use while I'm working. "Daphne's Delectable Cakes."

"Hi, hon. It's Myra. How are you?"

"I'm fine," I said, constructing a rose base onto the flower nail. "You?"

"Well, I just heard they got Yodel Watson's autopsy report back."

"Wow. That was quick."

"Yeah, it was, and apparently it raised more questions than it gave answers."

"What do you mean?" I switched to the petal tip and twirled the flower nail as I put the rose's petals in place.

"The autopsy report gave her cause of death as respiratory failure. It also said she had some gross hemorrhaging, some dead tissue, and something about bad kidney tubes."

"Ick. That sounds horrible. Where did you get the lowdown on the autopsy?"

"From Joanne Hayden. I saw her in the drugstore. She was buying hair dye. I *knew* that wasn't her natural color."

"Good ol' Joanne. I should've guessed." I put my second rose into the container beside the first one. "I really need to meet her. I've heard so much about her, I feel I know her already."

"Joanne says the police are afraid Yodel might've been poisoned."

I froze. "Really?"

"Yeah, and she said you were even being investigated to make sure it wasn't something in your cake that did her in."

"Myra, you *saw* that cake . . .you've *got* that cake! It hadn't been touched until you tasted the frosting. Did you tell Joanne that?"

"Yes . . . well, I tried to. But sometimes people can get sick from just smelling something, you know."

"Yodel Watson did not smell my cake! Besides, if she could've died instantly from merely smelling the cake, why didn't it kill me? Or you?"

"Oh, you've got a point. I hadn't even thought of that. So, you think it's okay then?"

"What? The cake?"

"Uh-huh. You know, I'd planned on serving it and the other two you made to my family tomorrow for Thanksgiving—"

"The cake is fine," I said angrily, interrupting. "But if you don't feel comfortable serving it—or the other two—bring them back over here, and I'll take them to Violet's house tomorrow and serve them to *my* family."

"No . . . uh . . . I think they'll probably be all right."

I stood up straighter and held my chin higher. "If it makes you feel any better, the Virginia Department of Agriculture and Consumer Services inspected my home and all my baking ingredients only a few hours ago."

"Honey, I'm sorry. I didn't mean to upset you. Joanne got me worked up is all."

"It's okay." I sighed. "It's got me worked up, too. I'm afraid these rumors will ruin my business before it even gets started."

As I continued making roses, my mind wandered back to my earlier conversation with Ben. Could someone here in town want to frame me? Or was I merely the scapegoat?

It was time to get some answers.

CHAPTER
five

I WAS FED up with Joanne Hayden. I didn't even know the
woman, and she was spreading rumors—dangerous rumors—
about me. I was going down to that police station, and I was
going to give Bill Hayden a piece of my mind.

If that didn't work, I'd go to the chief or the commissioner
or whoever was Officer Hayden's boss. I'd tell him how—
thanks to Bill's pillow talk—the entire department could very
well be facing slander charges if the situation was not rectified
immediately. I'd make the department issue a public apology.
That'd teach Bill *and* his wife not to be so quick to ruin someone's professional reputation on speculation and unfounded
accusations.

The yellow rose I was working on looked like a big, shapeless glob. I mashed it back into the icing bowl. With a growl of disgust, I realized I wouldn't make any progress on my roses until I resolved my anger. I covered my supplies and placed them inside the refrigerator for after I got back from the station.

I grabbed my purse and keys off a hook by the door, but before I could step off the porch, an attractive, fiftyish woman with a trim figure and shoulder-length, curly black hair timidly approached the house.

"Can I help you?" I asked. My voice was a bit terse partly due to my residual anger and partly because I'd reached my tolerance level for unexpected guests today.

"I . . . I'm Annabelle. I-is this a bad time?"

"Oh, of course not. I . . ." I sighed. "I'm just having a rough day."

"I'm sorry," Annabelle said. "I should've called first. I can come back."

"No, please," I said. "I'm the one who should apologize. Please come in." I stepped back inside and placed my purse and keys back on the hook.

"But you were obviously going somewhere."

"It can wait." I smiled. "In fact, it's probably best that it waits."

"This shouldn't take long," Annabelle said. "I haven't even been to . . . to Mother's yet."

"Do you have someone to go with you?"

Annabelle shook her head. "My husband wanted to come, but I insisted he and my daughters go on to his family's house for Thanksgiving tomorrow. Both our children are home from college and—" She closed her eyes.

"Please sit down," I said, gesturing toward the kitchen table. "Can I make you some coffee? Tea?"

"No, thank you." She took a napkin from the napkin caddy and pressed it to her nose. "I would like some water, though, if you don't mind."

"Not at all." I took a bottle of water from the fridge and sat a crystal tumbler and the bottle in front of Annabelle.

"Thank you." She filled the tumbler and drank deeply. "I hope you don't think my husband and children are being thoughtless, because they aren't."

I pulled out a chair. "Oh, of course—"

"I was adamant that they stay behind. They'll be here for the funeral on Saturday, but I wanted to go through Mother's things alone." She took another drink. "We've lived in Florida since the girls were small. They hardly know their grandmother."

I sat quietly, not sure what I could say or do to comfort her.

She forced a smile. "I guess I wanted my memories to myself." She let a shoulder rise and drop. "I wanted to be alone with her, with my thoughts, tonight and tomorrow." She lifted her eyes to mine. "Daffy, huh?"

"No." I smiled. "Sweet, thoughtful, certainly courageous, but not daffy."

"I don't know about courageous." She took another deep drink. "I'll probably rant and rave and cry and laugh like a complete lunatic."

"It's cathartic. The beginning of healing."

"You speak like you've been there."

I chuckled. "Suffice it to say I've had my share of lunatic moments." Suddenly parched, I got up to get myself a bottle of water. "Did you have any trouble finding me?"

"No. I was friends with the Pearces. Did you know them?"

I shook my head as I placed the water on the table and reclaimed my seat. "I only met them at the closing. They seemed nice."

"They're great. Did they tell you why they were selling their house?"

"They said they were moving to Arizona to be near their grandchildren."

Annabelle nodded. "When Chuck, my husband, was transferred, we asked both sets of parents to make the move with us. Chuck's did." Her face clouded. "I think Dad would have." She shook her head, sending her black curls bobbing. "But not Mother. She couldn't leave this . . . this viper's nest."

"I'm sorry," I said softly.

"Me too." She took another napkin, lifting her face heavenward as tears dripped from her cheeks.

I didn't know this woman well enough to hug her, but she was crying at my kitchen table. I squeezed her hand. "I'm so sorry."

"May I . . . use your bathroom?"

"Sure, it's—"

"I know," she said, hurrying down the hall.

Could this have been more awkward? I wished I knew what to do. . . what to say. . . what might bring Annabelle some comfort.

Annabelle came back to the kitchen, her face now free of makeup. "I used one of your washcloths. I hope you don't mind."

"Not at all. I only wish I could do something to help."

"You already have. You got the journal . . . didn't you?"

"I did. Be right back." I went to the bedroom and retrieved the journal and the key to Mrs. Watson's back door.

When I returned to the kitchen, Annabelle had sat back down and was refilling her water glass. I set the diary and the key on the table.

"Thank you," she said, putting the water bottle down. It

had left a wet spot on the table, and Annabelle wiped the puddle with a napkin. "Did you read any of it?"

I bit my lip. "I did. I tried not to, but I couldn't resist. I was curious about your mom's thoughts on my cakes."

Annabelle smiled. "That's all right."

"There was something in the book about Vern March," I said tentatively. I searched her downcast face for any sign of reaction, any clue that she knew what significance reading about Vern and my mother would have on me, but I could find none. Perhaps she didn't know of the affair. "He used to be a friend of our family. Any idea whatever became of him?"

She shook her head. "I have no idea. You might ask Joanne, though."

"Joanne?"

"Joanne Hayden. She's his granddaughter."

I gaped at Annabelle. "What? I never even knew Vern was married."

"Well, it didn't last very long. He married when he was sixteen. The girl was only fifteen, and she was pregnant. Her parents made them get an annulment."

"That's . . . that's too bad."

"Mm-hmm. You'd think with her pregnant, her parents would have insisted they remain married. Go figure." She took a drink of water. "It was a little boy. She—Joanne's grandmother—named him Jonah. Jonah March."

"And Joanne Hayden is his daughter."

I WAS STILL thinking about Joanne being Vern March's granddaughter after Annabelle had left so I went back to making my roses. This tidbit of information had made me rethink my decision to unleash my wrath on Bill Hayden. If Joanne Hayden did resent me, was it because she suspected my family of being responsible for Vern's disappearance and, ultimately, death? I wanted to call Violet and get her thoughts on the matter, but Mom and Dad would be there by now, and Vi wouldn't be able or willing to talk about Vern March with them around.

The phone rang, and I'd forgotten to put on my headset. By the time I'd put the flower nail in the Styrofoam block, the phone was chirping its second ring. On the third ring, the answering machine would pick up. I quickly grabbed the phone.

"Hello, Daphne's Del—"

"Yes, hello, Daphne. This is Steve Franklin."

"Hi, Mr. Franklin. Did the cakes sell well?"

"Yes . . . yes. I have a check for you at the front office. You can pick it up anytime."

"Thank you." My mood soared like a kite in a late March sky. "How many sold?"

"All of them."

There goes my kite, rising above the trees.

"After we took your logo off the boxes," Mr. Franklin finished.

My kite got caught in a power line.

"I . . . I beg your pardon?"

Mr. Franklin cleared his throat. "A few of our patrons appeared to be concerned about the cakes due to, uh, the . . . well, the unfortunate demise of Yodel Watson."

I clutched the phone so tightly my knuckles turned white. "Why?"

"They, uh, seemed to be afraid your . . . your product . . . had in some way . . . affected Mrs. Watson."

"That's ridiculous. Mrs. Watson was dead when I got there. She didn't even see the cake."

"Then don't worry. This will all blow over." He cleared his

throat again. "And when it does, Save-A-Buck will be delighted to offer your products again."

"With or without my logo?"

"Uh, we'll have to see about that, dear. Happy Thanksgiving."

With that, Mr. Franklin hung up.

I gave an outraged scream. I no longer cared whether or not Joanne March Hayden's condemnation of my family—in this case, me—was due to just cause. It was going to stop. I was going to *make* it stop.

I snatched the phone and called the police station. "Officer Hayden, please."

"I'm sorry," the nasal-voiced receptionist said. "He's out on a call right now, but—"

"Thanks." I hung up.

Once again I gathered my icing and completed roses to put into the refrigerator. I was going to that police station and I wasn't leaving until I got answers.

When I opened the refrigerator door, I spotted the casserole dish Mrs. Dobbs had asked me to give to Annabelle. I'd drop it off on my way. Maybe that'd give Officer Hayden time to get back to the station.

I SAW THE blue lights as soon as I turned onto Mrs. Watson's street. No red lights—which was good because that would indicate an ambulance or fire truck—but there were two sets of flashing *blue* lights. I parked my car one house down, retrieved my purse and the casserole, and walked to Mrs. Watson's house.

It suddenly occurred to me that if the police thought I killed Mrs. Watson with a cake, they might think I'd brought the casserole to do in Annabelle. Oh, well. I was here now. Besides, this might be the perfect opportunity to clear my name.

There was a police officer standing outside the front door, but it wasn't Bill Hayden. It was a woman, and she was talking into her radio. She stopped talking as I approached.

"Hello," I said. "I'm here to see Annabelle. Is everything okay?"

Stupid question, I know. Seldom are the police congregated at your house when everything is okay.

"I mean, is she all right?" I asked.

"She's fine. Your name?"

"Daphne Martin."

She radioed someone and announced my arrival.

Annabelle came to the door. "Daphne, hi."

"Mrs. Dobbs had given me a casserole for you. I forgot to give it to you earlier."

"Thanks." She took the casserole. "Can you come in?"

"Sure. What's wrong?"

"There's been a break-in. The glass was knocked out of the kitchen door."

I gasped when I stepped into the living room. The once immaculate room was now a disaster. The curio cabinet had been knocked over, tossing broken porcelain everywhere. Especially poignant were the dolls' faces staring up at me from the carpet.

"Watch your step," Annabelle said.

"I am so sorry," I whispered, my voice not willing to rise to the occasion. "Was anything taken?" I followed Annabelle through the living room and into the kitchen.

"I don't think so. But I would like for you to take a look around and make sure the house didn't look like this when you were here yesterday."

Officer Hayden was standing in the kitchen. "Wait a minute. She was here yesterday?"

"Yes," Annabelle said, setting the casserole dish onto the table. "I asked her to get something for me."

"Are you sure *she* didn't do this?"

"You may address me directly, Officer Hayden. And I can assure you I did *not* do this. I had no need to break in as Annabelle trusted me with a key." I lifted my chin. "Put that in your gossip pipeline and spread it."

He put his hands on his hips and took a step closer to me. "What do you mean by that?"

"I mean there's an awful lot of confidential information— much of it inaccurate—floating around town thanks to you and your wife."

"I don't like your tone." He swallowed, his Adam's apple jerking spastically.

"I don't like your veiled accusations."

Annabelle stepped between us. "Please. Can we not argue right now? I'd like to get this wrapped up."

"Of course." I took my first real look around the kitchen. Cabinet doors were flung open, and the countertops were piled with pans, canned food, cereal boxes, and cookbooks. I shook my head. "This kitchen was spotless when I was here yesterday. Is the entire house torn apart like this room and the living room?"

"Afraid so."

The policewoman joined us. "Johnson and McAfee are back from talking to the neighbors. Nobody saw anything."

Officer Hayden shot me a sharp look. "Figures."

I ignored him. "Annabelle, can I help you clean all this up?"

"I appreciate the offer, Daphne; I really do. But I'm so tired. The police have offered to board up the kitchen door for me, and after they leave I'm going to straighten up the guest room and leave the rest until morning."

"Aren't you worried about staying here alone?" I asked.

"I'll be fine." She smiled wanly. "I'll keep all the doors locked, including the guest room door. And I'll have my phone handy."

"If you need me tomorrow, please call me."

"I wouldn't dream of interrupting your Thanksgiving with your family."

"Dream of it," I said. "You'd be doing me a favor." I felt my conscience kick at that one, but I truly dreaded facing my mother tomorrow.

DRIVING HOME, I wondered if the person who'd trashed Yodel Watson's house had been looking for her journal. Had Annabelle not been so adamant about the book, I'd have thought the break-in had been engineered by junkies or perhaps vandals who'd read about Mrs. Watson's death in the newspaper. But it appeared nothing valuable had been taken. Plus, whoever tore up the house had been *angry*. I felt the fury the instant I saw the broken dolls. Most of the dolls appeared to be collector's pieces. A thief would've pawned the dolls, not destroyed them.

Was Annabelle right? Had someone murdered Mrs. Watson and later learned about her record of iniquities and come back to get it? I shuddered thinking of Annabelle in the house alone, wondering if the killer would try to break in again in order to get the book.

And now, thanks to Bill and Joanne Hayden, it would quickly become common knowledge that I'd gone to Mrs. Watson's house on Tuesday to pick up something for Annabelle. Would the killer figure out that the item I'd picked up for Annabelle was her mother's journal? With a gulp, I realized I'd better find out what had happened to Yodel Watson before I shared her fate.

As I was putting the key in my door, I heard a rustle in the bushes. I stood there with no weapon whatsoever and fumbled and dropped my keys. How stupid! I felt like the heroine in a horror movie. Next, I'd start to run and then trip and fall, giving the crazed maniac ample opportunity to kill me.

Keeping my eyes on the bushes, I bent and picked up my keys. It was still daylight—barely. Would someone actually attack me on my porch before it was even dark?

The rustling grew louder.

I jammed the key into the lock. Before I could turn the doorknob, I heard a plaintive meow.

I felt my limbs go weak with relief.

I opened the door and went into the kitchen. After a quick look around to make sure everything was as I had left it, I put some food out for the cat. She'd wait until I'd gone back inside before she'd come and eat. She, too, knew it paid to be cautious.

I shuffled to the living room and sank into my favorite chair. This week had been too much for me so far, and it didn't show any signs of improving.

On top of it all, I dreaded seeing Mom and Dad tomorrow. Mom for the obvious reasons, and Dad because I was afraid I might cry when I looked at his sweet, gentle face and knew what she'd done to him all those years ago. I still felt a need to share at least some of this burden before tomorrow. I got out my address book and phoned Uncle Hal. Aunt Nancy answered.

"Hi, Aunt Nancy. It's Daphne."

"Hello, darling. How are you? Enjoying the new home?"

"I love it. You should stop by and see it the next time you're down this way."

"You know I will."

"Listen, is Uncle Hal around? I have a question for him."

"No, dear. Actually, he's in your neck of the woods right now."

"He's in Brea Ridge?"

"Sure is. I'm surprised he hasn't been by to see you. He's been there since this past weekend."

"Since the weekend?"

"Yeah. He's with some of his hunting buddies. He'll be home tonight." She paused. "Is something wrong?"

"No. No, I just had a question about, uh, you know, getting the house ready for winter."

"Oh."

"And I wanted to say Happy Thanksgiving."

"You, too, darling. Give everybody our love and tell 'em we'll see them soon."

"I'll do that, Aunt Nancy."

As I hung up, her words replayed in my mind. *He's been there since this past weekend.*

CHAPTER

Six

I AWOKE THURSDAY morning with dread pinning me to the bed like a three-hundred-pound wrestler. I wondered what time it was but was afraid to look at the clock. It might be later than I thought. I might not have time to lie here and visualize every possible scenario that could take place at Violet's house today—none of them pleasant.

I burrowed deeper beneath the covers. I'd slept fitfully last night. I wondered why Uncle Hal was in town. It was deer season, so it was plausible that he'd actually spent the past few days hunting with friends. But I hadn't known he was here, and Violet hadn't mentioned anything about it, either.

Was it possible there was something more damning about

Uncle Hal in Mrs. Watson's book? Something I'd overlooked? Something he'd kill to avoid having revealed?

I gave myself a mental shake. Now I was being ridiculous. Even if Uncle Hal had been involved in Vern March's accident, it took place a long time ago. What difference could it possibly make after all these years? A tiny voice inside my brain whispered, *There is no statute of limitations on murder.*

I bolted upright. I had to get up and get over these foolish imaginings. Uncle Hal was not a murderer. I'd always seen him as a big, strong teddy bear, a protector, who'd never let anyone hurt me. Why, when he'd heard that Todd had taken a shot at me, he'd threatened to . . . to kill him. Of course, that was just anger talking. If anyone hurt Leslie or Lucas, I'd be out for blood, too. That doesn't mean I'd actually take someone's life. Right?

I said a quick prayer for strength and got out of bed.

I HAD DRESSED carefully, choosing black silk pants, a maroon satin shirt, black flats, and a string of gray pearls. I felt comfortable but knew—okay, hoped—I looked nice enough to pass Mom's scrutiny.

I slowly took the cake I'd made from the passenger seat. Thankfully, it was beautiful out so I didn't have to worry about rain. I bumped the car door shut with my hip and walked slowly up Violet's driveway.

Lucas and Leslie, their blond hair gleaming in the sunlight, flung open the door. They'd apparently been watching for me.

"We're so glad you're here!" Lucas shouted, tugging excitedly at his Virginia Tech jersey. "We've been waiting for you all day!"

I laughed. "But I'm early! It's not even eleven o'clock."

"We know," Leslie said, looking like a miniature pop star in her flared jeans and lacy top. "But it seemed like *forever*. Can we see the cake?"

"Yes. Come on, I'll put it on your mom's cake plate." I glanced around the living room and saw Dad sitting in Vi's plush blue rocker, watching the parade. In his tan cardigan and brown slacks, he looked alone and sad and pitiful, even though he broke into a huge grin upon seeing me. Okay, he actually looked like normal; but knowing what I knew made him appear sad and pitiful to me. "Hi, Dad."

"Hi, honey. You look like best-in-show at the county fair. Whatcha got there?"

"It's a chocolate cake with buttercream icing."

"Hmph. I might have my dessert first, then."

"Plus, this cake is *gorgeous*, Grandpa," Leslie gushed.

I smiled. "You haven't even seen it yet, silly girl."

"Still, I know it'll look as great as it tastes."

"Nuh-uh." Lucas shook his head. "I think it'll look good, Aunt Daphne, but it'll *taste* best."

"Well, stop arguing over it and give me a hunk of it," Dad said. "I'm starving."

"Oh, you're not," Mom told him, coming out of the kitchen. She looked at me. "I was beginning to wonder if you were still coming."

The woman I'd seen every day for the first twenty years of my life suddenly looked like a stranger. Her red lipstick seemed garish and her makeup too pristine. Although she'd always pre-ferred V-neck sweaters, the spice-colored one she wore today was a bit too low cut. Okay, she, too, looked absolutely normal, but knowing what I knew . . .

"I need to put this down," I said with a nod toward the cake in my hands.

"Yeah," Leslie said. "Come on."

I followed the twins into the kitchen, where Violet was adding sage to the dressing. The smell brought back memories of our grandmother mixing up dressing every Thanksgiving while I stood by her side and waited for a taste test.

"Happy Thanksgiving," I said.

"Happy Thanksgiving! Pretty outfit!" She smiled, her cheeks dimpling. "As soon as you set the cake down, would you taste the dressing for me? See if it has enough sage?"

There it was—the taste test. "I'd be honored."

Our gazes locked, and I bit my lower lip.

"I miss her, too," Vi said softly.

I put the cake on the table and dipped a spoon in the dressing. "It's perfect." I took the glass cake plate from atop the buffet.

"You might have to wash it off," Vi said.

I scoffed. "As if."

Lucas, unable to stand the suspense, opened the cake box. "Cool!"

"Ooooh, it's so pretty," Leslie said. "I love the flowers!"

I lifted the square cake—along with its doily and cake board—out of the box. "I thought you would. I also thought you might want to take the pearls and make necklaces for your dolls or something."

Leslie threw her arms around my waist. "Thanks, Aunt Daphne!"

"I want the piece with the most icing," Lucas said.

Mom came into the kitchen. "What's all the fuss about?"

"Daphne's cake," Vi said. "Isn't it pretty?"

Mom looked at the cake. "Mmm-hmm."

"Is there anything I can help with?" I asked, trying to shrug off the slight.

"Not now," Mom said. "Your sister and I have everything

taken care of." She flicked another glance at the cake. "I'll put this on the counter, out of the way."

"Thanks," I said, trying not to grit my teeth. "I guess I'll take cleanup duty. In the meantime, I'll go hang with Dad."

"Yeah," Lucas said. "Let's go watch the parade."

"They're gonna be showing horses in a minute," Leslie said.

We went back out into the living room. Jason, Violet's husband and the twins' father, had already joined Dad in front of the TV. With Jason's red hair and boyish freckles, I used to say he was "Richie Cunningham, all-American boy-next-door."

"Hi," he said, getting up to let Leslie, Lucas, and me sit on the couch.

"You don't have to do that," I said.

"I do if I don't want these guys climbing all over me. When you're around, everybody else takes a backseat." He sat down in a floral armchair that matched the sofa. "How's business?"

"Pretty good," I said, not wanting to get into the gory details of the past few days.

"Have you got some business cards?" Dad asked. "I'll take some home and hand them out up our way."

"I'll get you some out of the car before I leave," I said, wondering how many people would be interested in hiring a baker two hours away. "Thanks, Dad. I really appreciate your support."

"Well, I'm proud of you."

"By the way," I said, "I spoke with Aunt Nancy last night."

Dad nodded. "Hal get back home all right?"

"He wasn't back when I was talking with her. She said he was on a hunting trip."

"Yeah, he and the Duncan brothers went hunting out on Old Man Boyd's land."

"Is Mr. Boyd still alive?" Jason asked. "He was old even when I was a little boy."

Dad chuckled. "The Lord'll have to knock that one on the head on Judgment Day."

"Look, look, look," Leslie squealed. "Here come the horses!"

While we watched, Mom came in and announced that lunch was ready. Still, I knew who my allies were, and I sat right there with Leslie and Lucas until the horses went by. After all, it was only a few seconds. Then Jason turned off the television, and we filed into the kitchen.

Dad said the blessing, and we sat down around the table. I'd planned to sit next to Dad, but the twins sandwiched me between them. That was fine, too; I don't get to spend enough time with these sweet kids.

Unfortunately, it also put me directly across the table from my mother. Every time I looked at her, I thought of Vern March. I tried to avoid her, but it was still an awkward meal to get through.

After everybody had eaten as much of the main course as we could hold, Jason retrieved the cake and presented it with a flourish. "Thanks, Daph, but didn't you bring anything for the rest of the family?" He picked up his fork and pretended he was about to dive in.

"Dad, don't make me come over there," Leslie said.

Jason laughed as he got dessert plates and a serving knife.

"I get the first piece," Lucas announced.

"Nuh-uh. I do!" Leslie said.

"*I* get the first piece," Jason added, looking back and forth between his son and daughter.

He served himself the first slice and then wisely cut two slices so the twins could be served simultaneously. He gave the next slice to Dad, and then began to pass a piece to Mom.

"No, thank you," she said. "I'll just have a cup of coffee. I've had too much of this wonderful food to eat another bite."

She hates me. She's always hated me, a little voice whispered in my mind.

"I'll take it," Vi said, getting up to get Mom some coffee. "It looks yummy."

"It is," said Lucas, who'd already plowed through half his slice. "Can I have Grandma's piece?"

"Eat what you've got," Jason said, "and if you're still hungry, you can have more."

"Me too?" Leslie asked, icing at the corners of her mouth.

"You too." Jason grinned and handed me a plate. "Good thing you don't bring cakes over here every day or we'd all be roly-polies."

"Not me," Lucas said. "I get lots of exercise."

I put my arms around him and his sister. "Can I take these two home with me?"

"Yes!" Leslie cried. "Can we? Please, Mom?"

"We don't have school tomorrow," Lucas begged. "And we don't go to Grandma and Grandpa Armstrong's house until Saturday. *And* we've never spent the night at Aunt Daphne's new house."

"Please?" Leslie asked again.

Vi and Mom exchanged a glance. Mom appeared to be livid.

"But, guys," Violet said, "your grandparents are here."

"So?" Lucas swiped the back of his hand across his mouth. "We've been with them since yesterday, and we'll see them tomorrow when we get back home."

Leslie nodded her agreement.

I almost laughed out loud. When the twins team up, you'd better watch out.

Violet sighed. "Daphne, are you sure it's no trouble?"

"It'll be my pleasure," I said. "Besides, it'll give you and Mom a chance to hit those early-bird sales."

"Without dragging us along," Lucas mumbled.

"Yeah," Leslie said. "We can stay in a nice warm bed instead of being out in the cold with all those people who have diseases we could catch."

At that, I *did* laugh out loud. Dad did, too.

He loves me. He's always loved me.

AFTER DESSERT, I quickly went to the kitchen. I opened the dishwasher and returned to the dining room to collect the dirty dishes.

"We'll help you, Aunt Daphne," Leslie said.

She, Lucas, and I each carried a stack of dishes into the kitchen.

Mom followed us. "You children didn't help your mother and me with cleanup yesterday evening."

"That's because you all didn't have anything else to do," Lucas said. "We're helping Aunt Daphne so we can go to her house!"

With a look of irritation thrown my way, Mom announced she was going upstairs to read for a while.

"Come on," Lucas told me. "Let's get on the stick."

"DO YOU WANT to make Grandpa a bitty cake?" I suggested when we got to my house. "He can take it home with him tomorrow."

"Can we make a bitty cake for us to take home with us tomorrow, too?" Lucas asked.

"Of course." I smiled. "Let's get washed up."

Four feet thundered down the hall to the bathroom. I lagged behind and patiently waited my turn. I was hoping to set a good example, but as Lucas and Leslie jostled each other shoulder to shoulder and got water all over the vanity and the floor, I'm not sure they even realized I was there.

"Bitty cakes" are what I call six-inch round cakes. Often used for the last tier of a round wedding cake, six-inch single-layer cakes are perfect for small, intimate occasions, "just because" gifts, or little pick-me-ups. The children *love* them.

The kids dried their hands and turned to me with a triumphant and expectant gleam.

"Go into the kitchen and put on your aprons. I'll be right there."

I keep two red canvas aprons hanging on pegs next to mine in the kitchen for my junior bakers. They ran to the kitchen and left me to wash.

I wiped up all the water, washed my hands, and joined the children in the kitchen.

"Leslie, what job would you like?"

She smoothed her apron. "I wanna do the borders."

"Great. Lucas?"

"I wanna do something radical like Chef Duff from *Ace of Cakes*."

"No saws in my kitchen, mister."

He laughed. "I wanna paint with one of those sprayers."

"Well," I said, "I don't have an air gun, but I do have spray frosting."

"Awesome!"

"Can I try, too?" Leslie asked.

"No," Lucas said angrily. *"I'm* doing the paint. Besides, you already said you were doing the borders!"

"Maybe you can paint the borders," I suggested to Leslie.

"But her paint will get on mine!"

"Okay, how about if she paints the bottom borders? That way her paint won't touch your paint on the top of the cake."

"Fine," Lucas said.

"Is that okay with you, Leslie?"

"Yep!"

An hour later, we had two of the weirdest-looking bitty cakes I'd ever seen. But they were precious. Dad's cake had a turkey on it. I'd piped outlines for feathers, and Lucas had filled them in with different-colored spray frostings. I'd never seen a turkey with purple, green, blue, *and* orange feathers; but, hey, anything's possible. Especially when you're eleven. The turkey cake had a top white shell border and a bottom shell border with sections of yellow, pink, and light green.

The cake Lucas and Leslie made for themselves was even wilder. They put so much icing on it, I was afraid the poor cake might collapse. Leslie wanted flowers. I'd previously taught her how to make a rose, and she put three white roses on the cake and generously told Lucas he could paint them. He painted the roses blue, but apparently, three icing roses would not provide enough of a sugar rush, so he piped a mountain off to the side. At first he sprayed the mountain green. Then he decided a volcano would be even cooler if red dripped down the front, which more or less made the mountain look like a brownish glob.

"Eww," Leslie said. "That looks like poo!"

"Cool." Lucas laughed. "I get the poo piece!"

The three of us dissolved into a fit of giggles.

When we stopped laughing and started cleaning up our mess, Leslie paused to listen.

"I hear something."

"You're just trying to get out of working," I teased, putting Dad's cake into a box.

"No," Lucas said, "I hear it, too. It sounds like a kid crying."

"The cat. I forgot to feed her this morning."

"I didn't know you had a cat, Aunt Daphne!" Leslie exclaimed, as she and Lucas followed me out onto the porch.

"I don't exactly," I said. "She showed up one day, and I supposed she kind of came with the house."

"She's pretty," Leslie said.

Lucas squinted. "What's wrong with her eye?"

"I don't know. If I could catch her, I could take her to the vet. I might stop by his office on Monday anyway to see if I could give her some vitamins or something . . . you know, in her food."

The cat's hunger brought her a cautious step closer.

"Come on," I told Leslie and Lucas. "Let's sit over here on the step and be really quiet. Maybe she'll come and eat."

When the cat was confident we weren't close enough to catch her, she eased up to the bowl. She eyed us suspiciously one last time before crunching her food.

"What's her name?" Leslie whispered.

"I haven't given her one yet. I only found out she was here a few days ago."

"How do you know it's a 'she'?" Lucas asked softly. "It could be a boy."

"It could be," I said, "but I think it's a girl."

"Me too," Leslie said. "She's beautiful."

"Except for the eye," Lucas said.

Mentally, I had to admit they were both right. The cat, with her long gray and white hair and fluffy tail, was very pretty, but the one empty eye socket made you cringe and wonder what horrors she might have suffered.

"If she had a little black eye patch," Lucas said, "that would be cool."

"And a pirate hat," Leslie agreed.

Lucas's lowered voice took on the semblance of an English accent. "Aye, mate. Welcome to me crew."

"Cap'n Jack at your service." Leslie's accent was every bit as bad. She broke into a grin and resumed her natural voice. "That's it. We should call her Sparrow."

"Yeah." Lucas gave her a high five.

The cat looked up, poised to run if anyone made a move. We were still, and she resumed eating.

"Sparrow it is," I whispered.

I HAVE TO admit, I was exhausted when I took the children home on Friday. But it was a good tired, a happy tired. A just-got-back-from-vacation-and-need-a-rest tired.

Lucas and Leslie made a full-on frontal assault on their house at approximately 11:15 a.m.

"We made you a bitty cake, Grandpa," Leslie said excitedly. "It's not called a 'bitty cake' because you're like an old biddy or anything. It's because the cake is little."

Before Dad could respond, Lucas added, "It's for you to take home. We know Grandma doesn't make things like that for you."

"Where is this cake?" Jason asked quickly. "I'd like to see it."

"Aunt Daphne's got it," Lucas said.

"Yeah, but not because we argued over it or anything," Leslie said. "We just all decided it would be best if she carried it."

I showed the cake to Dad and Jason. Dad declared it to be the coolest turkey he'd ever seen.

"Do you like the borders?" Leslie asked.

"They're magnificent," Dad said. "Who did those? Daphne?"

"No." Leslie grinned. "It was me."

"Wow! I didn't know you could do that!"

"How about the turkey feathers?" Lucas asked. "I *painted* those like Chef Duff does on his show."

"This is incredible. A masterpiece. Are you sure I should eat it?" Dad smiled at me over the top of the children's heads. "Gloria, come here. You have to see this."

"What flavor is it?" Jason asked.

"Yellow," Leslie said. "Grandpa's favorite."

Lucas lightly elbowed his dad. "Don't worry, Dad. We've got one of our own."

"And it's truly a sight to behold," I said.

The kids started giggling.

I laughed, too. "I'll go back out to the car and get it."

"I'll go with you," Violet offered as she and Mom emerged from the kitchen. "I want to tell you about all the bargains we found."

"Come look at the cake we made," Lucas said.

"I'll see it in a minute, sweetheart. I need to talk with Aunt Daphne first."

Though she was wearing jeans and a silly sweatshirt, Violet's expression told me she was deadly serious. My mind went into automatic defense mode.

"What?" I asked sharply when we stepped outside.

"Mom's upset about the way you treated her yesterday."

"The way *I* treated *her*? She was the Frost Queen! She was ticked because I didn't arrive at daybreak to peel zucchini or whatever." I glared at Violet. "And you're the one who told me *not* to come early."

"I know, but you barely spoke to her."

"Do you blame me? Oh, wait, of course you do, or else we

wouldn't be having this conversation." I huffed. "But, then, you aren't the one she criticizes at every turn. You're the golden child."

"That's not true."

"She told you about her affair."

Violet took my arm and steered me toward the driveway. "Keep your voice down."

"How'd that come about, Vi? Were the two of you watching *Bridges of Madison County* when she happened to blurt out 'I did that'?"

"Don't be absurd."

"No, tell me," I said. "I really want to know."

"Okay, fine. She was talking to me about your divorce from Todd. She said she might understand it better if you were in love with another man but that she couldn't believe you'd rather be alone than with Todd."

"The man tried to kill me."

"I know that, Daph, but she doesn't think so. She thinks Todd was only trying to scare you."

I shook my head in disgust. "So, what? Mom says, 'I could see her leaving for someone else. I almost did that once myself'?"

"Basically, yes. And then we talked about it a bit."

"But neither of you felt compelled to share that information with me?"

"You had enough on your mind." Violet looked at the ground. "But I think it did Mom good to . . . to unload that burden."

"That burden? Oh, poor Mom, she had to shoulder the responsibility of cheating on our father by herself for all those years."

"It *was* a burden. She still feels guilty, not just for what she did to Dad and to us but to Vern March as well."

"You mean because Uncle Hal ran Vern out of town?"

"He beat up the man, Daph, and threatened to kill him."

"He was looking out for our family. Somebody had to."

"It was thirty years ago. Mom made a mistake. Can you please look out for our family *now* and let this whole thing rest?"

I sighed. "I don't think I can. Not until I know the truth."

Violet sighed, too. "What difference does it make?"

"I don't know." I rubbed my hand across my forehead. "It could explain why Joanne Hayden is trying to ruin my business, though."

"Joanne Hayden?"

I nodded. "She's Vern's granddaughter."

"Granddaughter?" Violet gasped. "I didn't even know Vern was married."

"There's more to this affair than meets the eye, Vi," I said. "There has to be."

CHAPTER
seven

I WENT HOME, put some food out for Sparrow, turned the porch light on, and headed toward the Blue Ridge Parkway and Uncle Hal. Sure, it was nearly a two-hour drive, but a relaxing road trip might do me some good. My telling Violet about Vern's marriage stopped our argument about Mom—at least for the time being—but I was still desperate for answers. I'd always thought Mom was devoted to Dad. There were times when I questioned her loyalty to me, but until Tuesday night, I'd never doubted her allegiance to him.

At least I was able to enjoy being with the children the night before. At first I worried about Annabelle's intruder coming after me, but then I realized I was being overly dramatic—the very thing I'd accused Violet and the other townspeople of being. How could anyone, with the exception of Annabelle, possibly know I'd had the diary? And even if they did, why would anyone think I still had it now that she was back home for the funeral?

The service was tomorrow. I planned to go; I wanted to be there for Annabelle. I have to admit, though, I had other, less altruistic reasons for going. I was secretly hoping Joanne Hayden would be there. I wondered what she looked like—whether or not she resembled Vern. I wondered how she'd act when we finally met face-to-face.

I was also hoping Ben would be there. I wondered how he'd spent Thanksgiving. With his parents probably. They'd been like an extra set of parents to me when Ben and I were growing up.

When I got to Uncle Hal and Aunt Nancy's house, her car was gone but his pickup truck was in the driveway. I knew that traditionally Aunt Nancy spent the Friday after Thanksgiving shopping, and then she put their Christmas tree up on Saturday. Uncle Hal was a couch potato on Friday, resting up for Saturday tree duty. Hopefully, the couple remained true to form and I hadn't wasted a trip.

I parked on the street to avoid blocking the driveway should Aunt Nancy come home. Taking a deep breath, I got out of the car and walked to the front door. I rang the doorbell and heard Chester the Chihuahua come barking to the door. Uncle Hal ineffectively told Chester to be quiet as he opened the door.

"Hey, girl!" Uncle Hal said, his face breaking into a smile. "What brings you by?"

"Well, you didn't drop in when you were down my way, so I had to come see you."

"Come on in." He scooped Chester into his beefy arms so the tiny white dog wouldn't run outside.

"Hi, Chessie." I patted the dog's head before taking off my coat and draping it over the back of a chair.

"Nancy's out shopping."

"I figured she would be. I'm here to see you."

Uncle Hal sat down on the couch. "Sounds serious."

"It is." I sat on the overstuffed chair where I'd hung my coat. "It's about Mom."

He frowned. "She sick?"

"Not the way you mean."

"Daphne," he said, but his admonition lacked any serious wallop.

He looked so much like Dad. Same white hair, same blue eyes. He was just a heavier, stockier build. I looked away. "Tell me about Mom and Vern March."

"Sounds like you already know."

I looked back at him. "Did you hear about Yodel Watson's death?"

"I heard."

No wonder Uncle Hal was such an excellent poker player. Who could read that face?

"She kept a journal," I said. "Her daughter asked me to get it for her."

Still no reaction from Uncle Hal.

"I . . . uh . . . read about Mom and Vern."

"What'd the book say?"

I let my gaze wander away from my uncle. I couldn't stand to say the words while looking at a man who resembled Dad so much. "That they were having an affair. That Mom was planning to divorce Dad." The tears started falling before I'd even realized they were there.

Uncle Hal crossed the room and pulled me to my feet and into a hug. "I'd hoped you'd never find out."

I sniffed. "It's all true? All of it?"

He nodded.

"How could she?" I asked. "How could she do that to him? To us?"

"I don't know, baby."

When I pulled away from Uncle Hal, Chester was at our feet. I picked him up as Uncle Hal and I sat back down.

"I just don't get it." I snuggled Chester. "For her to do that and then to lecture me when I divorced Todd."

"He got off easy for what he did to you," Uncle Hal said. "If I had my way—" He shook his head. "But, yeah, Gloria had no right to pass judgment. I told her so, too."

"Does Dad know?"

"I don't think so. I didn't tell him, and if he'd heard it from anyone else, I'm sure he would've talked to me about it." He squinted and tilted his head. "You ain't planning to tell him. Are you?"

"No. It would only hurt him." I sat Chester on the floor and he trotted over to lie at Uncle Hal's feet. "I wouldn't hurt Dad for anything. I wish I hadn't found out myself."

"I wish you hadn't, either. Did you tell Violet?"

"She already knew. Believe it or not, Mom told her."

"I take it the two of you are on opposite sides of the fence on this one."

I nodded. "I want to confront Mom. Vi says I should let it go."

"Your sister's right. Let this mess stay buried in the past, where it belongs."

"I'm not sure I can," I said. "I *needed* her to be there for me when I was going through my divorce with Todd. That entire ordeal—having Todd arrested, testifying at his trial and sentencing hearing, facing not only him but the media—" I nearly choked on my frustration. "She wasn't there for me, Uncle Hal, because she felt *I* was betraying my husband."

"Don't let this eat you up. It'll only end up hurting you worse. Thirty years ago, I did everything in my power to protect my brother's family. Dredging up the past now . . ." He closed his eyes. "Trust me. It's better if you don't."

"How—" I swallowed. "How did you protect us, Uncle Hal?"

He opened his eyes but stared up at the ceiling. "I ran Vern March out of town."

We both fell silent then. The only noise was Chester's toenails clicking on the hardwood floor when he spotted a toy and went to retrieve it.

Finally, I spoke. "He must not have cared very much about Mom, then."

"I can be fairly persuasive—or I could be, back in the day." Uncle Hal's voice was softer now, tired. He gave me a wan half smile. "And I always took care of my baby brother. Even though there's not that much difference in our ages, I prided myself on being the big brother, the protector."

"I know." I grinned, although I felt an almost overwhelming urge to cry again. "To me you were always Batman to Dad's Robin." I had to lighten the conversation before Aunt Nancy came home to find me bawling. Okay, to be completely honest, I had to change the subject before I asked questions I wasn't 100 percent sure I wanted answered.

"So," I said, "is Aunt Nancy doing her part to help the economy today?"

Uncle Hal gave a chortle that held more than a hint of relief. "Depends on whose economy we're talking about. I don't doubt she's boosting the retailers' economy, but I might be eating peanut butter sandwiches for a month."

"You know better," I said, laughing.

"Yeah," he admitted. "We could live on yesterday's leftovers for two weeks."

We chatted about the family then—Vi, Jason, Lucas and Leslie, as well as Uncle Hal and Aunt Nancy's children and in-laws. We shared funny stories for a half hour or so, and then I stood and put on my coat.

Uncle Hal walked me to the door. "That other matter . . . it's over, right?"

I nodded.

"Good." He kissed my cheek. "Be careful driving home."

BEFORE GOING HOME, I stopped by the Save-A-Buck to pick up my check and the glass cake plate I'd used for my display. Juanita was leaving as I went in. She took my arm and pulled me back outside the store.

"I'm so sorry for your troubles," she said. "I know your cake did not poison that lady."

"Thank you. Hopefully everyone else will realize that, too."

"I pray that they will. You are a good person." She smiled. "I bought one of your white cakes, and my family enjoyed it very much."

"I'm glad."

"This will pass." She nodded. "It will pass."

A lump gathered in my throat. I barely knew this woman and she was treating me like a lifelong friend. "Thank you."

Juanita left and I went on into the store. En route to the office I was stopped by a diminutive old lady with two iron-gray braids hanging to her waist. The pigtails made me wonder if Willie Nelson's mother might still be living—in southwest Virginia.

"I understand you found Yodel's corpse." For such a small woman, she certainly did have a booming voice. Every head in sight turned our way.

"I . . . yes. I did." I kept my voice low, hoping she'd take the hint. She didn't.

"I heard she was poisoned."

"I don't know how I can make this any clearer. The woman didn't even see the cake I—"

"Oh, no, I don't think it was you. I just wonder who the police think did the old gal in. Has anybody brought my name into this?"

I frowned.

"I'm China York." She stuck out her hand.

I shook her hand, noticing she had a strong grip for a seemingly ancient woman. She also had calluses; she was clearly still a hard worker.

"Me and old Yodel had quite a round at church a few years back. I thought it'd only be fair for me to know if I'm a suspect."

"I'm not privy to the police investigation," I said, wondering if I should refer her to Joanne. "But I don't see why you'd be a suspect, Ms. York. An argument at church is hardly a motive for murder."

"Right." She grinned. "I've got an alibi in case I get hauled in for questioning."

"That's always good to have . . . I guess."

"You bet. Well, good luck with your business. Things'll likely pick back up once Yodel's in the ground."

I stood slack-jawed as Ms. York spun around and walked away.

I finally made it to the office and collected my check and cake plate. Mr. Franklin had put the cake plate in a Save-A-

Buck bag, presumably so no one would see me leaving with it. Heaven forbid anyone think the Save-A-Buck had sold possibly tainted cakes. This, despite the fact that Save-A-Buck had merely taken my name off the cakes and sold them anyway. If Mr. Franklin had been truly concerned, he'd have dumped my cakes in the garbage. He knew they were good, but I'd been tried and convicted in the court of public opinion. He and his store could not openly associate with me until that conviction was overturned. From a business standpoint, I could understand this logic. From a personal standpoint, this was merely another stab in an already gaping wound.

I was weary and bone tired when I got home. I wanted to take a bath, have a cup of hot tea, get into my favorite pajamas—

That's where my thoughts—and plans—were interrupted by the inevitable knock on the door. Could I get away with not answering it? Probably not. My car was in the driveway, my lights were on, and with one recent murder, someone would probably call the police if I ignored the knock.

I went to the front door and took a look through the peephole. Myra. I stifled a groan.

Maybe she wouldn't stay long—and maybe there really is a Bigfoot.

I opened the door.

Before I could greet her, Myra said, "Honey, you look awful." She placed her hand on my forehead. "You're not hot. Do you feel sick? Could it be something you ate yesterday?"

I smiled and led her into the living room.

"I'm just tired is all," I said, dropping onto the couch.

Myra sat in the pink-and-white gingham chair, kicked off her shoes, and tucked her feet under her. "I only dropped in to tell you how good your cakes were. Everybody loved them. Carl Jr. even took what was left of the spice cake home with him."

"Good. Thanks for sharing that with me. It seems some people in town think I'm the Confectionary Killer."

"I hate that, sweetie. That's probably why you feel bad. Nerves. But this will blow over. You'll see."

"So I've been told. According to China York, 'things'll pick back up once Yodel's in the ground.'"

"China's never been one to mince words. Don't be offended. It's her way."

"Is she always so cold?"

Myra pursed her lips. "Don't know that I'd call her cold." She cocked her head. "Hard-nosed. Is that the word I'm looking for? And she sure ain't two-faced. She didn't like Yodel when Yodel was living; she ain't gonna pretend to like her now that she's dead."

"She asked me if she was a suspect. Why would she think I'd know?"

"Because you found the body. It's only natural you'd be kept in the loop—unless the police thought you killed Yodel, which I don't think they do."

"Why in the world would I be kept in the loop? I'm not next of kin. I'm not involved in the investigation. I don't think I'm a suspect, even if Joanne Hayden wants everyone to think I am."

"Why do you say that?"

"I think she's trying to ruin my business."

"Joanne can be pretty vocal," Myra said, "but I don't know why she'd do that. What could she possibly have against you?"

"I don't know. What do you know about her?"

She shrugged. "She and Bill got married right out of high school, which wasn't all that long ago. They have a daughter in elementary school."

"Before that, I mean." I leaned forward. "Who are her parents?"

"Jonah and Peggy March. Why? Would they have it in for you for some reason?"

"I don't know. Perhaps I'm just being paranoid. Maybe Joanne is concerned about the health and well-being of the community and thinks a cake decorator would make everybody get fat." I sighed. "Do her parents live around here?"

"Her mother does. Her daddy's dead." Myra clicked her tongue. "Killed himself a couple years after his daddy, Vern, died."

I nearly fell off the couch. "What?"

"Uh-huh. Poor Jonah had kind of a rough life from what I hear, and he was always on the gloomy side. Depressed, I reckon you could say. Vern died in a car wreck, and I guess Jonah lived with that for as long as he could. Eventually, he shot himself."

"Man. No wonder she doesn't like me. She must hate my entire family."

"Who? Joanne? Why?"

I looked at Myra, realized I'd said too much, and quickly tried to claw my way out of the pit I'd tumbled into.

"B-because of Vern," I said. "My uncle Hal . . . argued with Vern, and then Vern left town. If he hadn't moved away, he might not have had the accident."

"Now, honey, you don't know that. I firmly believe that when your number's up, your number's up. He was destined to die when he died. Take my great-aunt Mamie. She smoked a pipe for as long as anybody in the family could remember. Everybody thought she'd die from lung cancer or something. But not long after her one hundredth birthday, she died in a horrible motorcycle accident."

"Your one-hundred-year-old great-aunt Mamie drove a motorcycle?"

"Oh, no, honey—that'd be nuts. She hitched a ride on the back of one when she was on her way to the store to get some tobacco." Myra examined her thumbnail before resuming her narrative. "We'd all been telling her for years not to smoke, but nobody ever thought to warn her not to hitchhike. You couldn't tell that old lady a blessed thing anyway, though. She thought she knew it all, and she was gonna do whatever suited her. Still, when her number was up, it was up. It just so happens it was Great-Aunt Mamie's destiny to ride out of this world on the back of a hog."

"I guess." I needed a minute to collect my scattered thoughts. "Would you like something to drink? Tea, maybe?"

"No, thanks, dear. Now, you said Vern and your uncle argued about something. What was it?"

"Uh—" I forced out a laugh. "You tell me. It was about thirty years ago."

"I've only lived her for twenty-three." She chewed her bottom lip a moment. "I'll tell you who would've known—Yodel. That woman made it her business to know everything about everyone."

"Too bad I can't ask her."

"Yeah, but there's bound to be someone else who knows. I'll ask around."

"No! I mean, it's not all that important. Like I said, it was a long time ago, and I'm probably being paranoid. I've had a rough week."

"You sure have, sweetie. I'll go now and let you get some rest. Call me if you need anything."

"I will, Myra. Thanks."

After she left, I abandoned my notion of relaxing in a warm bath. Instead I found myself drawn to the computer.

I opened it to my homepage—my website. I had no new

visitors, forum posts, or requests for information. I hadn't really expected any, given the holiday weekend, but a nagging voice in my head wondered if the lack of interest in my site was actually due to my now murderous reputation.

I surfed on to some genealogy sites, hoping to find something—anything—about Vern or Jonah March. I found both men's Social Security death records. The information was basic and useless: name, last known residence, date of birth, and date of death. There was no cause of death listed, no spouse or family members named. The record pretty much stated "this person existed and then died."

I searched for over an hour. I found nothing on Vern March's marriage or on Jonah March's birth. Despite my search, I failed to see what difference this knowledge would make anyway. How could Vern's wife affect Joanne's feelings toward me and my family? It had to be that Joanne despised us because Uncle Hal ran her grandfather out of town, taking him away from his family.

I rested my head on the back of my chair and tried to recall whether Vern had ever mentioned a son. I realized I was a kid myself—a stupid, blind, naive, trusting kid—when Vern was spending so much time at our house but I'd have remembered if Vern mentioned a son. Of course, family was obviously not at the top of either of their priority lists, unless it was starting a new one together.

I closed my eyes, and suddenly it was like a movie trailer in my mind. I saw Uncle Hal telling me, "I can be pretty persuasive."

CHAPTER
eight

A T 2:00 a.m., I'd woken up on the couch with a stiff neck and then had gone to bed with my clothes still on. I'd tried to make up for last night by soaking in the tub this morning, but the water had gotten cold long before I'd worked out the kinks in my aching muscles. I could use a hot stone massage, and I promised myself I'd get one as soon as this mess was behind me.

While I was in the tub, I had the oven preheating and a batch of yeast dough rising. Now the dough was ready to be kneaded. I decided to take cinnamon rolls to Annabelle and her family before the funeral. Besides, it was nice to be able to take some of my frustrations out on the dough. Afterward, I put the dough back into the bowl, covered it with plastic wrap, and ate my breakfast while the dough rested.

I rinsed out my cereal bowl and put it in the dishwasher. I took the dough from the bowl and rolled it into a rectangle before brushing the dough with butter and liberally sprinkling a cinnamon–brown sugar mixture on top. I rolled the dough up and scored it in one-and-a-half-inch increments with a knife. Using unwaxed, unflavored dental floss, I cut the dough—floss somehow cuts it more neatly than a knife. I then put the rolls into a greased pan with their sides touching and put the pan in the oven.

It was a relaxing process for me. The kitchen was the one place I always felt in control. I smiled to myself and headed to the bedroom to change. The last thing I needed was to be late. But before I got there, my phone rang. Somehow I knew instantly that it was Ben.

"Hey," he said. "How was your Thanksgiving?"

"It was nice. Leslie and Lucas came home with me to spend the night. We had a blast once it was just the three of us," I laughed. "How about you?"

"Mine was good. Doesn't sound as much fun as yours, though. Sally and I went to my mom and dad's. They sold their house and bought a condo in Jonesborough a few years ago. Nowhere for us to sleep there anymore so we came home last night."

"That's . . . wonderful. I'm sure your parents enjoyed having you there."

"Oh, yeah."

"I'm sorry to rush off the phone," I said, "but I'm getting ready to go to Mrs. Watson's funeral."

"That's actually why I called. I'm going and thought if you were, too, I could come by and pick you up."

"Are you sure? I need to drop off some cinnamon rolls to Annabelle first."

"No problem. I know you hate these things and that you're probably feeling kind of awkward about the whole situation."

My jaw dropped slightly. He still knew me after all those years. "Thanks," I said softly.

"I'll be there in about half an hour?"

"Okay." He hung up and as I set my phone in its cradle, I couldn't help but wonder if I'd soon be meeting the elusive Sally.

As soon as Ben got there, I noticed he was alone. Okay, as soon as he got there, I noticed that he looked terrific in his dark brown suit. It was sort of a mahogany color, I guess you could say, and it somehow brought out the blue in his eyes. *Then* I saw that he was alone.

"Where's Sally?" I asked as casually as I could.

"Home."

"She didn't want to come?"

"Uh, she probably did, but it's hardly appropriate." He was looking at me as if trying to decide whether I was under the influence of alcohol, drugs, or both. "I did tell you Sally's my dog, didn't I? She's well behaved, but I don't think she'd be welcome at the funeral home."

"Oh, right." I could feel myself blushing from the tips of my toes to the top of my head. "I'll just put these cinnamon rolls in a tin, then, and we can be on our way."

ALL THE WAY to Annabelle's—or rather, Yodel's—house, Ben looked like he was trying to keep from laughing. I knew this from the covert glances I made in his direction. I mentally smacked myself for making such assumptions.

We arrived at Mrs. Watson's house to find that Annabelle

and her family were the only people there. Mrs. Watson's siblings, sister-in-law, and friends had agreed to meet at the funeral home and then come back to the house after the service. It gave us a nice opportunity to meet Annabelle's husband and daughters, though. While Ben and Mr. Fontaine made small talk in the living room, Annabelle and I stepped into the kitchen. She thanked me for the rolls and placed them on the table.

"How are you?" I asked. "Was it good for you to go through your mother's things alone?"

"It was." She smiled. "You know, especially when you grow up and move away, the distance between you and your mother often seems more than physical. At times she was like a stranger to me."

"I know the feeling."

"But I found so many things—trinkets, cards, notes, photos—that reminded me that I was never far from her heart." Her eyes glistened with unshed tears. "It meant so much."

"I'm sure it did." I wondered what I'd find if I went through my mother's things. Would I find precious keepsakes that would warm my heart, or would I find old love letters from Vern? Or from someone else?

Annabelle checked her watch. "I need to be going."

"I thought I'd attend the service . . . if that's okay."

"Of course, it is. Thank you, Daphne. You've been such a good friend to me."

I smiled at her and gently took her by the elbow. "Come on," I said. "Let's go."

BEN AND I drove behind the Fontaine family. When we arrived there was still some time before the funeral began and people were milling around, offering condolences and sharing stories. Ben excused himself to go and talk with someone he knew.

I spotted some people I knew as well. Mr. and Mrs. Dobbs sat in a pew near the front, both looking somber and unapproachable. Candy sat in the pew behind them, and given Myra's tale about Mrs. Dobbs's feelings toward her husband's employee, that might explain the bad vibes emanating from the couple.

Candy caught my eye and waved excitedly. I waved back, and she motioned for me to sit with her. I held up my index finger to signal "in a minute," and she nodded. I wasn't at all inclined to find myself in the middle of a Dobbs family feud.

Thankfully, Myra came up beside me. Her black dress—complete with black hat and veil—was very, well, *Dynasty*. For some reason, an image of Great-Aunt Mamie on "the hog" came to mind. Her funeral must have been quite an event.

"Hi, honey. You feeling better today?" she asked.

"A little." I looked around the crowded church. "I'm second-guessing my decision to come, though. I wanted to support Annabelle, but I don't have a clue as to who most of these people are."

"See that big man with the thin, white comb-over? That's Yodel's brother, Tar. He's talking to Joanne Hayden, and that's Tar's wife chatting with Bill."

Joanne wasn't at all whom I'd pictured. Of course, I'd pictured her pretty much as a stick figure with a head that was mostly mouth. But in reality, she was short and trim and had long, dark-blond spiral curls. Her back was to me, so I couldn't see whether or not she had an outrageously large mouth, but I doubted she did.

Myra scanned the crowd. "Melody's dead, but that's Harmony—Yodel's middle sister—over there in the loud floral dress, talking to the preacher." She clucked her tongue. "Harmony should've known better than to wear a print like that to a funeral, especially her sister's funeral. I know styles are limited for women her size, but I also know they have some beautiful clothes nowadays for extra plus-sized ladies."

I was barely listening to Myra as I stared at Tar and Joanne. It was now time to introduce myself.

"Excuse me, Myra."

I made my way over to Tar and Joanne. Neither of them noticed me.

"I haven't laid eyes on your grandmother," Tar said, "in . . . Lawd, I reckon, forty years or better. How is Gloria?"

Gloria?

"Don't ask me. I met the woman one time in my entire life, and that was by accident."

Tar shook his head. "That's a shame. Maybe y'all can get to know each other sometime."

Joanne scoffed. "There wasn't room in her life for my dad; I doubt there's room for me."

I turned and made my way back through the crowd as quickly as my suddenly spinning head would allow. I saw Ben, grabbed his arm, and steered him toward the vestibule.

"I have to leave." My breath came in labored spurts. "I've . . . got to . . . get out . . . of here."

"Are you all right?"

"No. If you . . . want to stay . . . I'll call Vi."

"I wouldn't hear of it. I'll take you home."

"DAPHNE, CALM DOWN. You're hyperventilating."

I handed Ben my door key. "Actually, I'm . . . having . . . a full . . . fledged . . . panic attack."

"Do you need to go to the emergency room?"

I vigorously shook my head and opened the car door. What I needed was to wake up from this lousy nightmare.

"Wait. Let me help you." Ben came around to my side of the Jeep and took my hand. "You look like you're about to faint."

If I wasn't afraid I really might pass out, I'd do a damsel-in-distress number to see if Ben would sweep me into his arms and carry me inside. It would be my luck for him to let me drop onto the porch and split my head open. Just because I finally figured out Sally is a dog didn't mean Ben was ready to be my knight in shining—or even tarnished—armor.

He unlocked the door and ushered me inside to the sofa. "Be right back."

He quickly returned with a bottle of water. "Do you need something stronger? I noticed a diet soda in the fridge. Or I'd be happy to make you some coffee or tea, if you'll tell me where to find everything."

"Water is fine, thanks."

Ben twisted off the top and handed it to me before sitting beside me on the couch. I took a sip. The cold water soothed my throat and sent an icy refreshment through my body. I was able to concentrate on slowing my heart rate and getting my emotions in check.

"Feeling better?" Ben asked.

I nodded.

"Want to tell me what freaked you out?"

"Yes and no," I said with a weary smile.

"You don't have to."

"While I'm reluctant to air my dirty laundry, I'd like your help in getting some answers."

"I'll do whatever I can."

"Even if it's something that winds up being off the record?"

"Of course. Do you think I'd help you only if there was a story in it for me?"

"No." I rested my head against the back of the sofa. "I hope you get a great scoop out of this. I just pray it doesn't involve anyone in my family." I went on to explain about Yodel's journal and admitted my reading about my mother and Vern March.

"Which is why you were interested in what happened to him," he said, piecing together quickly.

"Exactly. Violet confirmed the affair, and so did Uncle Hal. Uncle Hal even admitted to running Vern out of town in order to save our family." I took another drink of water. "Then I found out that Joanne Hayden is Vern's granddaughter. I never even knew Vern had a family."

"So Vern was married when he and your mother were . . . together?"

"I don't think so. It's my understanding that he married young and the girl's parents had the union annulled, even though she was pregnant."

"Did the girl raise the baby or give it up for adoption?"

"Ordinarily, I'd think the girl raised the child, but I'm wondering if maybe Vern did. The child did bear his surname." I looked down at my clasped hands. "Then today at the church, I heard Tar Watson asking Joanne about her grandmother. He said, 'I haven't seen Gloria in forty years.'"

I looked up at Ben to gauge his reaction. At first there wasn't one, but then understanding flooded his face.

"You think the Gloria they were talking about is your mother?"

"That's what I need to know. Jonah March could've been my half brother. Joanne might be my niece."

"Come on, Daphne. Do you honestly believe your mother could keep something like that a secret?"

"She kept the affair a secret," I reasoned.

"An affair is one thing. A child is an entirely different matter."

"I know, but still. Mom didn't grow up here. She could've had the baby and given him to Vern and no one here would know who the mother was." I tried to stop my shaking hands. Ben noticed and reached for me, settling his hand on top of mine.

"If a single man had suddenly showed up with a child, the gossip mill would've been running so hot it would've caught fire."

"I know," I said, "but what if he refused to reveal the mother's identity?"

"It would have made the gossip hounds even hungrier. They'd have eaten poor Vern alive if he didn't tell them."

"Then what if he made something up?"

"You do realize you're grasping at straws here, don't you?"

"Maybe I am, but what else am I supposed to do? Call my mother and ask her if she and Vern March had a child together before she married Dad?"

Ben shrugged.

I huffed out a breath. "I can't do that. She doesn't even know I know about the affair. Plus, I need to protect my dad."

"You said Violet knows about the affair, too. Would she know if there's more to it?"

"Maybe. That's where I'll start. But wouldn't she have told me everything she knows already?"

Ben inclined his head. "She didn't tell you about the affair until you asked her about it."

"Good point." I sighed, frustration etched across my face.

"So, provided Violet can't or won't provide answers, you want me to help you discover whether you and Joanne Hayden share . . . DNA."

"Do you think you can do it?"

"Probably. Anything else you need my assistance with?"

I squeezed his hand. "I want you to help me find out who poisoned Yodel Watson."

MY FIRST ORDER of business after Ben left was to call Violet.

"Did you go to the funeral?" she asked without any preliminaries.

"I went to the church, but I didn't stay."

"Why? Did someone say something?"

"No one came up and accused me of poisoning the deceased, if that's what you mean. But I did overhear something that threw me for a loop."

"What?" she inquired. I waited a moment before answering.

"Is there anything about Mom's affair with Vern March that you neglected to tell me?"

"Such as?" There was an edge creeping into Vi's voice.

"Did she know him before?"

"Before what? Before he and Dad started hanging out?"

"Yes."

"Not that I know of." My sister sighed loudly. "Daphne, why can't you simply leave this alone?"

"I heard Joanne Hayden and Tar Watson talking about Joanne's grandmother—Gloria."

"So what? Mom's not the only person in the world with that name. It's not like . . . Jehoshaphat or something," Violet said.

"No, but it's not like Mary or Anne, either. What if Mom was the girl Vern married when they were teenagers? What if they had a child together?"

"And you call *me* dramatic? Don't you think we'd have known if we had a half brother, Daph?"

"Not if Vern and his family raised the baby."

"You think Mom would've had a baby and never had anything to do with him?"

"I don't know," I said, suddenly feeling defeated. The emotional and physical effects of the past week were settling over me like a damp wool blanket. "I merely wondered if it were possible. Maybe I'm trying to come up with a more compelling reason for Mom to have considered leaving us other than the fact that Vern was Mr. Wonderful."

Violet was quiet for a couple seconds, and when she spoke again her voice was softer. "I know all this has been rough on you. You learned something pretty shocking about Mom and that was compounded by your other trauma. In a few days, when your judgment isn't so . . . cloudy . . . maybe you can accept what happened and move on."

"So you don't think there's any way Jonah March was our half brother?"

"No, I don't. Hey, why don't you come over and have dinner with us? We're having lasagna."

"Thanks, but I can't tonight. I'm exhausted."

"I understand."

"Vi, maybe when my judgment *is* less cloudy, maybe you, Mom, and I could go to a spa for the day and she could explain the whole Vern March attraction to us."

"Maybe. You rest up, okay?"

"Thanks. I'll try," I promised. With so many thoughts running through my mind, it was the best I could do right then.

I HUNG UP convinced that if Mom and Vern had been married as impetuous teens, Violet knew nothing about it. Unlike Violet, however, I thought the union—and the child from that union—was a strong possibility. I just needed to confirm my suspicions.

I phoned Uncle Hal, hoping he might have some insight.

"Hi," I said when he answered. "Are you busy with the Christmas tree?"

"Not at the moment. Your aunt decided she needed *another* string of lights and headed off to town."

"So we've got a few minutes."

"A few. When I change the subject, you'll know we're done. I take it you haven't let this matter with your mother rest?"

"It's more like it won't let me rest, Uncle Hal." I told him what I'd overheard at the church and Violet's reaction.

"Honey, once again, I'll have to agree with your sister on this one. A baby is a lot harder to hide than a fling."

"A marriage isn't."

"If the girl was underage and her parents had it annulled, it is."

I huffed. "I need to know if you think Mom was ever married to Vern March."

Uncle Hal was silent.

"Joanne told Tar that Gloria wasn't involved in her dad's life and that she'd only met the woman one time," I continued. "Do you think it's possible Joanne's 'Gloria' is Mom? That Mom's past with Vern is what made her consider leaving Dad?"

"Well, the main thing is to weatherproof your windows. You lose more warm air around your windows than you realize."

My heart dropped. "Aunt Nancy's back."

"Sure is, honey."

"You never told her?"

"I don't see a need for that. You just put some weather stripping around your windows and at the bottom of your doors, and that'll help you save on your heating bill."

"Okay, Uncle Hal. Thank you. Give my love to Aunt Nancy."

"You bet."

I was running out of energy very quickly. It was dead end after dead end. As a result, I finally took a warm, relaxing soak in the tub. My thoughts, however, didn't slow. Both Violet and Uncle Hal had been a wash—pun intended. Neither could confirm or deny that Mom and Vern March had a past prior to their affair. I supposed I could ask Joanne, but I hoped to exhaust all my other options first. Myra had said that Jonah March's widow, Peggy, still lived in town. Maybe I could pay her a visit. But on what pretext?

I got out of the bathtub and was drying off when the phone rang. I hurried to the bedroom to answer it. It was Uncle Hal.

"Don't have but a second," he said in a low, gruff voice. "But I remember something. I found out about your mother's affair when a woman called and told me. She said not to let Vern ruin another family."

"*Another* family? Who was she?"

"I don't know. She said what she had to say and hung up. Maybe she was Vern's former wife."

"Thanks."

"I'm probably wasting my breath, but leave this alone . . . please. You might uncover something no one wants revealed."

"Unfortunately, Uncle Hal," I said, "that's a chance I have to take."

CHAPTER

nine

Sunday was a wasted day. I wore slouchy old clothes and watched tear-jerker movies. I failed to give my website a much-needed update. In fact, I didn't log on to the computer at all. I didn't phone anyone. I just vegged in front of the television and tried to forget my problems. No such luck. If you're ever trying to forget your problems, *don't* watch TV. The gardening channel did a show on poisonous plants growing in your own backyard. Many of the women's channels had infidelity-themed movies, and the crime channel did a special on wrongly accused people getting justice after spending years in the penitentiary.

Even the most inane things made me think of either Yodel or Mom and Vern. Or both. Take the commercial of the woman serving brownies to a group of friends, for example. My first thought was, "I wonder which of the men she's seeing behind her husband's back?" Then, "I wonder if those brownies have been laced with poison?"

All in all, the day was a morbid little pity party.

I awoke Monday with new resolve. This day was most certainly not going to be wasted. I even made a list of an impossible number of tasks to complete. If I got as many as half of them done, I'd be ecstatic. With the list in my jeans pocket, I headed out before 9:00 a.m.

My first stop was Dr. Lancaster's office. It was the easiest thing on my list. Dr. Lancaster was our town's only veterinarian, and I hoped he could give me some advice on how to help Sparrow.

When I stepped through the door, I saw that a half-grown Saint Bernard was taking up the majority of the small waiting area.

"Hello!" I flashed a smile at his owner—a tall, athletic-looking woman with streaked blond hair pulled into a ponytail.

The puppy bounded over to reciprocate my greeting. I bent and rubbed his furry head.

"You're so precious!" I said with a laugh as he licked my other hand.

He truly was adorable, big and ungainly with hair that was still mostly puppy fuzz.

"What's his name?" I asked his owner.

"Linus." She smiled. "He has a blue blanket he drags around all over the house."

I laughed and kissed the top of Linus's head. "What a sweetheart. He doesn't have any brothers or sisters who need a home, does he?"

"I'm afraid not."

I nodded. I really wished he did. I'd even call the dog Charlie or Lucy. I was lonely. I could use a terrific puppy to cuddle on the sofa with. Suddenly, an image of Ben came to mind, and I straightened up and addressed the receptionist.

"I have a stray cat at my house. She's missing her left eye, and is awfully skittish. I'd like to help her if I can."

"Let me see what Dr. Lancaster thinks," the receptionist said. "He's in the back right now, but he should be done any minute."

I looked around as I waited. There was a gray parrot sitting in a cage beside her desk. "That looks like Banjo, Mrs. Watson's parrot."

"It is." She looked at the bird. "Animal control brought him here because he has a respiratory infection. Don't you, Banjo? Poor baby."

Banjo didn't reply, merely bobbed up and down on his perch.

"Mrs. Watson must've been crazy about him," I said.

"Why do you say that?"

"She apparently let him have the run of the house."

The receptionist raised her brows. "Where'd you get that impression?"

"I once saw a yellow stain on Mrs. Watson's carpet. I thought it was, you know, parrot pee."

The woman laughed. "I don't know what you saw on that carpet, but parrot urine is clear, like water. Mrs. Watson actually wasn't terribly fond of poor little Banjo. He had belonged to her husband, and I think she only kept Banjo out of a sense of obligation. I can't imagine her letting him out of his cage at all, much less to run around the house."

"Oh. What will happen to him now?" I asked.

"If no one in Mrs. Watson's family wants him, he'll be available for adoption. Are you interested?"

I cocked my head and considered the bird for a moment.

He stared back at me with what appeared to be thoughtfulness.

"I've never had a bird before."

"They're not too hard to take care of."

Dr. Lancaster opened the door dividing the waiting area from the exam area. He had white hair sprouting from his head like an unruly weed growing in all directions. Tortoiseshell glasses framed his heavy-lidded brown eyes.

"Is Linus here for his rabies shot?" Dr. Lancaster asked.

"He is," the receptionist replied, "but first, this lady has a quick question for you."

I briefly explained about Sparrow and her eye. "Could I give her some medicine or vitamins or something in her food?"

"Does the eye appear to have been recently injured, or is it inflamed?"

"From what I can tell, the socket appears to be empty, but it doesn't look like an open wound."

"Good. Without seeing the cat, I can't provide any particular suggestions as to her care. If you continue feeding her and perhaps use bits of meat to help you gain her trust, hopefully you can catch her and bring her in."

"I'll try to do that. What about vitamins?"

"If you'd like to give her some, Dobbs should have some decent ones in stock."

"Thank you."

Dr. Lancaster turned and nodded at Linus's owner, and she led him through the door toward the exam rooms.

As I turned to leave, the receptionist called to me. "Do you think you'd be interested in adopting Banjo?"

"Probably not. Having never had a bird before, I just don't know that I could take care of him properly."

"Well, if you change your mind, let us know."

"I will."

I opened the door and stepped out into the chilly November air, almost running headlong into Walt Duncan. I recognized Mr. Duncan because he'd looked exactly the same for the past twenty-five years. It was the perfect opportunity to check on Uncle Hal's hunting story.

"Good morning, Mr. Duncan."

"Mornin', young-un." He squinted. "Why, hey, howdy! You're Jim's oldest, ain't ya?"

"I sure am." I smiled. "I'm Daphne."

"Daphne! That's it! Hal said you'd moved to town. You doin' all right?"

"Just fine. How'd you guys do on your hunting trip?"

"Fair to middling. Me and my brother bagged a ten-pointer Saturday morning."

"Wow. That should keep you well fed for the rest of the winter." Don't think about Bambi. Don't think about Bambi. "How did Uncle Hal do?"

"Didn't get a dad-gum thing." Mr. Duncan chuckled. "Of course, he was only with us Friday. He left early Saturday morning."

"He did?"

"Yep." He spat a stream of tobacco juice onto the pavement. "He had to go to the doctor or something."

"Oh. How about that?" So where was Hal Saturday and Sunday? I nodded at Mr. Duncan's pet carrier. "What've you got there?"

"My grandson's snake. The boy had to go to work today, so bringing the snake to the doctor for its annual checkup fell to me."

"That doesn't sound like a fun job."

"Ah, I've had worse."

"It was good seeing you, Mr. Duncan."

"You, too, darlin'. Tell your daddy I said howdy."

"I sure will."

Mr. Duncan ambled into the vet's office. I got in my car and squeezed the bridge of my nose between my thumb and index finger. So, Uncle Hal *hadn't* been with the Duncan brothers for the entire weekend. He'd left early Saturday morning. But if he'd truly had a doctor's appointment, why wouldn't he have gone home?

I was hesitant to call Uncle Hal again. I didn't want him to think I was checking up on him. And it *was* possible he'd begun feeling ill Friday night and had decided to go to a doctor or the emergency room Saturday morning. It was a possibility, albeit an unlikely one. Plus, if Uncle Hal had been feeling ill, Mr. Duncan would've said "He got sick Friday night" rather than "He had to go to the doctor or something." I'd have to look into this one without Uncle Hal's help.

I got out my list and added "check with area doctors" to the bottom. While I had the list out, I double-checked the address for Peggy March I'd gotten off the Internet. Lucky for me, she hadn't remarried. I supposed she had her hands full raising Joanne by herself.

THE WHITE HOUSE was small, but it and the lawn surrounding it were as tidy as could be. Most of the leaves had been raked and disposed of; the few that remained looked as if they'd been artistically placed rather than having blown off the trees. I saw a curtain move in one of the two dormer windows. My presence had been noted, but I wasn't sure it would be acknowledged.

I got out of the car and walked on the smooth stepping-stones to the front door. I'd think they would be slippery when the weather turned colder, but by the looks of the rest of her home, I imagined Peggy March would be outside with a bag of rock salt by the time the first snowflake hit the ground.

I rang the doorbell and wiped my palms on my thighs. I was getting more nervous by the second and didn't want to offer a sweaty hand if she was the handshaking type. I took a deep breath, and the door slowly opened.

If I'd been allowed only one adjective with which to describe Peggy March, it would have had to be "dainty." When she stepped out onto the porch, I felt like a giant standing before her. She was barely five feet tall and appeared no heavier than a whisper. She looked as if a good stout wind would blow her away. Her hair was a golden blond, and I could see strength and determination in her hazel eyes.

"Can I help you?" she asked.

"I hope so. My name is Daphne Martin. I just moved to town about a month ago and wanted to reconnect with some of my parents' old friends in the area." I smiled.

Peggy eyed me with suspicion, not that I could blame her. The story sounded lame even to me.

"Do you know Vern March?" I asked.

"I was married to Vern's son, Jonah." She opened the door. "Why don't you come in and tell me what you're *really* doing here?"

Part of me wanted to turn and run back to my car. The part of me that sought the truth—no matter how painful it might prove to be—stood tall and stepped into the house.

Like the home's exterior, the interior was pristine. It looked like a page out of a magazine.

"Are you an interior designer?" I asked.

"No. Would you prefer to talk in the kitchen or in the living room?"

"Either would be fine."

She led me to the kitchen, where the decor was a retro black and white. "Coffee?"

"No, thank you."

She got herself a cup—black—and sat down at the gleaming white table with the black-and-white-checked cloth. She looked at me expectantly, and I sat down across from her.

What was I doing here? From where did I think Joanne got her hatred of our family in the first place? What was I hoping to gain?

"Well?" Peggy asked, obviously perturbed.

I folded my hands in front of me. "I suddenly feel the need to apologize . . . though I don't know why."

Peggy simply stared at me. She apparently knew why I should apologize, but she wasn't forthcoming about it.

"I'm here to find out if your husband was my half brother."

She nodded. "I figured that was it." Now that Jonah's skeleton was out of the closet and lying on the table between us, Peggy proceeded at a more leisurely pace. She took a sip of her coffee. "Sure you won't have a cup?"

"Positive. Thank you."

She cleared her throat. "Tell me what you know."

"A few days ago, I learned my mother had an affair with Vern when I was a little girl, about thirty years ago. She even consulted a divorce attorney; she was going to leave us."

Peggy nodded. "Go on."

"Then at Mrs. Watson's funeral, I overheard your daughter talking with Tar. He asked about Joanne's grandmother . . . Gloria." I took a deep breath. "My mother's name is Gloria."

"And you're here to find out if your mother is *the* Gloria."

"Yes . . . at least I think I am."

"Why don't you just ask her?"

"She doesn't know I know about the affair, much less anything that might've happened between her and Vern prior to it."

"I'll tell you what little I know about my father-in-law's past."

"Thank you." I gave her a half smile. It was all I had in me right then.

She pressed her lips together.

"You don't think much of my mother, do you?" I asked.

"I don't think much of Jonah's mother. I believe they might be the same person—Joanne is convinced of it—but I don't know for certain."

"I understand Jonah was born when Vern and . . . and Gloria were very young," I said, nudging her to continue.

"She got pregnant in high school. It wasn't as common then as it is these days. They—Vern and Gloria, that is—paid some lady to pretend to be Gloria's mother and sign a consent form so they could be married. Vern was crazy about her, I know that much."

So was Dad.

"When the happy couple began telling people they were married," Peggy continued, "Gloria's parents took their daughter home and had the marriage annulled."

"Did they know she was pregnant?"

Peggy nodded. "They sent her somewhere—to a relative, I suppose—to have the baby."

"But I heard Vern wound up with the baby."

"He did. He threatened Gloria's parents that he'd take out an ad in the paper and tell the whole sordid story if they didn't let him have Gloria and the baby." She took a drink of her coffee, wrinkled her nose in distaste, and pushed the cup aside. "They compromised. He got the baby."

"But what about Gloria? Didn't she want the baby?"

"From what I understand, she'd gone off the deep end by

then. She spent some time in a mental institution," Peggy said.

"A mental institution?" My mother was crazy but I couldn't imagine her in a straitjacket.

"Uh-huh. She had some sort of breakdown."

"Well, I don't doubt that. Afterward did she—"

Peggy was shaking her head before I could finish my question. "She never met Jonah, at least, not until he was grown."

My eyes widened.

"Vern brought your mother to meet Jonah when Jonah was nineteen. We were newlyweds." She gave me a half smile. "I suppose marrying young runs in the March family."

"And Vern told Jonah that my . . . that Gloria . . . was his mother?"

"No. He merely introduced her as Gloria Carter and said they were contemplating a future together."

I felt my anger at my mother start to burn all over again. How could she do that? How could *he*? How could they pretend she had no obligations and was free to pursue a future with another man? She had a nine-year-old and a six-year-old daughter at home who needed her, who depended on her. My breathing quickened. "I don't remember Vern that well. How could . . . how could they?"

Peggy put her hand over mine. "I'm sorry." I believe in that instant she realized that I was almost as much a victim as Jonah. "Maybe they thought it was all right because they were picking up where they'd left off all those years ago."

"But that didn't make it right for Violet and me. It didn't make it right for our dad. And it didn't make up all those missed years to Jonah."

"I know, sugar. I know."

CHAPTER

ten

I CHECKED MY e-mail when I got home later that day. There was one message in my in-box. I started to delete it because the address began "sweetcandy4u." But then I saw "Cake" in the subject line and decided to take a chance and open it.

I was glad I did. It was from Candy at the pet shop. She wanted to order a birthday cake for a *special male friend*. I e-mailed back asking her to call me at her earliest convenience so we could discuss cake flavors, designs, and how many people the cake should serve.

After sending the e-mail, I went straight to my cake books. I doubted Candy knew what type of cake she wanted, other than one that would look pretty and taste delicious. I realize that's what everyone is looking for in a cake, but it's up to me to help my client make an informed decision. Since it had been a few days—days that felt like years, come to think of it—since I'd taken a specific cake order, I thought I should reacquaint myself with the basics. Besides, looking at cake books was comforting to me.

First I looked at the serving charts. I personally can't hold fast to the numbers suggested on the charts, but they do provide a good starting point.

If she wanted something simple, as far as decorations go, then she could have pretty much any flavor of cake she thought her friend would like. If, however, she wanted a three-dimensional or sculpted cake, we would need to go with something with a firm-textured batter like a pound cake. I wrote down some options I thought Candy might like.

When she called, I was prepared for her.

"I'm so glad you've got the time to make a cake for my friend," she said. "I want it to be something really, really special."

"All right. Tell me a little bit about him. What flavors does he like?"

"Well, he loves chocolate."

"Milk, white, or dark?"

"All of it. He's what you might call one of them chocaholics." She giggled.

"Okay. Great." I was taking notes as we talked. "Is he a coffee drinker?"

"Why, he is! Are you sure you don't know him better than I do?"

I laughed. "I hardly think so. What do you think of a mocha-flavored Madeira cake with chocolate buttercream icing?"

"Coffee and chocolate? That sounds scrumptious! He'd love that."

"Good. Now, tell me what else he likes."

"He likes me."

She laughed, and I joined in. I wondered if my laugh sounded as hollow to her as it did to me. I was trying not to be judgmental about Candy's relationship with Kellen Dobbs, but it was hard, especially given my current circumstances.

"He likes animals," she continued. "He likes to play chess and—"

"Chess?" I interrupted.

"Uh-huh. I try to play with him, but I'm not any good."

"What if I make a square cake with white and dark chocolate squares, like a chessboard, with milk and white chocolate chess pieces?"

"You can do that?"

"I sure can," I said, hoping she wouldn't be disappointed with the final product.

"That sounds positively perfect!"

"When is your friend's birthday?"

"In two days. Can you work me in?"

I started to tell her, "I positively can," but I was afraid that would sound ungracious. Instead, I let a simple "yes" suffice. Candy asked me to deliver the cake to her at work on Wednesday, and I told her I'd be there by midmorning.

After talking with Candy, I went into the kitchen to melt some chocolate. I got out my chessmen molds and put some milk chocolate chips in a glass bowl. Luckily, I'd bought chess piece molds a couple years ago to make a chessboard cake for Dad. While I melted the chips in the microwave, I got out my Mocha Madeira recipe, my favorite blue mixing bowl, and my three-inch-deep, nine-inch-square cake pan.

As soon as the chocolate was melted, I spooned it into the molds, tapped the molds on the countertop a couple times to remove air bubbles, and then set the molds in the refrigerator.

Before I could get out the batter ingredients, my phone rang. It was Ben, inviting me to dinner. I knew I had a lot to do but I accepted his invitation anyway and put away my mixing bowl. I could make the cake tonight or tomorrow morning and still have plenty of time to decorate it, especially with half my chess pieces already hardening in the molds.

Ben had mentioned steak so I figured we'd be going to Dakota's; it was the only steakhouse in town. That meant I should dress casually. But I wanted to look good so I gave my clothes and makeup more consideration than usual. I chose a white silk wrap sweater and black wool pants. Casual yet sophisticated.

I tried to go for the "smoky eye" look with my makeup but wound up looking raccoonish and had to wash my face and start again. This time I went with a more natural look for my face and eyes and added color via a dark red lipstick. Much better. More Elizabeth Taylor, less Rocky Raccoon. Not that I was Elizabeth—*The Last Time I Saw Paris*—Taylor, by any stretch of the imagination, but now I doubted I'd be accused of turning over the neighbors' trash cans at night and foraging for food.

THE BLACK-CLAD HOSTESS led us to a booth in the back and announced that our server would be with us momentarily.

"So tell me about your day," Ben said.

He looked handsome—even more so than usual—and I wondered if he'd taken a little extra time with his appearance, too, or if he had simply come straight from work. With men, you can never tell. He wore dark jeans, a crisp white shirt, and a brown tweed sport coat.

"Are you sure you don't want a stiff drink before I start telling you about my day?" I asked. "Better yet, let's start with *your* day."

"There's not that much to tell. Got up, went to work, took a beautiful woman to dinner. That's about it so far." He grinned. "I did do a little digging into Vern March's past, though."

I leaned forward. "What did you find out?"

"Hi!" A voice I didn't recognize interrupted our conversation.

I looked up as a dark-skinned young man approached our table. He had a tribal tattoo on his right biceps, a silver ring through his left eyebrow, and the smile of an angel.

"I'm Jarrod, and I'll be your server this evening. What can I get you folks to drink?"

We gave Jarrod our drink order and after he left our table, Ben told me what he'd learned about Vern. It seems Vern divided his time between Brea Ridge and Scott County, where his parents had lived. He'd gotten a job here when he was sixteen and that's when he met Gloria.

Ben shrugged. "And I guess you know the rest of the story."

"I do, and I don't," I said. "There are so many blanks. For instance, Peggy March told me Gloria spent time in a mental institution after having the baby. That doesn't fit what I know about Mom. She's been through a lot of tough times, but she doesn't crumble."

Jarrod returned with our drinks so Ben was spared from giving me his opinion on my observation. We ordered our food, and Ben abandoned the subject of Gloria and Vern.

"So how *was* your day?"

"I got a cake order," I said, hoping to appear nonchalant.

He smiled. "That's super."

"It is. I was beginning to wonder if anyone in this town would ever order a cake from me again."

"Who's the intrepid customer?"

"Candy from Dobbs's Pet Store. I'm making her a Mocha

Madeira cake to look like a chessboard with chocolate chess pieces."

"Sounds delicious. When does it need to be done?"

"Wednesday morning."

He nodded with mock graveness, a devilish smile playing about his lips. "I might have to go by the store Wednesday about lunchtime and pick up some treats for Sally."

"She didn't say the cake was for Mr. Dobbs."

He laughed. "Bet she didn't say it *wasn't* though."

"She said the cake was for a friend."

Ben tried to hold in his laughter again, and in that moment he reminded me of Michael Landon—Little Joe trying not to laugh at Hoss and get punched, failing usually.

"What?" he asked when I kept staring at him. "It's the town's worst-kept secret."

"What about his wife? Do you think she knows?"

"She'd have to be blind or stupid not to know—and take my word for it, Janey Dobbs is neither."

"Wonder why she doesn't divorce him, then?"

He shook his head. "Maybe she loves the guy. Or maybe it's a money thing, or a matter of pride. Who knows?"

"I feel sorry for her." I opened my mouth to elaborate but Jarrod arrived with my filet mignon and Ben's prime rib. When he left, neither Ben nor I was inclined to resume the subject of the Dobbses' marital woes. It appeared we'd both grown tired of that heavy conversation for the time being.

"Tell me what's been going on with you for the past twenty years," I said.

"I went to college not knowing what I wanted to be when I grew up. Other than rich, of course. You see how well that worked out." He winked and took a bite of his baked potato, which was swimming in butter and sour cream.

"When did you figure it out? What you wanted to be, I mean?"

"In my first writing class my sophomore year of college. It was a great class. Tough, but in a way that made me think. It was a challenge, but it was a joy to wrestle with rather than merely another cruddy class to slog through."

"I take it you had several sloggers?"

"Almost all my classes were sloggers."

I laughed. I knew the feeling. Business school was the same way for me.

"During those tumultuous college years," I began, "was there a Lois Lane to your budding Clark Kent?"

Ben chewed slowly. After he'd swallowed, he didn't answer straightaway. I was starting to think the question had made him so uncomfortable he wasn't going to answer it at all. I decided it was best to change the subject.

"The food here is excellent."

"It is," Ben agreed. "There was a girl in college. I fell fairly hard for her, but to her we were only friends. I watched her go from boyfriend to boyfriend hoping she'd one day realize I was the man of her dreams. That day never came. Instead she dropped out of school and married her chemistry professor."

"I'm sorry."

He shrugged. "I guess it wasn't meant to be. Sometimes lifelong bachelorhood is in the cards we Clark types are dealt, right?"

"Who knows? The right girl could be out there yet." I took a drink of my soda and wondered whether or not I should've said that. I didn't want Ben to think I was casting myself in the role of his "right girl." On the other hand, I didn't want to quell any interest he might have in me, either.

We dug into our meals and made small talk until we were

finished eating. It wasn't until Ben and I were on our way back to my house that I approached the other thing I'd wanted to ask him.

"Um, Ben? Do you have any friends on the police force . . . besides Bill Hayden?"

"Yeah, I have several friends on the force. Why?" He glanced at me from the corner of his eye. "Did you get a speeding ticket or something?"

"No. Actually, I learned that parrot pee is clear."

"And that's a crime?" He raised an eyebrow at me.

"Of course not," I said, rolling my eyes. "There was a stain on Yodel Watson's living room carpet. I figured the parrot had been out of its cage and had an accident, but today I found out that parrot urine is clear like water. It wouldn't have left a stain."

"Then what do you think caused the stain?"

"That's what I want one of your police friends to look into. What if that stain was made by whatever poison killed Mrs. Watson?"

"But I thought Mrs. Watson died in her den."

"She was found in the den. She wasn't necessarily poisoned there." I playfully slapped his arm. "You're a reporter. You should know this CSI stuff."

He chuckled. "Okay. I'll see if the substance was tested. If not, maybe they'll go ahead and run a tox screen on it."

"See? I knew you knew that CSI stuff." My smile faded. "If the kind of poison that killed Mrs. Watson could be determined, maybe I could put this nightmare behind me."

Ben couldn't stay after taking me home. He said he had to get up early and all that jazz. I heard Sparrow mewing as I went inside, so I put on a coat, grabbed a couple slices of prosciutto, and went back out onto the porch. I sat down on the top step, and the cat peered at me from around the side of the house.

"Come here, Sparrow," I encouraged softly. "I've got a treat for you." I tore off a piece of the prosciutto and tossed it near the edge of the porch.

Sparrow crept tentatively toward it, watched me for a second, and then gobbled up the meat. I tossed another before she could run away. She snatched it up and practically swallowed it whole.

When I tossed another piece of the prosciutto, I made sure this one landed about a foot closer to me than the previous two. With a wary look, Sparrow advanced and ate this morsel. I quickly tossed another. Again, I made sure it was a little closer to me. The cat stared at me for several seconds. Then her hunger triumphed over her suspicion, and she advanced. Piece by piece, I fed her the rest of the prosciutto. I didn't urge her any closer, though. For now this first step toward trust was enough.

Oddly enough, that made me think of Ben. Trust was hard for me. Of course, I'd known Ben for so long and had trusted him implicitly when we were younger. But now that I'd been hurt so badly by Todd, I was gun-shy—literally. I'd trusted Todd with my life, and he'd almost taken it.

I WENT INSIDE and took a warm bath, all the while thinking of what I should be doing rather than soaking in the tub. I should be making Candy's cake. I should be calling Uncle Hal to ask him if he's feeling better after having to go to the doctor during last week's hunting trip. I should be at the police station asking them myself to test that stupid yellow stain in Yodel Watson's living room. I should be in my mother's face asking her if she was also Jonah March's mother. And I should also be calling her a hypocrite for deriding my decision to leave Todd, a man who'd abused me in every way possible since our so-called honeymoon.

Daddy had never mistreated her. He'd loved her—and me and Violet—and he'd never been unfaithful to her or slapped her or shot at her or locked her in a bathroom. I know he hadn't. He'd never been anything but a good husband and father. And she'd betrayed him. She'd betrayed us all. She was *still* betraying me.

As I wept into my bath towel, the telephone rang. I almost expected it to be Mom, my thoughts were so focused on her. Instead, it was Dad. "Honey? No need to panic but I'm in the ICU right now." I gasped. "No, no," he continued. "It's okay. Your mother just had a minor heart attack." My throat dried up. I knew he was downplaying it for my benefit.

"What happened?" I croaked. "Is she going to be all right?"

"Oh, sure, I believe everything will be fine. They're evaluating her overnight to see if they think she needs any surgery."

"You mean, like bypass surgery? Isn't that dangerous?"

"The doctor doesn't anticipate your mother needing it, sweetheart. It's just a precaution," he said. "They're not ruling anything out until they know more."

"As soon as I hang up, I'll throw some clothes in an overnight bag and—"

"No need for that," he said, interrupting. "It's late, and I don't want you driving this time of night, especially when you're upset. Just wait and come in the morning. If anything changes, I'll let you know."

"Are you sure?" I didn't like the idea of him being there all alone but he was the stubbornest man I knew.

"Positive. I don't want to have to worry about you making a two-hour drive tonight," he said.

"Okay, but if you need me, call and I'll be on my way."

"I know you will."

"I love you, Dad."

"I love you, sweetheart."

"Tell Mom I love her, too."

He agreed and promised to keep me updated. After I hung up, I slipped out of my robe, put on my favorite pajamas, and went into the kitchen to await Violet's call. Dad had called me first, which I found a bit odd—Violet and Mom were much closer than Mom and I. Maybe that's why Dad called me first; he thought Violet would take it the hardest. She probably would. My eyes welled up with tears, but I fought them back.

I took my apron from its hook and dropped it over my head. I tied it as I walked over to the counter to retrieve my headset. I got out my baking essentials, recipe, and ingredients, and I mixed up Candy's Mocha Madeira cake. I needed to do *something* to distract myself. Baking was my therapy.

I WAS POURING cake batter into my painstakingly prepared square pan when the phone rang again. When you're doing therapeutic baking, you know, everything must be precise.

"Hello! Daphne's Delectable Cakes!" I used my most professional, chipper voice when I answered the phone, even though I knew the caller was most probably Violet. It was, of course, and I wondered at myself—even became irritated at myself—for attempting to sound so nonchalant.

"It's me," Violet said.

I could tell she'd been crying, and I felt even lousier than I had to begin with.

"Dad said he called you," she said.

"He did."

"Do you think she'll be all right?"

"Of course I do." I put the pan into the oven and set the timer. "You know Mom. She's as healthy as—" I couldn't think of anything healthy. For the life of me, no clichés, no platitudes, nothing whatsoever came to mind. "She'll be fine."

"I wanted to go up there tonight, but Dad told me not to."

"He's right, you know. He has enough on his mind without worrying about his two girls driving up there this time of night."

"That's exactly what he said."

"Just try to get some rest," I told her. "We'll go up first thing in the morning. Can Jason take the kids to school?"

"Yeah. That'll be no problem. Are you sure we don't need to go tonight?"

"I'm positive. If Dad had thought we should be there, he'd have asked Jason to bring us tonight."

"That's true." She paused. "Are *you* okay?"

"Oh, sure, I'm fine. I'm getting some baking done."

"I know you're more upset about this than you're letting on. I'll come and stay with you if you need me to. That way I'd be there already and we could—"

"Don't be silly. You need to be home with your family tonight, and I have work to do. I'll see you in the morning."

"Okay, then . . . if you're sure."

"Positive. Good night."

"Good night."

I hung up the phone and sank to the floor. I pulled my legs to my chest and sobbed until the oven timer went off.

CHAPTER eleven

VIOLET ARRIVED at my house around six the next morning. Her face was peaked, and there were deep, purplish circles under her eyes. That's one advantage I have over her, being the dark complexioned sister. Still, the instant she saw me she told me *I* looked tired.

"I knew we should've gone to the hospital last night," she said. "Neither of us got any sleep anyway."

"Nah, I had to get caught up on my baking. In the cake pan there on the island is my client's cake, and her chocolate decorations are in the fridge. All I have to do now is make the chocolate buttercream, frost, and decorate." I gave Vi a smug smile.

"And that's the only thing that kept you up last night?"

I lost the smile. "No, but I don't think you want me to re-hash all my Mom-related angst, do you?"

She frowned. "Not really."

"Then let's go. And we'll listen to my *Mega Hits of the Eighties* CD all the way there."

She almost smiled at that. "Can I sing?"

"For as long as I can stand it."

"Mom *is* gonna be okay . . . right?"

Closing my eyes, I nodded. "This is her twisted way of getting back at me for Thanksgiving." I opened my eyes. "I didn't pay enough attention to her then, so she's forcing me to pay attention to her now." I jerked my head toward the door. "We'd better hit the road."

Violet did sing all the way to the hospital. I even joined her on a couple songs from the Go-Go's and the Bangles. Our mood turned somber, however, when we got out of the car.

We walked toward the hospital's main entrance. Several small groups were clustered outside, some smoking, some talking in grave whispers, some weeping. Did I mention I hate hospitals? Even when I go to visit someone who's had a baby—a joyous occasion—the air of suffering and dread that lingers over a hospital depresses me.

I glanced at Violet. "She's going to be okay." Was I trying to reassure my sister or myself?

At the front desk, we asked for Gloria Carter and were told she was moved out of the Coronary Care Unit and into a private room this morning. That was a relief. We strode to the elevator feeling better already.

Mom was sleeping when we got to her room. Dad, Uncle

Hal, and Aunt Nancy were there. Dad told us in a hushed tone that Mom was doing much better.

"Since your girls are here, Jim, I'm going to get a cup of coffee," Uncle Hal said. "Anybody need anything?"

"I'll walk with you," I said. "I could certainly stand to stretch my legs after the long drive, and I'd love a soda. I'm sure Vi would like one, too. Daddy, do you need anything?"

"A coffee would be nice." He reached for his wallet.

"I've got it." I turned to Uncle Hal. "Lead the way."

"So how's Mom really?" I asked when we were in the elevator.

"I knew this was more an inquisition than a soda run." He smiled and shook his head. "Honest to goodness, she is doing fine. She'll probably get to go home tomorrow."

"Great. What about you?"

"We're tired. We've been here all night. Now that you and Violet are here, Nancy and I will go home and get some sleep. Jim should, too."

"I'll try to make him go."

"If anybody can make Jim do anything, it's you, baby girl."

I smiled briefly. "Thanks. But when I asked about you, I meant your health in general." He looked at me confusedly. "I bumped into Mr. Duncan yesterday, and he told me you had to leave the hunting trip early to go to the doctor."

Uncle Hal scowled. "Walt Duncan needs to keep his mouth shut about things that don't concern him."

"Apparently, this did concern him. And it concerns me, too. Are you okay?"

The elevator doors opened and a young nurse got on. We said a polite hello and then fell silent. At the lobby, we got out of the elevator.

As Uncle Hal and I walked to the cafeteria, I revisited the subject of his health.

"About that doctor's appointment—"

He sighed. "This is between you and me, all right? Not even your Dad knows."

"All right." Now he was scaring me a little. Uncle Hal tells Dad everything.

Then I remembered Mom's affair with Vern. Well, almost everything.

"I went to a hospital in east Tennessee to have a CT scan."

"What's wrong? I mean—"

"I've been having a lot of severe headaches, so I went to my regular doctor a couple weeks ago. He said I needed a CT scan, and I told him I was going out of town and would prefer to have the CT scan there."

"Why?"

"You read Yodel Watson's journal. You saw how information in a small town can be made to sound like something out of a tabloid." He scoffed. "I was hoping that having the test run four hours away would enable me to be the one to determine what and when and who I tell about it."

"Makes sense. Do you know anything yet?"

He shook his head.

"Well, your secret's safe with me. And I'm here if you need to talk." I fished money for the vending machine out of my purse.

"Have you decided to put your mother's ancient history to rest?"

I fed a dollar into the soda machine. The machine spat it back out. I shrugged off Uncle Hal's question by urging the machine to accept my money.

When the machine had taken my dollar and I had made my selection, I turned back to my uncle. "Has Mom ever been in a mental institution?"

Eyebrows raised, he answered, "Not that I know of. Where'd that come from?"

"Just wondering if insanity runs in the family." I grinned.

"I don't know about your mother's side, but quite a few of mine and your dad's people are certifiable."

"Yay!" I giggled. "It's good to know I'm not alone then." I got Violet a soda while Uncle Hal got coffees for himself and Dad.

By the time we got back up to Mom's room, she was awake and Violet was standing by her bed, holding her hand. Uncle Hal passed Dad his coffee, and I set Vi's soda on the table.

"How're you feeling?" I asked Mom.

She slowly rolled her head toward me. "I'm tired. How are you, honey?"

"I'm all right."

She turned back to Violet. "Are my grandbabies doing okay this morning? Are they having trouble readjusting to school after the holiday?"

"Not too much. They're getting awfully eager for Christmas break, though."

I sat down in a vinyl orange chair, sipped my soda, and got comfortable being invisible.

A few minutes later, Uncle Hal and Aunt Nancy convinced Dad to let them take him home for some much-needed rest.

"The girls will be here," Aunt Nancy said. "Everything will be fine, and Gloria needs you to be sharp and well-rested for her when she comes home."

Dad must've been exhausted because he didn't require a lot of arm twisting. He kissed Mom, Violet, and me, and left with Uncle Hal and Aunt Nancy with a forced smile.

Once the crowd in the room thinned out, Mom dozed off again. Violet went down to the gift shop to get Mom some magazines. I drank my soda and watched Mom sleep.

Her face looked more peaceful—and younger—than it did when she was awake. How many times had I looked at that face as a little girl and wanted to look just like her, to be just like her? And yet I never measured up. I still didn't measure up to my mother's standards. Violet was the petite, porcelain-skinned beauty who shared our mother's interest in gardening and romance novels. It was Violet who watched *Gone with the Wind* with Mom for the umpteenth time while I shot pool with Daddy. Of course, Daddy and I were close, but I'd always longed for a mere smidgen of the closeness Violet shared with Mom. It was Violet who had the storybook marriage and had given Mom grandchildren. It was to Violet that Mom had confided her affair with Vern March.

Tears were flowing down my cheeks unheeded now. I stood and took a tissue from Mom's hospital nightstand. Her eyes fluttered open.

"Daphne, darling, it's all right."

I gulped and gave an awkward nod.

"I'm going to be fine," she said. "Really."

Again I nodded. Then, barely realizing what I was saying, the words tumbled from my lips. "Why didn't you tell me about Vern March?"

Mom squeezed her eyes shut, her face crumpling in pain. As tears fought their way through the iron slits, she whispered, "I was afraid you'd judge me too harshly."

Her vulnerability left me incapacitated to unleash the rage and resentment I'd been feeling toward her. I couldn't even ask the questions I knew I deserved to have answered. Instead I went to her side and held her hand.

That's how Violet found us when she returned from the gift shop. "What's wrong?" she asked sharply, piercing me with an accusatory glare.

"Nothing," I said. "Mom and I got a tad emotional, that's all."

Looking as if she couldn't quite believe me and as if she should've known better than to leave me alone with Mom, Violet opened the bag and presented Mom with a diverse selection of magazines. I released Mom's hand and resumed my place in the ugly orange chair. Almost immediately, I became invisible again.

I was about to nod off when a hospital cafeteria worker brought Mom's lunch. The food smelled scrumptious. That or I was just really hungry. When Mom removed the metal cover to reveal the plate underneath, the meal's blandness was apparent. A grilled chicken breast had been drained of the slightest hint of succulence. Steamed carrots and peas could possibly have been made palatable by a pat of butter, but Mom didn't even have butter for her roll. A cherry gelatin jiggled around some fruit enmeshed in its center.

Violet and I exchanged looks. Both looks clearly shouted, "Ewww!" Okay, to be more accurate, my look shouted, "Ewww!" Violet's look shouted, "Nasty gross!" which was one of her favorite phrases as a teen. You have to say it like a Valley girl, which she did, even though we couldn't have gotten any farther from the Valley if we'd tried. Still, I think you get my point.

"Mmm," I said, not sounding the least bit convincing. "While you start on that, we'll stretch our legs."

Violet eagerly followed me out into the hall and several feet away from Mom's open door. "She can't eat that! It's nasty!"

"Nasty *gross*," I said, correcting her. "But it might be all she can have. Whatever the case may be, we definitely cannot eat in front of her."

"You're right. What're we gonna do?"

"We'll eat in shifts. You go first—say you're going to check your messages or something. She'll buy that; you're important." I ignored Vi's grimace of protest and/or martyrdom. "Meanwhile, I'll check with the nurse to see if there's anything not falling into the cardboard food group that Mom can eat."

"Good thinking. And I do need to call Jason and let him know how Mom is doing. I'll get a sandwich while I'm at it."

"Take your time," I told her.

"Aren't you hungry?"

"I was until I got an eyeful of Mom's lunch."

"Yeah." She scoffed. "Way nasty gross."

We both laughed as Violet went to the elevator, and I headed toward the nurses' station.

"Um . . . hi." I gave the nurse at the desk my most charming smile. "I'm Gloria Carter's daughter. I'd like to get a treat of some kind for her dessert."

"Did she not get dessert with her lunch?"

"She did. And I'm sure—" I'm such a lousy liar. "I'm sure the gelatin will be great, but—"

"No, it won't." The nurse gave me an apologetic smile.

Oh, good. We were beyond pretense. I didn't have to try to tap-dance around my request now. Or did I?

The nurse continued. "We're not necessarily concerned with gastronomic delights right now. If we were, your mother could have whatever she wanted. Our main goal is to get her well again."

I nodded, duly chastened. "I just feel so bad for her. Isn't there anything that would taste good *and* be good for her?"

The nurse cocked her head. "Does she like blueberries?"

"Loves them."

"In the cafeteria, on the first floor, they have small containers of plain yogurt with blueberries. She can have one of those."

I beamed like the light on a miner's helmet. "Thank you. Thank you so much."

I hurried downstairs and got Mom's dessert. She was still

picking dejectedly at the chicken breast when I returned to her room.

"Is it good?" I asked.

"Not bad."

"Try this." I placed the yogurt and blueberries on her tray.

She stole a furtive look at the door.

"It's okay. The nurse approved it." I winked at her.

She set the top aside and plunged her spoon into the yogurt. At first taste, her eyes closed in delight.

I caused that expression. I made her happy this time. Not Violet.

As soon as that thought flitted through my mind, it was hounded by guilt.

"Thank you," Mom said between bites, and I felt another wave of self-congratulatory pleasure. But then the demons in my head took me in a different direction.

Why did you think I'd judge you too harshly? Retaliation, perhaps, because you've always judged me so harshly, held me to standards I could never attain? Why was I never good enough, Mom? Why could I never earn your love or respect or admiration?

All the questions I longed to ask remained in my head, swallowed like a bitter pill as Mom smiled and took another bite of her yogurt. I smiled back at her. I may not do many things right as far as my mother is concerned, but I hit the ball out of the park on this one.

Violet came back and I went to have some lunch, glad I could escape for a few minutes. Before I could reach the elevator, though, I heard shoes click-clacking quickly down the hall. I turned and was surprised to see Violet hurrying toward me, a delighted smile spread across her face.

"This couldn't wait," she blurted.

I smiled, too. Her excitement was contagious. "What? Tell me."

"I spoke with Annette at the office, and a house buyer accepted my clients' offer!"

"That's fantastic!" I gave her a hug.

"Yep. I'm thrilled. With the housing market as volatile as it has been, this is great." She smiled again. "Well, enjoy your lunch."

"I sure will."

I left the hospital and had lunch at a nearby sub shop. It was after the lunch rush now, and the restaurant wasn't at all crowded. I called Ben from my table at the back of the dining room.

"Hi, Daph," he said when he answered his phone. "Did you get my message?"

"No. I'm not at home." I explained about Mom. "She's doing well, though, and might even get to go home tomorrow."

"Oh, wow. I'm glad she's okay. I had just wanted to let you know someone from the police department's crime lab will be going to Yodel's house to get a sample of that yellow stain today or tomorrow."

"You're not actually Clark Kent, are you?" I asked playfully.

"No, but I'm flattered if you're saying I'm super."

"You're getting there, Ben. You're getting there."

WHEN I RETURNED to Mom's room, she and Violet were watching a sitcom. I sat down and watched the rest of the show with them—and then we watched another. The only comments we made were about the shows. It was a comfortable and companionable way to spend the afternoon. I knew those feelings couldn't last, however; Mom or I was bound to say or do something to hurt, offend, or anger the other, unintentionally though it may be—so I was grateful to see Dad, Aunt Nancy, and Uncle Hal walk through the door.

I wanted to shout, "Hallelujah! Get me out of here before something bad happens!" Of course, that thought alone was enough to ensure that if something bad did indeed happen, my conscience would not be clean.

Still, when Dad suggested Violet and I "get on home before it gets dark," I jumped at the chance. With kisses and hugs all around, I was at the door with my purse in hand before Violet had finished saying good-bye to Mom.

"You didn't have to be in such a rush to leave," Vi said as I backed out of the parking lot.

"Yes, I did. I have a cake to finish and deliver tomorrow morning."

"Oh, yeah. Sorry. I forgot." She frowned. "Do you want me to drive? You know, so you won't be too tired to work when we get home?"

"No, I'll be all right, but thanks for offering."

"You're welcome. If you need me to take over, just let me know."

We were silent for a few minutes.

"Mom looked good, don't you think?" Violet asked. "Her color, I mean."

"Yeah, she looked like everything's going to be fine."

"I hope you're right."

"I'm your big sister. I'm always right." That's what I said, but my brain argued that I'm most assuredly *not* always right. In fact, it immediately recalled a half dozen times I had been absolutely, unequivocally, slap-your-hand-to-your-forehead wrong. As my mind began to reel off even more wrongs, I wished it would shut up. I turned on the CD player to drown it out and gave Violet a reassuring smile. To illustrate how not worried I was, I joined Cyndi Lauper in a chorus of "Girls Just Wanna Have Fun."

Violet chimed in, and we sang and bobbed to the CD for the next twenty miles. The car even got into the act. It began thumping and pulling to one side.

Saucer-eyed, Violet turned down the volume. "What's that?"

"I'm afraid we've got a flat tire."

I pulled onto the shoulder. Sure enough, the front driver's-side tire was flat. I opened the trunk and took out the jack, praying no one would run me over while I replaced the flat tire with my spare.

A black Mercedes pulled in behind my car. As visions of lounge lizards and rich chain-saw maniacs danced in my head, Violet raced up beside me.

Lovely. Together the two of us might have more of a fighting chance, but if Richie Rich turns out to be Freddie Krueger and kills Violet, that's just one more thing for Mom to blame on me.

CHAPTER

twelve

INSTEAD OF a homicidal maniac, Janey Dobbs got out of the car. She shaded her eyes with her hand. "Daphne? Daphne Martin, is that you?"

I let out the breath I wasn't aware I'd been holding. "Yes! Yes, Mrs. Dobbs. It's me and my sister, Violet."

"Thank goodness I recognized you," Mrs. Dobbs said. "You can't change that tire here on the side of this busy interstate highway. You'll get hit by a car or one of those tractor trailers."

"The thought had crossed my mind."

"You two grab your things and lock the car, and I'll drive you to a service station." I thanked Janey and did as she suggested.

Fortunately, we were able to find a garage that was still open after 6:00 p.m. and willing to tow my car and repair the tire. Unfortunately, I could've probably bought a small, third-world country for the same cost, plus maybe a quart of tequila.

Violet and I sat down in the dusty waiting room. To my surprise, Janey Dobbs joined us.

"Thank you for bringing us here," I said. "But, please, don't feel obligated to wait. I'm sure you—"

"Of course I feel obligated to wait! What if they're unable to fix your car? How will you get home?"

"Well . . . thank you," I said, "if you're sure . . ."

"We're lucky you came along," Violet added. "What're the odds someone we know would be driving along that stretch of interstate at the very moment Daphne's car broke down?"

Mrs. Dobbs laughed as she pushed her curly, brown hair back off her forehead. "It isn't such a long shot. I prefer to think of it as serendipity."

"So do I." I smiled. "What fortunate coincidence brought you in this direction today?"

"Oh, I wanted to get out and enjoy some of the sites before winter sets in. That giant guitar thing, for one."

"You know, I've never been there. I've always thought it would be interesting to go."

"Me too," Violet said. "Maybe you and I could take the kids there one day."

"How old are your children?" Mrs. Dobbs asked.

"They're eleven. Twins—a boy and a girl."

"That's marvelous. Kellen and I never had children. I've always regretted it." She gave a quick, sad shake of her head as if that would dislodge her melancholy. "Do take the children to the guitar museum. I think they'd thoroughly enjoy it."

"Thank you. I will." Violet gave Mrs. Dobbs a warm smile. Of course, thoughts of her children always brought out Vi's biggest, brightest smile. Mine, too, come to think of it.

The mechanic, Mr. Burly—sorry, Mr. Addison, though he looked like a Mr. Burly to me—came into the waiting room wiping his hands on a blue paper towel. "We've got you ready to roll again, Ms. Martin."

"What happened to the tire?" I asked. "Did I run through some broken glass or something?"

"I don't know. You had a small puncture, but the object wasn't embedded. We patched it, and the patch should last for the life of the tire."

"So I won't need to buy a new tire when I get home?"

"Not unless you run over some more sharp objects on your way." Mr. Burly laughed at his own joke, and the rest of us smiled out of politeness.

While he wrote up his invoice, Mrs. Dobbs stood. "Girls, I'm glad I was able to help."

"So are we," I said. "Thank you so much. If I can ever return the favor, let me know."

"I'll hold you to that," she said, waving an index finger through the air.

"Please do."

"Violet," Mrs. Dobbs said, "it was a pleasure meeting you, dear."

"Trust me," Violet said with a laugh, "the pleasure was mine."

Mrs. Dobbs left, and Mr. Burly handed me the bill. I gave him my credit card, and when he gave it back along with a receipt, Violet and I got in the car to resume our strange journey home.

"I can give you some money on the tire repairs and to help with gas," Violet began.

"Nonsense. Christmas is coming up. Buy me a vacation house on Lake Tahoe, and we'll call it even."

"Ha-ha. It was lucky for us Mrs. Dobbs came along, huh?"

"Yeah. Talk about your uncomfortably weird coincidences."

"What do you mean?"

"The cake I'm delivering tomorrow is for Candy, a girl who works at Dobbs's Pet Store."

"Huh. That is a coincidence. I wouldn't call it 'uncomfortably weird,' though."

"I would because the *real* coincidence is that Ben thinks the cake is for Mr. Dobbs." I cut a glance her way. "I think it is, too."

"And? Lots of people buy cakes for their bosses."

"But everybody in town thinks Candy and Mr. Dobbs are having an affair."

"Just because—"

"Yodel Watson said she caught them. It was in her journal—I found it."

Violet emitted an angry growl. "I wish that stupid journal had gone up in flames the night that old battle-ax died. It was filled with nothing but hatred, gossip, and bitterness. And *bitterness* is all that book has left in Mrs. Watson's wake."

"I know. I'm sorry I brought it up. It's just, if Candy is having an affair with Mrs. Dobbs's husband . . ." I sighed. "I don't know."

"That's right. You don't know. You're making a cake for a client. You have nothing to feel guilty about."

"But it seems like I'm condoning their affair."

"You aren't condoning anything, except maybe your business. A client called and asked for a cake and you made it, right?"

"Right."

"Did your client say, 'This cake is for my married boss, and I'm buying him a cake because we're having a torrid extramarital affair'?"

I giggled. "No."

"Okay. End of guilt."

"You've got a lot of wisdom for a baby sister, you know that?"

"Yes. Yes, I do." With that, she turned on the CD player and cranked the volume.

I WOKE UP early to get cracking on Candy's cake. By now I had all my chess pieces completed, and they were in the refrigerator awaiting placement on the cake. I opened the freezer and took out the baking sheets holding the white and dark chocolate I had melted before going to bed last night. Using a heavy cardboard pattern and a small, sharp knife, I cut the chocolate into one-inch squares. I placed the baking sheets in the fridge until I was ready to place the squares on top of the cake.

I then whipped up the chocolate buttercream frosting and divided it into two bowls. I thinned one bowl to medium consistency for piping the cake's borders. I carefully added enough water to the first bowl to render the icing a little thinner for frosting the cake.

I put a cake icing tip into a sixteen-inch featherweight decorator bag and added a generous amount of thin-consistency icing. I turned the bag to where the tip would leave a combed effect to the sides of the square Mocha Madeira cake.

Before I could begin icing the cake, the telephone rang. I hadn't put on my headset since no one normally called this early. A knot gathered in the pit of my stomach as I put aside the decorator bag and answered the phone. I hoped nothing had happened to hamper Mom's release from the hospital.

"Daphne, good morning. I hope I'm not calling too early."

There was a vague familiarity to the voice, but I couldn't place it. I was just happy this call wasn't about Mom.

"Not at all," I said.

"I trust you and your sister had no further problems getting home?"

Janey Dobbs. "We sure didn't. I can't tell you how much we appreciated your help last night."

"Why, you're welcome. I'm glad I was around!" Janey paused. "So, I recall your telling me to let you know if you could ever return the favor?"

"That's right; I did."

"If this is too short notice, don't you hesitate to say so, but today is my husband's birthday, and I wondered if you could make him a cake."

I hesitated.

"It wouldn't have to be anything fancy, and I wouldn't need it until late this afternoon."

"What kind of cake does Mr. Dobbs like?"

"Oh, anything will do. A small white sheet cake with white icing and a few flowers of some kind would be marvelous."

I had some peach and yellow roses in the freezer, so I could pull this off, no problem. "Would you like there to be any writing on the cake?"

"Yes. 'Happy Birthday with Love to My Darling Kellen.'"

That would sure fill up a quarter of a sheet cake. "Okay, Mrs. Dobbs. When and where would you like the cake delivered?"

"Could you bring it to our house at around five thirty this afternoon?"

I told her I could, and she gave me directions to the house.

After talking with Mrs. Dobbs, I washed my hands and resumed work on Candy's cake. If both cakes were indeed for Mr. Dobbs, he would be getting two *very* different cakes—one "positively perfect" and one "anything will do."

For some reason, the prospect of making the "anything will do" cake left me feeling a little sad.

At 10:00 A.M., I delivered the chessboard cake to Dobbs's Pet Store. I noticed that since my last visit, a bell had been installed above the door. I imagined they were getting tired of being, well, surprised.

"Can I help you?" Mr. Dobbs asked. His voice sounded a tad gruff, and I wasn't sure whether he was coming down with a cold or was aggravated about something.

Before I could respond, Candy scurried to the front of the store, put her arm around me, and rushed me down the hall to a back room.

"She's here to see me, Kel," she called over her shoulder. She gave me a conspiratorial wink. "Right here."

She flipped on a light, and I saw that she'd brought me to a kitchenette/lunchroom. I placed the cake box on the table. Candy was practically hopping up and down in anticipation, so I decided to have a little fun with her.

"Would you like to see the cake?"

"If you don't open that box, I'm gonna bust!"

I laughed and opened the box, hoping the cake would meet her expectations.

Candy let out a squeal of delight and pulled me into the tightest bear hug I'd ever received from such a small person, with the exceptions of Violet's twins. "It's positively perfect!" She let me go so she could look at the cake again. "Oh, I love it! I do!" She put her hands over her mouth, and I could tell she was fighting back tears. "Oh, Daphne, this is the prettiest cake I've ever seen. Look at the rook, and the knight, oh, and the queen!"

"So you're happy with it?"

"Happy? Honey, I couldn't be more tickled! Thank you. Thank you so much." She hugged me again. "Let me get you a check."

After her reaction, I'd have almost given her the cake for free. But Violet was right; I was running a business. I closed the cake box and waited for Candy.

She returned to the room almost as radiant as a bride. "You do such good work." She handed me a check. "I'm gonna tell everybody I know."

"Thank you."

"No, thank *you*. I can't wait to see . . . my friend's face when he gets a load of this cake."

I couldn't help myself. I had to say, "He should certainly be pleased with how much thought you put into this."

"Oh, honey, you're the one that did all the work. I just wanted something he'd be happy with, you know?"

I smiled. "I know."

I left the pet store and drove home to work on Mrs. Dobbs's "anything will do" cake. It was obvious Candy truly cared about Mr. Dobbs. Did Mrs. Dobbs suspect their affair? If so, that could explain her lackadaisical attitude about his cake. All she'd seemed to be particularly interested in was the message: "Happy Birthday with Love to My Darling Kellen." Was Mr. Dobbs toying with the affections of both women? Did he care for Candy? Or was he merely having his cake and eating it, too?

I know, I know. Bad analogy.

Mrs. Dobbs's cake was in the oven when Myra dropped in. I took off my apron and joined her in the living room, bringing both of us a diet soda.

"How've you been?" I asked, sitting on the sofa and placing my drink on a coaster on the side table.

"I'm good. How about you, sweetie? I saw Jason at the gas station, and he told me about your mother."

"I'm fine. Mom's getting there. She'll probably get to go home today." I took a sip of my soda. "I'm not sure, though. I haven't heard from Dad yet."

"You keep me posted, and let me know if there's anything I can do."

"Thank you, Myra. I will."

"You look tired. Are you getting enough rest?"

"No." I set my glass down. "Can I confide in you?"

Myra leaned forward and suddenly reminded me of an eager puppy expecting a treat. "You know you can confide in me, dear. And whatever you tell me in trust will stay right here in this room."

"All right. Remember when we talked about Mr. Dobbs and how Janey doesn't like him working with Candy?"

"Yeah."

I clamped my lips together as I tried to decide how to phrase my question.

"Go on," Myra urged.

"Do you think Candy and Mr. Dobbs are having an affair?"

"Of course I do. The whole town does. Don't you?"

"I don't know. I thought maybe it was possible that Candy had a crush on Mr. Dobbs but that he didn't feel the same way."

Myra scoffed. "Darlin', you've seen Kellen Dobbs. Do you think he's one to make a younger woman's heart go pitter-patter?"

"I wouldn't believe he could make anybody's heart go pitter-patter. He certainly doesn't do a thing for me. Still, Candy must see something in him."

"Yeah. She sees dollar signs. She's hoping he'll leave Janey for her."

"But you told me everything belongs to Janey."

"It does. That don't mean Kel has told Candy that."

"Then you think Mr. Dobbs is playing Candy for a fool, stringing her along?"

Myra gave me a half smile. "If the girl is having a fling with a married man, she's a fool already, don't you think?"

"For some reason, I feel sorry for her. I think she really cares about him." I told Myra about the cake. "She was so excited. She reminded me of a little girl at Christmas. She was a cake decorator's dream client."

"Maybe she does have feelings for the man." Myra cocked her head. "But I still say she should've known better than to get involved with him. She'll wind up with a broken heart and no job when old Kel decides to move on. Just you wait and see."

"Do you think Mr. Dobbs loves his wife or that he just stays with her for the money?"

"You don't cheat on somebody you love, Daphne."

"No, you don't." It was inevitable for my thoughts to stray to Mom and Dad. Did she love him? Was it possible her infatuation with Vern March had been a passing fancy or that she'd felt some sense of obligation to Vern because of their past history? Because of their son?

I took another drink of my soda and tried to get my thoughts back to Mr. and Mrs. Dobbs. "How did those two get together in the first place?"

"Kel and Janey? Oh, honey." Myra arranged herself into a more comfortable, this-might-take-a-while position. "You see, Janey was dating this young man who was in a band. His name was Elvis. He—"

"Elvis? Janey Dobbs was dating Elvis Presley?"

"No, not that Elvis. This was Elvis Collins. He played bass guitar, and he wasn't all that good. The only reason he was even in the band was because of his brother Phil. Phil played the drums and was the band's lead singer."

My jaw dropped. "Phil Collins? Janey Dobbs dated Phil Collins's brother?"

"Yes, she dated Phil Collins's brother, and no, he wasn't *that* Phil Collins. These were a bunch of second-rate musicians who never amounted to much."

"Gotcha," I said with a nod.

"Anyway, Janey was pretty much dating a bum. Meanwhile, an industrious young fellow was working for Janey's father in the snack-food plant. He was in the accounting department. The boy knew how to manage money, and Janey's daddy took a shine to him."

"I'm beginning to see where this is going," I said, "but the majority of kids—in the United States, at any rate—would hate anyone chosen for them by their dad."

"True, but Janey was not the majority of kids. She was a relatively plain girl who'd rather die than be cut off from Daddy's money."

"And Kellen?"

"He'd had a rather lean upbringing. Now, all of a sudden, everything he'd ever wanted was within his reach." She shrugged. "He'd probably never been in love and figured he could grow to love Janey as easily as he'd come to love her family's fortune."

"Did he ever fall in love with her?" I asked.

"That's a question I can't answer, honey."

Just then the oven timer rang to let me know Mrs. Dobbs's cake was done.

* * *

IT WAS ALMOST dark, and it was difficult to drive while reading the directions to the Dobbses' house. Eventually I turned onto Maple Lane. It was a dead-end street, and Mr. and Mrs. Dobbs lived at the very end of it. I followed the winding driveway up a hill that made me wonder how Mr. Dobbs ever made it into town on slick winter mornings. And then I was in front of the house.

No one could accuse the Dobbs of living in the low-rent district. While the other houses on the street had been impressive, the Dobbses' house was by far the grandest. The house was a two-story brick colonial that was six windows wide in the front. Given that the bottom windows were picture windows, I decided the two front rooms must be the living room and dining room.

Of course, this was merely conjecture on my part. I had two way-smaller-than-picture windows in my living room and *no* windows in my dining room. I did, however, have plenty of windows in my kitchen. I figured Mrs. Dobbs did, too, though. I mean, doesn't everyone have windows in their kitchen?

I realized I was stalling and parked the car midway around the circular drive. I took the cake box from the passenger side and walked up to the front door. Mrs. Dobbs must've been watching for me; I didn't even have to ring the doorbell.

"Right on time," she said, opening the door with a broad smile. "I do admire punctuality. I have a bit of a reputation for being late myself."

"I've been known to be late a few times," I said with a laugh. "But when it's for a client, I make an extra effort to be early or at least on time."

"That's good of you. Please come in."

I preceded her into a wide foyer illuminated by a four-tier chandelier.

"Right this way, dear," Mrs. Dobbs said.

I was right about the dining room; it was one of the rooms with the enormous picture windows. The furniture was cherry, there was a table for eight, a hutch, and a side buffet. A brass and crystal chandelier hung above the table and shone on a white chrysanthemum centerpiece.

The table was set for two, but not at either end. One place setting was at the head of the table, and the other was to that person's left, as if one person took a deferential position to the other.

I gently set the cake on the table. "It appears Mr. Dobbs's birthday celebration is going to be an intimate occasion." I smiled.

"I do hope so, Daphne. I—" She looked away. "I hope so." She looked back at me. "I'm having Dakota's deliver dinner."

"Dakota's delivers?"

She gave a tight smile. "We have an arrangement." She glanced at the brass clock in the center of the buffet. "In fact, the young man should be here any minute."

"Would you like to look at the cake before I go?"

"Oh, no, dear. I'm sure it's lovely. If you'll leave me your business card, I'll have my accountant send you a check."

"This one's on me."

"Nonsense. I'd feel terrible if you didn't allow me to pay you."

I took a business card from my purse and handed it to her. "I appreciate your business, Mrs. Dobbs."

"You're quite welcome. I've heard you do marvelous work."

"Really? May I ask from whom? I mean, I haven't been in town that long."

"Yodel mainly. Yodel Watson. She might not have let on to you, but she was impressed with your work."

"Thank you. I appreciate your sharing that with me."

Mrs. Dobbs looked at the clock again. "I do hope Kellen gets here soon." She lowered her eyes. "He's so very dedicated to . . . the store."

"I'm sure he'll be here as soon as he can." I moved toward the foyer, and Mrs. Dobbs walked me to the door.

"Do have a safe drive home."

"Thank you, Mrs. Dobbs. Good night."

As I left, Mrs. Dobbs was standing in the doorway. I didn't know whether she was watching me leave or waiting for her husband to come home. Either way, I could feel myself beginning to harbor some hostility toward Kellen Dobbs.

CHAPTER

thirteen

O N THURSDAY, I awoke with a sense of purpose. I'd talked to Dad the night before and knew Mom was home and doing well, but the ghost of Jonah March would not give me a minute's peace. I had to find out if my mother and his mother were the same person. Most people—I'm thinking Violet here—would ask, "What difference does it make? The man is dead and gone." But it made a difference to me. I wanted to know if Jonah had been my half brother, if Joanne Hayden was my niece.

Since Mom's episode, I doubted I could ever ask her anything about Vern March or an illicit pregnancy without making her heart explode, an event that would not only kill her but more than likely ruin the very bra she'd hoped to be buried in. Two major strikes against me in one fell swoop.

Please forgive me for being so flippant about my mother's health. I do love her, but making these jokes and laughing to myself about her condition makes it seem less real somehow. I'd be devastated if she were to die, so I simply choose to make that possibility absurd.

Anyway, I knew I couldn't talk with my mother about the issues weighing on my mind—not to mention my heart—so I decided to look through public records. But where to start? Vern had been buried in Scott County. Something Ben had told me led me to believe he'd had family there. It made sense that he and Gloria would leave this town to get married, especially if they were going to falsify the license by having someone pose as Gloria's mother. Scott County seemed to be my best bet.

I fed Sparrow, filled a travel mug with coffee, and headed toward Scott County. I figured that by the time I got there, the courthouse would be open.

The fiery reds and golds and muted greens of the autumn leaves had all turned brown as I drove along. Not many leaves were actually left on the trees, of course—only a few hung on, ignorant of their futility. Those stark, naked trees spoke to my soul as they lifted their limbs to heaven, seemingly entreating God for mercy. I, too, longed for His mercy. What would it do to me, how would it change my life, if I found out my mother had been married to Vern March and that they had had a son?

THE SCOTT COUNTY courthouse loomed before me as I parked my car near one of the lot's three-globed lamp stands. The building seemed to get even larger as I approached. I imagined Vern and Jonah March looking down on me from the octagonal tower atop the courthouse.

"That's Gloria's daughter," I imagined Vern saying. "She's here to learn the truth."

I could practically hear Jonah's mocking laughter. "Is she now? Is she really? The truth ain't always what it's cracked up to be. You can still get back in your car and go home, little girl."

I *could* go home.

It's odd that, in my mind, Jonah's ghost had called me a little girl. Or maybe it wasn't so odd. I did feel like a child—vulnerable, alone, or getting ready to sneak a peek into her mother's purse, afraid of getting caught. But I wasn't taking a peek into a purse. I was confronting the past. And I wasn't afraid of getting caught but of what I'd find.

You can still get back in your car and go home, little girl.

I looked back at my car, red paint sparkling in the sunshine, and then glanced up at the tower once more. I took the steps at the left side of the courthouse, squared my shoulders, and walked through the door.

I asked for assistance from a smartly dressed blond woman who ushered me into a large records room.

"The marriage records from 1960 will be in this cabinet, filed alphabetically."

"Thank you."

She left, and I began looking through the M's. Within five minutes, I'd found the record.

> March, Vernon P.
> Cline, Gloria A.

Cline. Not Beeson, Mom's maiden name.

Tears of relief pricked my eyes. I blinked rapidly and read the rest of the document.

Jane S. Cline had signed the consent form as Gloria's

mother. Yet I knew Gloria's mother had not consented to the marriage. Not that it really mattered to me at this point. My mother had not been married to Vern March, and she was not Jonah's mother. I could now go home and put this part of the mystery to rest.

As soon as I got home, I called Violet. "Can you talk?"

"I've got a few minutes. What's up?"

"I went to Scott County this morning. Our mom was never married to Vern March. It was Gloria *Cline*."

"Great. See? I knew you were worrying yourself for no reason."

"And you weren't worried? I really was afraid Jonah March was our half brother, Vi. I wonder if I should let Peggy and Joanne know they have Gloria Cline—not Gloria Carter—to blame for all Vern's problems."

"Well, she wasn't responsible for *all* of them. Remember, Uncle Hal *did* run the man out of town."

"With good reason. I have to place the blame for that squarely on Vern and—well, mostly on Vern."

"Yeah. I'm glad your fears were put to rest, sis."

"So you truly weren't worried at all?"

"I've already made peace with Mom's past, Daphne. She made a mistake, but then, haven't we all? Maybe now you can let go of it, too."

"Maybe. I mean, I hope so. Do you think I should tell Peggy March about Gloria Cline?"

"I guess so," Violet said. "Maybe somehow it'll ease her mind, too."

"Yeah. I'll talk with you soon."

We said our good-byes, and I hung up the phone. I nearly

wet my pants when I turned and saw Myra standing in the doorway.

"I knocked," she said, "but you didn't answer. Since the door was open, I came on in. Hope you don't mind."

"N-not a bit."

"Didn't mean to eavesdrop, but I heard you saying something about Gloria Cline."

"Do you know her?"

"Not really. But I know her sister . . . and you do, too."

I frowned. I had no idea who she meant.

"Janey Dobbs. Janey was a Cline before she married Kellen. Do you recall my telling you about the snack-cake factory? It was Cline's Cakes and Snacks."

My brow furrowed as I tried to put the pieces together. To no avail, naturally. "I heard Gloria Cline once spent time in a mental institution," I said, hoping the conversation would spark something.

"Spent time?" Myra snorted. "She *lives* there. From what I've heard, Janey's sister has been in the nuthouse since she was eighteen or nineteen years old. Some boy broke her heart, and she had a nervous breakdown or something."

"That's crazy."

"Uh, yeah, that's why she's in the loony bin."

"No, I mean, we all have our teenage heartbreaks. Was something wrong with her to begin with?"

"You mean, did she have what folks used to call a delicate condition? Something like that?"

I nodded.

"I don't know, but you'd think so, wouldn't you? If they locked up everybody who's ever been heartbroken, very few of us would be out wandering around."

"I sure wouldn't be."

"Me, either."

I couldn't help but wonder if there was more to Gloria's story than I knew. I silently cursed myself for reading every Victoria Holt novel ever written and tried to put Gloria out of my mind.

LATER WITH MYRA gone, I listened to my answering machine messages. The first was from Candy:

"Daphne, it's me, Candy. I positively cannot thank you enough for the wonderful cake you made. I've saved you a piece of it, so you come on by the store and get it, okay? Thanks again, sweetie. You do great work. I'm tellin' everybody!"

Candy apparently was sincere with regard to being head of my marketing department. The next call was a potential client.

"Hello, Ms. Martin. I'm Belinda Fremont, and I'm planning a party for my precious Guinevere. I'd like to talk with you, so give me a call as soon as possible."

She left her home and cell numbers. Surely I'd be able to reach her at one of them.

The final message was from Ben.

"Hi, Daph. Give me a call when you get in. Thanks."

I called Belinda Fremont back first. She answered promptly but refused to discuss business over the phone.

"Please bring some cake samples and your portfolio to my home at 143 Wedgwood Street at three thirty p.m. today."

"All right. I look forward to seeing you then," I said as brightly as I could, even though I was panicking inside.

I'd been so depressed over the Yodel Watson situation and its effect on my business that I'd neglected to stock my freezer with as many sample cakes as I should have. I looked at the clock. It was a quarter past eleven; I'd have to work quickly.

I checked the freezer and found a square spice cake on

hand. I set it on the counter to thaw. Candy was saving me a piece of the Mocha Madeira—that was two samples. I needed three more sample cakes to provide Mrs. Fremont with an ample variety of choices.

I hurriedly thumbed through my cookbooks and came up with an almond pound cake, a strawberry cake, and a chocolate peanut butter cake. I mixed like mad. While the cakes were baking, I made cream cheese and chocolate frostings. The cream cheese was for the spice cake, and the chocolate was for the chocolate peanut butter cake. Luckily, I had a batch of vanilla buttercream in the fridge that would work nicely with the almond pound cake and the strawberry cake.

By two thirty, my kitchen was a disaster area, but I had four two-by-one-inch cake samples to present to Mrs. Fremont. I put the samples on a lace-pattered cake square in a Daphne's Delectable Cakes box, grabbed my portfolio off the desk in my office, and rushed out to the car. I carefully placed the cake samples on the passenger seat and leaned the portfolio against the box to further cushion the samples.

That's when I realized I was still wearing my apron. I decided I didn't have time to unlock the door and hang it up, so I just folded it and laid it on the backseat. I got in the car and was put in the precarious position of having to hurry but having to also be very careful. If you've ever had to drive a woman in labor to the hospital, or drive an animal in labor to the veterinarian's office, then you know what I mean.

My first stop was Dobbs's Pet Store. I experienced a mental speed bump when I noticed the rather large iguana standing on the counter. Thinking four cake samples was probably enough, I started back out the door.

Candy had already spotted me, though. "Hi! Come on back here."

I glanced nervously toward the counter.

"Aw, she won't hurt you," Kel said. "She's been under the weather lately anyhow."

"Put her in her cage or at least hold her a minute," Candy said. "Daphne's scared of her."

With a look that told me Kel much preferred animals to people, he scooped up the lizard and cradled her against his chest.

"Thanks." I followed Candy to the back.

"Boy-howdy, your cake was a hit." Candy handed me a small plastic container. "It was all I could do to save you that tiny piece."

"You didn't have to save me a slice, but it was sweet of you to think of me."

"Gosh, you're welcome. Once the customers found out that cake was back here—" She looked down at her turquoise sneakers. "I reckon you know the cake was for Kel."

"I figured as much. Back when I had a *real job,* I always made the boss a nice birthday cake."

She raised her head and smiled. "You did?"

"Of course. Especially since his birthday was around performance review time!"

We both laughed.

"I was afraid you'd think bad of me if you knew the cake was for Kel." Her cheeks flushed pink.

I shook my head. "How could such a thoughtful gesture make me think poorly of you?"

Candy gave me one of her now anticipated hugs. I took my cake, darted past Kel and his scaly beast, and got into the car. I drove about a mile before pulling off the road to transfer the Mocha Madeira cake into the box with my other samples. I'd have hated for Candy to look out the shopwindow and wonder what I was doing with the cake she'd so painstakingly preserved for me.

I'd told Candy the truth—I didn't think poorly of her. The more I got to know her, the more I felt that she—and Mrs. Dobbs, for that matter—were victims of Kellen Dobbs's manipulations.

I'D BEEN IMPRESSED with the Dobbses' house; I was impressed with Belinda Fremont's *driveway*. A burnished plaque on the gate assured me I was at the right place—143 Wedgwood. I drove onto the white and terra-cotta bricks, half wishing I'd washed my car before coming here so my tires wouldn't dirty up the intricate design. I put down my window and pressed the intercom call button to my left.

"Yes?" responded a male voice.

"I'm Daphne Martin. I have a three thirty appointment with Mrs. Fremont."

"Of course."

The wrought-iron gates opened to allow me entrance to the magical kingdom. I drove slowly up the patterned drive until an elegant white *hotel* appeared before me.

Remember how I said no one could accuse Janey and Kellen Dobbs of living in the low-rent district? Belinda Fremont could. And I don't even want to hazard a guess at where that puts me on the social measuring stick.

When I got closer to the entrance, a man in tan slacks and a brown sweater walked down the stairs.

I rolled down my window once again. "Mr. Fremont?"

He chuckled. "Hardly."

I recognized his voice as that of the gatekeeper.

"I'll carry your packages inside," he continued, "and then I'll park your car. Please leave the keys in the ignition."

"Yes, sir. Thank you."

Valet parking? Maybe this *was* a hotel! Was I supposed to tip this man?

I followed him up the steps and into a Victorian-style sitting room. He sat the cake box and my portfolio side-by-side on a round table in the middle of the room.

"I'll tell Mrs. Fremont you're here." He grinned. "Good luck."

He left the room before I could ask what he'd meant by that. I went to stand by the fireplace, where a small fire knocked the chill off the room. I'm no historian by any means, but the love seat and high-backed chairs made me think they were done in the Louis XIV style. The paintings on the walls and the photographs on the mantel were of people dressed in the style of the early 1900s. The women had parasols and dresses with cinched waists and bustles. The gentlemen wore bowlers and had ridiculous mustaches.

"Hello!" boomed a cheery voice from the doorway. "I'm Belinda Fremont."

"I'm Daphne—"

"Yes, I know. Let's see what you can do." She strode over to the table and opened my portfolio.

What struck me about Belinda Fremont was that, despite her cultured voice and her lofty demeanor, she seemed young—no more than thirty-five, I'd venture. Of course, plastic surgery can make anyone look young, but she didn't have that restriction of facial movement many plastic surgery patients end up with. Nor did she have a turkey neck or crone hands. If only she'd take off her shoes so I could see if she had old-person feet.

Still, I thought she probably was as young as she looked,

which made me feel like a failure somehow. Idiotic, I know, but your emotions will rear up in the strangest of places.

"Nice," Mrs. Fremont was saying as she flipped through my cake photos. "That's cute. Pretty. Intriguing." She turned to me. "I'm assuming the samples are in the box?"

"Yes, ma'am," I answered with a smile.

"Let's take them into the kitchen and try them."

I followed her down the gleaming hardwood hallway, resisting the urge to look down at my reflection to make sure there was nothing in my teeth. She led me to a kitchen that was just plain drool-worthy, not only for the smells coming from the various pots on the stove and/or the three—yes, three—ovens, but for its sheer enormity. I could bake and decorate—not to mention store all my stuff, and buy lots more stuff to store—until I passed out from glee. I was feeling light-headed already, and that was only from considering the possibilities.

I noticed that both Mrs. Fremont and her cook, whom I hadn't seen previously, were staring at me. Suddenly I realized I was gazing around the room with my mouth wide open. I closed my mouth and smiled shyly at Mrs. Fremont.

"What?" she asked.

"It's just . . . your house . . . it's incredible."

She smiled. "Thank you. It's modeled after Crane Cottage on Jekyll Island. You know, off the coast of Georgia. Are you familiar with it?"

"Yes," I said. "I've vacationed there."

"You'll recall, then, that Crane Cottage is the largest of the private residences."

I nodded. Good thing I had no desire to interrupt because talking about her home was obviously one of Belinda Fremont's favorite pastimes.

"Like Crane, this home was built in the Italian Renaissance

style. I even have a replica of the courtyard out back. I'll show you before you leave, provided it's still light enough outside to appreciate it."

"Thank you. I'd enjoy that."

"We have lighting in the summer, of course, but not during the fall and winter months. Perhaps if things work out well, you can do something else for us." Mrs. Fremont opened the box. "Plates and forks, please, Hilda."

The rotund cook was quick to comply with her employer's request. Before you could say "cake samples," there were half a dozen delicate china dessert plates sitting on the table with a dessert fork and a linen napkin to the right of each one. I deconstructed the box so I wouldn't damage the samples as they were being lifted out, and, with a small smile, Hilda handed me a silver cake server. I put the five samples on five of the plates, wondering if Belinda Fremont had expected six samples or if Hilda was merely playing it safe. It didn't matter now—I had what I had. I was starting to get aggravated at myself for feeling so nervous and inadequate here.

Mrs. Fremont tried each sample as I told her what type of cake it was and explained some of the cake's properties— texture, ease of design, complementary flavors, and so on. Then she tasted each sample again. Forty-five minutes later, she'd narrowed it down to the almond pound cake and the strawberry cake. Twenty minutes after that, she chose the almond pound cake.

I took a notebook out of the back of my portfolio and began taking notes. "How old is your daughter?"

"My daughter?" Mrs. Fremont barked out a laugh. "Is that what you think?" She laughed again, though I noticed Hilda didn't even smile. "Come with me. It's time for you to meet Guinevere."

CHAPTER

fourteen

I FOLLOWED BELINDA Fremont up the white and walnut staircase to the second floor. At the top of the stairs, we turned left into a dimly lit hallway.

"This is their suite," Mrs. Fremont explained.

"Their?"

"Guinevere and her friends. They each have a separate room but visit in their sitting room when they're so inclined."

"Oh."

We stopped at the second door on the right, and Mrs. Fremont opened the door.

"Quietly, please," she whispered. "Guinevere prizes tranquility."

The room was decorated in pink with ivory accents. Against

the far wall was a daybed flanked on each side by a round table. The tables were covered in the same material as the daybed's coverlet. On each table, a lamp provided a soft glow. Frilly pillows, stuffed animals, and toys were scattered over the floor.

The darkness and silence made me wonder if Guinevere was ill. But why were there cages with various colors of paper bedding scattered throughout the room? Shouldn't a sick child avoid pets? The room was empty, though. Maybe Guinevere was in the sitting room with her friends.

I spotted a particularly interesting stuffed animal lying in the middle of the floor. It reminded me of Cousin Itt of Addams Family fame. But instead of long, brown hair, this creature had orange and white hair flowing in all directions and completely obscuring its features.

"How cute!" I stepped forward to pick it up so I could get a better look at it. I think at this point Mrs. Fremont yelled, "No." I'm not completely certain because It let out a loud shriek.

"Excuse us," Mrs. Fremont said, picking It up. "I'll see you back downstairs in the sitting room."

I scampered back downstairs. In the foyer, I ran into the valet. His lips were twitching with suppressed amusement.

"Hilda tells me you thought Guinevere was Mrs. Fremont's daughter."

"Yeah." I grimaced. "I take it Guinevere is the furry thing I made scream?"

At this point, he did laugh. "I'm afraid so. Guinevere and her friends are Satin Peruvian guinea pigs."

"I've been told to wait for Mrs. Fremont in the sitting room, but you might want to stay close by. I imagine you'll be bringing my car around soon."

I went to the sitting room and perched on an uncomfortable chair. My portfolio had been returned to the round table in the middle of the room—by Hilda, I presumed. I'd only been waiting about ten minutes when Mrs. Fremont joined me.

I stood. "I'm so sorry."

"It's all right. You merely startled her. I suppose I should've warned you . . . though I had no idea you'd attempt to . . . what *were* you doing?"

"I just wanted a closer look. Again, I apologize. Guinevere is the first Satin Peruvian I've ever seen in real life."

At that, her eyes lit up. "You're familiar with the breed?"

"Not terribly, but I do know they're adorable." I forced as genuine a smile as I could.

Mrs. Fremont bubbled with laughter. "They are, aren't they? When you bring your designs next week, you can get better acquainted with Guinevere and her friends."

"How many friends does she have? So I, uh, can plan for the party?"

"There's Lancelot, Morgan, Arthur, Beatrice, and Merlin. They'll need something of their own, of course, and then we'll need a cake for the fifty to seventy-five humans in attendance."

"Of course."

"You can bring your ideas and designs back on Tuesday."

"Three thirty?" I asked.

"Perfect."

I lingered for a moment. "May I ask if you were referred to me by Candy, from Dobbs's Pet Store?" For some reason, I couldn't see Candy and Belinda Fremont chatting it up.

Mrs. Fremont placed a hand to her chest. "Oh, no. It would have to be a dire emergency for me to set foot in Dobbs's Pet Store."

"Really?"

"Really. I was referred to you by Annabelle Fontaine, Yodel Watson's daughter."

ANNABELLE ANSWERED ON the third ring, sounding out of breath.

"Is this a bad time?" I asked.

"No. I was on the porch when I heard the phone ring, so it just took me a minute to get inside."

"Is the weather still lovely there in Florida?"

"It sure is. What's going on in the Old Dominion?"

"I got a new client today, and I wanted to call and thank you for the referral."

"Then Belinda did call you. Good." She laughed softly. "Or is it?" she added somewhat mischievously.

"It is," I said hesitantly, "although the task she's set before me will be challenging."

"I can only imagine. Belinda can be demanding and a wee bit eccentric, but she's fair-minded. And she knows *tons* of people. If she's happy with your work, she'll send plenty of business your way."

"What do you know about Guinevere?"

"She's one of the guinea pigs, right?"

"Right."

"They're like children to Belinda. And all her Peruvians are champions."

"Champions?" I was beginning to feel like Yodel's parrot, Banjo, but I couldn't seem to help myself.

"Yes, champions recognized by the American Cavy Breeders Association. Belinda has photographs and ribbons above the fireplace in their sitting room."

Those things need a fireplace? I chuckled to myself.

"How long have you known Mrs. Fremont?"

"Since grade school."

So Mrs. Fremont was older than she'd appeared. Maybe if I impressed her with my cake, she'd take me to the Fountain of Youth in her courtyard.

"Has she always been—"

"Rich?" Annabelle finished for me.

"I'm sorry. That's none of my business."

"Be that as it may, the answer is yes. She was born rich and married richer, so there you go."

"What's Mr. Fremont like?"

"He's warm and has a wicked sense of humor. He travels a lot, though. But I'm sure he'll be at Guinevere's party."

"Ah . . . okay. Well, how are *you*?" I asked. "I know getting back home has probably helped."

"It has helped, and I'm doing well. I have my days, you know, but overall I'm okay."

"Have you heard anything from the police?" I asked tentatively.

"The last I heard, they'd found a suspicious stain in Mother's living room and were going to test it." She sighed. "I hope Dr. Lancaster is able to find Banjo a good home. If you don't mind, would you check on that for me?"

"I'll be happy to. Thank you again for referring me to Mrs. Fremont."

"You're quite welcome. I hope you'll still feel that way when you've finished the job," she said, clearly holding back a laugh before saying good-bye and hanging up.

Nothing like a parting shot to fill one to the brim with confidence.

I went into my office and took a couple books off the shelf. Belinda Fremont seemed to be all about extravagance, so I thought Sylvia Weinstock might have just the sort of cake I was looking for.

I put on a jacket and took my books, a book light, and some cat treats out onto the porch. I sat down and Sparrow eased out from under a nearby bush.

"Hi, Sparrow," I cooed quietly, tossing a treat in her direction.

She ran to the treat, snatched it up, and raced back to the edge of the bush to eat it.

I threw the next snack a bit closer to me and opened up *Sweet Celebrations: The Art of Beautiful Cakes* by Sylvia Weinstock with Kate Manchester. I thumbed through the book and tossed cat treats, pretending to ignore the cat, until I found what I was looking for. It was on page 89—a three-tier cake decorated with marzipan fruit and gum paste flowers. The cake would serve eighty to a hundred people, and I could easily come up with something for the guinea pigs to coordinate with the cake.

I caught a movement in the corner of my eye. It was Sparrow. She'd moved to within two feet of me. I dropped a treat at my side. She got it and then retreated but stayed scarcely beyond arm's reach until I dropped another treat. I smiled. We were getting there.

WHEN THE NIGHT air became chilly, I went inside to the kitchen. I cut the two cakes I'd made earlier into sample sizes and put them in the freezer, but I couldn't refreeze the spice cake. Even though there was a slice out of it—maybe *especially* because there was a slice out of it—I knew precisely what to do with it.

I called Myra. "If you've got some decaf coffee, I've got spice cake."

She invited me right over.

The warm glow of Myra's porch light beckoned as I strode carefully from my yard to hers. When I rang the doorbell, Myra opened the door and took both my jacket and the cake. She hung my jacket on a coatrack near the door and took the cake into the kitchen.

"I'm glad you came over," Myra said. "After Thanksgiving, when everybody goes back home, I get the lonelies for a few days. This is exactly what I needed."

"Me too." I smiled. "There's a piece missing from the cake, though. I had to provide a sample for a new client."

"A new client! That's great, honey." She put dessert plates, forks, cups, and saucers on the table. "Is somebody getting married?"

I pulled out a chair and sat down. "No. It's a birthday party . . . for a guinea pig."

Myra's eyes got huge, and I started laughing.

"Are you kidding?" she asked.

I was still laughing so hard that all I could do was shake my head. Myra started laughing, too. Before we knew it, tears were streaming down both our faces.

Myra caught her breath first. "You're making a spice cake for a guinea pig's birthday?"

"No. As a matter of fact, I'm making her an almond pound cake."

This set off another eruption of giggles.

At last I wiped the tears from my cheeks. "Actually, it's even more absurd than that. Do you know Belinda Fremont?"

"Mrs. Belinda 'Mansion on the Hill' Fremont?"

"That's the one."

"I don't know her, but I do know *of* her."

"Please don't think poorly of me for poking fun at one of my

178   Gayle Trent

clients, Myra. I have the utmost respect for Mrs. Fremont, but this is the strangest project I've ever taken on!"

Myra carried over a coffee carafe and placed it on the table between us. Then she sat down. "So you really are serious? About the guinea pig's birthday party?"

"I am. I need to prepare some sort of cake for the guest of honor and her five guinea pig friends and another cake for fifty to seventy-five of her human guests."

Myra poured coffee into our cups. "Must be some guinea pig."

"I'd never seen one like her. According to Annabelle Fontaine, all of Mrs. Fremont's guinea pigs are champions."

"Like show dogs?" she asked as she served the cake.

"Yes, except they're show . . ."

"Pigs."

I grinned. "Pigs who live high on the hog, believe me. They each have their own bedroom."

Myra cut her fork into her slice of cake with a wistful expression on her face. "Wonder what I'd have done with my money if I'd been born rich instead of beautiful?" She winked and took a bite of cake.

"Do you know anything about a feud of any kind between Mrs. Fremont and the Dobbses?"

Myra slowly shook her head. "No. Why?"

"I asked Mrs. Fremont if Candy recommended her, and she said it would have to be a dire emergency for her to set foot into Dobbs's Pet Store." I dug into my piece of cake.

"I don't know," Myra said, "but let me make a few discreet inquiries."

* * *

I HAD A nice visit with Myra, and by the time I got home, I had a plan for Guinevere's "cake." I went into my office and logged on to the Internet. Within half an hour I had a pattern and step-by-step directions to make a willow basket, and a list of foods guinea pigs like to eat.

I took a sketch pad from my right-hand drawer and began to lightly pencil my basket onto the center of the paper. I added sprigs of timothy hay, apples, green bell pepper slices, raspberries, baby carrots, kiwi slices, grapes, strawberries, and blueberries. If I incorporated some of the same fruits into the floral arrangement on the cake, the basket and cake would complement each other beautifully.

I got my coloring pencils and began tracing and filling in my pencil drawings. I was pleased with my concept and, for the moment at least, felt sure that Belinda Fremont would like it, too.

The phone rang. It was Ben. I hoped he was merely making a social call, but there was more to it than that.

"I got a call from my friend at the police department," he said. "They got the lab report back on that yellow stain."

"What was it?"

"You have to promise what I'm about to tell you will go absolutely no further."

"Yeah, yeah. Scout's honor."

"I'm serious, Daphne. It's important that this information doesn't get leaked. My friend trusted me, and I'm putting both his friendship and my credibility on the line by telling you this."

"I won't tell a soul. I promise. Now, what was it?"

"Snake venom."

"Did you say 'snake venom'?"

"That's what I said."

"But it's November. Aren't snakes supposed to be hibernating or something right now?"

"If they're wild, yes."

Then I remembered Kellen Dobbs milking the rattlesnake and gulped. "Do the police think somebody put a snake in Mrs. Watson's house to scare her or, you know, to kill her?"

"Mrs. Watson's death is being officially ruled a homicide. That's something else I need you to keep between us, though. I've been promised an exclusive when the perpetrator is caught."

"How can you be so calm about this? Somebody right here in our town is going around killing people with snakes."

"That's the other odd thing. While respiratory failure due to poisoning is the cause of death, there was no evidence at the autopsy of a snake bite. There was a suspect puncture wound on the back of her neck, but there was only one wound, not the two wounds you'd expect from a snake bite."

"This whole thing is simply bizarre, don't you think?"

"Yeah, I do think it's bizarre. And I have the exclusive—the *exclusive*—and I'm not only talking about the local newspapers."

I huffed. "I get that you're excited about that, but there's a lot more to be taken into consideration here. What about Anna-belle, Mrs. Watson's daughter? Have the police told her?"

"I'm sure they have. I figure they'd want to ask if her mother knew anyone who might've had a snake."

"How do you know something like that? I met a woman today who I wouldn't have dreamed owns six guinea pigs, but—"

"You met Belinda Fremont?"

"How'd you know?"

"How'd I know you were talking about Belinda Fremont, or how'd I know she has six guinea pigs?"

"Both."

"She's the only person in town, as far as I know, who has six guinea pigs. And since she's friends with the *Chronicle*'s owner, the paper makes a fuss over it every time one of Mrs. Fremont's pets wins one of those cavy things."

"But still, if you met Belinda Fremont on the street, would you say, 'Now there's a guinea pig owner if I ever saw one'?"

"If I talked with her for five minutes, I would."

"Good point."

"And, Daphne, I know your heart is in the right place, but *please* don't discuss any of this with Annabelle Fontaine."

"All right. But what if she calls and wants to discuss it with *me*?"

"Daphne." There was a scolding-dad tone in his voice. I found it terribly aggravating.

"Never mind," I said, with just a hint of a growl. "I won't blow your precious exclusive and, in fact, I wish you'd never told me."

"I—"

"You don't even have to bother to say it, Ben. I know you wish you hadn't told me, either. I have to go. I've got work to do."

He tried to say something—to apologize, most likely—but I cut him off again, said good-bye, and hung up. What *was* I supposed to do if Annabelle called? Of course, if *she* told *me* what happened to her mother, then I wouldn't be breaking my word to Ben. Would I?

CHAPTER

fifteen

I TOOK MY gum paste kit into the living room, opened the armoire, and turned on the television. I sat on the floor and placed my kit on the coffee table. There was a game show on TV, but I wasn't paying much attention to it as I laid out a kitchen towel on the table. I then took out my rose petal cutter, oval cutter, calyx cutter, orchid cutter, and ball tool so I could get started. I'd already colored some gum paste light green for the kiwis and grapes and dark green for the calyxes, and I had some white and pink marbled gum paste for the roses and orchids. I figured that even if Belinda Fremont decided she didn't like my design idea, I could still use the pieces for something. When stored properly, gum paste decorations can keep for months. Besides, working with the dough would calm my frazzled nerves.

I decided to start with the roses. I rolled a piece of gum paste into a marble-sized ball and then began to flatten it into a teardrop shape.

I thought about Ben. After hearing how excited the newspaper owner got about Mrs. Fremont's Satin Peruvians winning a cavy championship, I could see why Ben would want meatier articles. This article on Mrs. Watson's murderer could be a boon to his career.

Mrs. Watson had said in her journal that Ben wanted to work for one of those "fancy" newspapers in Knoxville or Charlotte. But Ben was forty years old. If he'd wanted to work for a bigger newspaper, he'd have left here years ago.

I flattened the smaller part of my teardrop-shaped dough into a round petal and then curled the petal around itself to form the center bud. I stuck a bamboo skewer into the bottom of the bud and then stuck that into a block of Styrofoam.

I tried desperately to understand Ben's position. If he wanted to report grittier news stories, why hadn't he gone to a bigger city, rather than spend his entire career here? Was he working on a novel? Had he been hoping all these years that some fantastic story would come along and propel him to journalistic stardom?

I took my mini rolling pin out of the kit and rolled out a square sheet of dough. I rubbed a dab of cornstarch onto my rose petal cutter and made a petal. I covered the rest of the sheet with plastic wrap. Placing the petal in my left hand, I took my ball tool in my right hand and rolled it around the petal, ruffling the edges slightly as I went.

I also found it odd that even though Annabelle was friends with Belinda Fremont, who had to be one of the richest people in town, there was no mention of any "Belinda" in Mrs. Watson's journal. Of course, I hadn't read the entire book—the

Gloria Carter story had kind of stopped me in my tracks. But I'd have thought Mrs. Watson would write about her daughter's friend fairly frequently.

On the other hand, the journal wasn't your typical journal. It was more a tabloid. In fact, the only place I'd even seen Annabelle mentioned was in connection with the story about Myra and Carl at the steakhouse. Violet was right about that book—it was filled with hatred and bitterness, and nothing more.

But was the book enough to make someone kill Yodel Watson?

I placed my petal over an inverted egg cup to rest and then cut another petal. Once again I rolled the ball tool around it, ruffling its edges.

I made a mental inventory in my head. As far as I knew, who had something against Mrs. Watson?

Fred, the produce guy, hated Mrs. Watson because she got him demoted at work. Plus, Fred has some mental problems and—as I had witnessed firsthand—some extreme anger issues. I decided to go to Save-A-Buck tomorrow and ask Fred if he had a snake. That's not *that* unusual a question, is it?

Kellen Dobbs and Candy had a grudge against Mrs. Watson because, although every other person in town *guessed* the two were having an affair, Mrs. Watson had seen proof of that fact with her own two eyes. Mr. Dobbs might have been afraid Mrs. Watson would tell Janey. A divorce would ruin Mr. Dobbs financially. *And* Mr. Dobbs has plenty of snakes and knows how to milk venom from them. He seemed the most likely suspect.

I replaced my resting petal with the new one on the egg cup and attached my finished petal to the rosebud. I cut another petal and started the entire process again.

Who else would want to kill Yodel Watson, though? I

needed to cover all the bases. An image of Uncle Hal floated into my mind. But why would Uncle Hal want to kill Mrs. Watson after all these years? Even though there is no statute of limitations on murder, Uncle Hal hadn't killed Vern March.

Someone had.

I hate when my mind argues with me. While I had to agree that it *appeared* someone had tampered with Vern's car, causing the brakes to fail and thus causing his accident, Vern's death had been ruled exactly that—an accident. It was never proven that anyone put a hole in the car's brake lines.

Besides, if Uncle Hal had wanted Mrs. Watson dead, he's had plenty of opportunities over the years. Why would he do it thirty years after the fact?

Or maybe Ben killed her. Maybe because he was tired of waiting for that fantastic story to happen and decided to create his own, wherein he would help solve the crime and be a hero.

Maybe I killed her. Maybe I was so sick of her incessant criticisms of my cakes that I put snake venom in . . . nope. I can't come up with anything to implicate myself. She didn't touch the cake I made. Now, if I could convince the rest of the town that I'm innocent, maybe I could grow myself a thriving business.

And maybe Belinda Fremont could help me do precisely that.

I'D BARELY FINISHED putting away my flowers, fruit, and gum paste supplies when Myra called.

"Hi, darlin'," she said, excitement practically jumping through the phone line. "You busy?"

"No. What's going on?"

"Well, after you left, I called Tanya Talbot of Tanya's Tremendous Tress Taming Salon to make a hair appointment for tomorrow."

"Tanya's Tremendous Tress Taming Salon?" That was a mouthful.

"Yeah. Tanya's mother is an English teacher and told her people seemed to remember catchy titles with alliteration."

"I'd hate to have to answer the phone in that salon."

"It's okay. They just say, 'Tanya's, can I help you?' But I didn't call to tell you I made myself a hair appointment. I called to tell you that Tanya knows all about the Dobbs-Fremont feud."

My eyes widened. "She does?"

"Oh, honey. You see, when I called, I told Tanya I wanted my hair to be pretty for Christmas, what with all the parties and everything going on. Then I said, 'Speaking of parties, Belinda Fremont is having a birthday party for one of her guinea pigs. Isn't that sweet?' And Tanya said, 'Sweet . . . yeah.' She said it like that, too, like she didn't think it was all that sweet. I'm not so sure it is, either, but hey, Belinda Fremont can do whatever she wants with her money."

"I'm with you there."

"So then Tanya said, 'It's all I can do to throw together birthday parties for my kids.' I said I remembered them days sure enough and then drew Tanya back to talking about Belinda because, honey, if there's anybody who's Yodel Watson's successor in the gossip department, it's Tanya Talbot. So I said, 'I wonder where she gets stuff for those little guinea pigs of hers? I've heard she won't shop at Dobbs's.' And Tanya said, 'That's the truth. She wouldn't give Kel Dobbs air if he was stopped up in a jug.' I asked why and she told me she went in there one time and there was a pitiful little hamster cowering in a cage getting ready to be devoured by this big ol' snake!"

"Ewww. That is pitiful," I agreed, "but maybe the poor hamster was sick or something . . . and the snake *had* to eat."

"Who knows, but to hear Tanya tell it, Belinda Fremont lit into Kel Dobbs and let him have it with both barrels. She accused him of feeding all those little creatures to his snakes and said she'd have him boycotted by the American Cavy Breeders Association, the American Rabbit Breeders Association, the Humane Society, and everybody else she could think of."

I brought my hand to my chin. "I wonder what Mr. Dobbs thought of that."

"Apparently, he didn't back down. Tanya did say he lost some business because of it, though."

"I guess he did. I mean, the snakes have to eat and they sure don't eat snake chow or whatever, but you'd think he'd feed the snakes when his shop was closed so it wouldn't upset his patrons."

"You'd think," Myra said. "Still, from what I've always heard of Kellen Dobbs, he's gonna do what he's gonna do whether people like it or not."

I GOT UP early the next morning. It seemed to be my new routine. Get up, get dressed, and get out of the house before 7:00 a.m. This particular morning, though, I wanted to catch Peggy March before she left for work.

She was certainly surprised to see me.

"I'm really sorry for coming by so early. I won't take but a minute of your time," I added, as she took a curler out of her hair and looked at her watch. "I only wanted to tell you what I learned about Vern March's wife."

"Come in," she said, "but I have to finish getting ready."

"Of course. I'll talk from the hallway."

I followed her down the hall, where she went into her bathroom and closed the door all but a crack.

"I went to the Scott County courthouse yesterday. Vern was married to Gloria Cline, not my mother, Gloria Carter."

"Good for you, dear. I know you're relieved." She paused. "Cline . . . Cline . . . why does that name sound familiar?"

"Cline's Cakes and Snacks?" I ventured.

"Oh, right."

"Gloria is—was? Well, I'm not sure she's still living. Anyway, Gloria is one of the snack-cake Clines, I guess you could say."

The bathroom door slowly opened and Peggy stood there with a mascara wand in her hand. "Are you telling me that Jonah—and now Joanne—could be, well, provided for?"

"It's certainly something you should look into, Mrs. March."

She smiled. "Believe me, I will. Thank you. Thank you for coming and telling me this."

I nodded and saw myself out. I hoped Peggy would benefit from my news about Gloria Cline. I didn't know whether or not Gloria was still living, but either way, it could be a good thing for Joanne. She stood to gain either a grandmother or some shares in a snack-cake franchise. And now she no longer had a reason to hate me. I still got mad enough to bite a nail in two when I thought of my little visit from the Department of Agriculture, though.

I wanted to go by Dr. Lancaster's office next, but I knew it wasn't open yet so I headed over to the Save-A-Buck. Juanita was there in her usual cheery frame of mind. She smiled broadly and waved when I walked into the store. I got one of the half carts since I didn't need too many groceries. Just my staples again—confectioners' sugar, shortening, and cake flour.

I caught a glimpse of Fred stocking in the soup aisle and

decided tomato soup and a grilled cheese sandwich would be delicious for lunch.

"Good morning," I said as I approached.

Fred grunted in my general direction. I, naturally, took that as an invitation to chat.

"Fred, do you know anything about snakes?" I asked sweetly.

He put the can he was stocking on the shelf and turned to me. "A little bit. Why?"

"I've got a friend who's on the outs with Mr. Dobbs because he only feeds his snakes live rodents. Is there anything else snakes will eat?"

"I get frozen."

"Excuse me?"

"For my snake. There's a company I found online that sells frozen mice."

"Oh. Maybe I'll mention that to Mr. Dobbs, then. Thank you, dear."

"Whatever. 'Course, he has different kinds of snakes in his store and stuff. They might not eat already dead mice." He scrunched up his forehead. "In the books I've read, though, they say it ain't good to feed live rodents to snakes because the snakes could get hurt."

"The *snakes* could get hurt? That's hard to believe."

Fred narrowed his eyes.

"I believe you, Fred, but . . . wow. I never knew that. What kind of snake do you have?"

A smile crept across his face. He clearly loved his pet.

"A ball python."

"Do they make good pets?"

"Yeah. I've had Rusty for five years, and he ain't been to the vet but one time and that was just the other day," he explained.

"Is he okay?"

"Yeah, he was constipated is all."

Eww . . . too much information.

"You have to keep an eye out for that." He laughed. "I had to work, so my papaw had to take him. Papaw wasn't too thrilled about that, let me tell you."

"Papaw's skittish around Rusty, huh?"

"Sure is."

"Wait a second." The gears in my head were churning at full speed. "I ran into Walt Duncan taking his grandson's snake to the vet. Is Mr. Duncan your papaw?"

"Sure is."

I smiled. "Small world."

"Yep, but I wouldn't want to have to paint it." He chuckled. "Stole that from Steven Wright. You know, the comedian?"

"Good one," I said, pushing out a laugh. I waved to Fred, grabbed a can of tomato soup, and moved on to the baking supplies aisle.

I wondered if I'd just gotten a peek at the "old Fred" Mr. Franklin had talked about—Fred before the car accident had ruined not only his personality but his life. And Fred was Walt Duncan's grandson? Who knew?

At least now I could rest assured that Uncle Hal didn't somehow use Fred's snake to kill Yodel Watson. Pythons aren't poisonous; they're constrictors. The autopsy said death by poisoning, not strangulation.

I was still trying to wrap my mind around the fact that Fred was Mr. Duncan's grandson as I put the sugar and cake flour into my cart. If Fred's snake was a python, then that ruled him out as a suspect in Mrs. Watson's murder, too. Unless, of course, Fred knew other snake owners who had venomous snakes. I'd have to give Uncle Hal a call to see what he knew about Fred.

BANJO GREETED ME as soon as I walked into Dr. Lancaster's office.

"Come in!"

I smiled. "Hi, Banjo."

"Come in!"

"Good morning," the receptionist said. "How can I help you today?"

"Annabelle Fontaine wanted me to check with you on the status of a new home for Banjo."

"We haven't found anyone yet. In fact, we're thinking of keeping him here in the office. Someone is here every day— even when the office is closed—to feed and check on the animals."

"Oh, it would be nice if he could stay here."

"Yeah." She pulled a string, causing a tiny bell in Banjo's cage to ring. "He's really growing on us. He's such a sweetheart. Aren't you, fellow?"

"Cash, check, or credit card?" Banjo asked.

The receptionist and I both laughed.

"See? He's learning new words here and everything," she said.

"I'll be sure and pass that along to Annabelle. She'll be delighted Banjo is doing so well." I tilted my head. "May I ask you a silly question?"

"I don't know if I'll be able to answer it or not, but feel free to ask."

"Someone told me you shouldn't feed live rodents to pet

snakes because the rodent could hurt the snake. Is that true?"

"Yes, depending on the size and type of snake and the size of the rodent. What type of snake do you have?"

"I don't. I have a friend who has a major grudge against Kellen Dobbs for feeding live rodents to his snakes, so I'm just interested."

"Is your friend Belinda Fremont?"

I nodded.

"Dr. Lancaster sees Mrs. Fremont's Satin Peruvians. She's discussed the matter with Dr. Lancaster, and he's tried to speak to Mr. Dobbs about it on more than one occasion."

I frowned. "I'm guessing speaking to Mr. Dobbs didn't do any good?"

She shook her head. "No big surprise there, though. Mr. Dobbs does what he wants."

"Somehow, I've gathered that. Well, thanks for the update on Banjo. Keep me posted on any changes in his whereabouts, would you please?"

"I sure will."

My FINAL STOP of the morning was Dobbs's Pet Store. The bell above the door heralded my arrival, but neither Candy nor Mr. Dobbs came to greet me. That fact, given what I'd read in Mrs. Watson's journal, made me feel incredibly awkward. There was no way I was going looking for them. Hoping to stay as far away as possible from any . . . inappropriate pet shop behavior, I walked over to the snake cages.

The snakes looked harmless at the moment, either coiled up or stretched out unmoving in their aquariums. I wondered if they were sleeping. Since they don't have eyelids, it was hard to tell.

"What can I get for you?"

I started at the sound of Mr. Dobbs's voice. Not only was it loud, but it was nearly touching me. I could feel his breath on the back of my neck. I slowly turned.

Mr. Dobbs wasn't allowing me any personal space whatsoever, especially since the snakes were now at my back. I took a step sideways to put some distance between us.

"They're fascinating, aren't they?" I asked, jerking my head toward the snakes. "I heard something about snakes this morning that I found hard to believe."

"What's that?"

"I heard you should never feed your pet snakes live rodents because the rodents can hurt the snakes."

"Did you come here to question me about what I feed my snakes, or did you come to buy something?"

"I came to get some vitamins for my cat," I said.

"Good. I hoped you weren't sticking your nose where it doesn't belong." He stalked into the cat supply aisle and returned with a bottle of chewable vitamins. "Here. On the house. Consider it a gift for not getting involved in things that don't concern you."

CHAPTER

sixteen

WHEN I got home, there was a basket of flowers on my porch step. I quickly got out of the car so I could take a closer look and find out whom they were from. They were beautiful—yellow mums, white roses, orange lilies, purple asters, red carnations, and yellow daisies. I plucked the card from its holder. It read: *Sorry I hurt your feelings. I do trust you and hope you'll let me buy you dinner this evening. Ben.*

I smiled to myself before unlocking the door and going back to the car to get my groceries. It had been a wild morning, that was for sure. I put away the groceries and checked my answering machine. There were four new messages.

The first was from Violet. "Hi, it's me. Call me when you get a chance, okay?"

The next message was from Ben, saying essentially the same thing.

The third message was from Mr. Franklin at Save-A-Buck. "Good morning, Ms. Martin. I was wondering if you could do a few cakes for the store. I understand you are doing a birthday party for Mrs. Fremont, so if you don't have time right now, then perhaps you can do them once you have finished with the party. Please give me a call so we can discuss. Thank you so much, and have a great day."

That was odd. I thought he didn't want any more of my cakes until Yodel's murderer was found. I had to force myself to listen to my fourth message and not call Mr. Franklin right away.

The final message was from Candy. She was nearly whispering. "Hi. I heard what Kel said to you this morning, and I'm ever so sorry he was rude. He can be plumb darn touchy sometimes. I'll give you a call back later on, okay?"

I called Mr. Franklin back first.

"Ms. Martin," Mr. Franklin's voice boomed when he came on the line. "Thank you for calling back so promptly."

"You're quite welcome. What can I do for you?"

"I realize you're currently obligated to Mrs. Fremont, but—"

"How do you know that? I only met with Mrs. Fremont yesterday, and we don't even meet to go over my design ideas until next week."

"Right . . . well, good news travels fast, as they say."

"Obviously."

"Now then, might you have time to prepare some cakes for Save-A-Buck?"

I was still irritated with him. Within nine days, I'd gone from being a pariah to being the It girl of baking. But I wasn't going to turn my back on this opportunity. "Sure, I can make some cakes for Save-A-Buck. How many would you like and when do you need them?"

"Could you get me ten cakes—the same as you brought the last time—by next weekend?"

"I can do that, Mr. Franklin."

"Thank you. If you could bring the cakes to the store on Friday morning, that would be wonderful."

"Shall I put them in plain white boxes?" I asked, grimacing to myself.

"Excuse me?"

"As opposed to boxes bearing my logo."

"Heavens, no, don't use plain boxes. We'll be delighted for our customers to know Save-A-Buck is a patron of Daphne's Delectable Cakes." He paused. "Friday, then?"

"All right, I'll see you then." I had to admit I was confused, but I certainly wasn't going to complain.

I called Ben next. I know the dating experts would've probably told me to make him wait, but . . . aw, heck, I didn't want to. I'm forty years old. Who has time to play mind games?

We made plans for dinner and, despite my run-in with the testy Mr. Dobbs, I found myself in a delightful mood. After talking with Ben, I tried Violet. Her phone went straight to voice mail so I left her a "tag you're it" message. Since Candy had made it apparent she didn't want me to return her call, I started toward my office to get my Save-A-Buck records.

Two cakes for clients this week, a potential new client with a lot of clout, and a cake order from Save-A-Buck complete with logo boxes. And a date with Ben this evening. I was feeling extremely pleased with the way this week was progressing. Violet's call back made things even better. I sat down in my office chair.

"Hi, Daph," she said. "Jason has to go out of town for a couple days for a work conference, and the kids and I were wondering if you'd like to come for a sleepover tomorrow night."

"I'd love to! We haven't done that in ages."

"Terrific. Lucas and Leslie will be thrilled."

"Where's Jason going?" I inquired.

"Chicago. He'll be back on Monday."

"Good. Oh, hey, I passed along the Cline information to Peggy March. She seemed happy about it."

"It surprises me that she never looked into the matter herself. If you had a child and both her father and grandfather were dead, wouldn't you want to know if she had any other family out there?"

"I don't know. Maybe not if I wanted to keep the child to myself. Maybe Peggy figured Joanne had her and that was enough. Or maybe she felt Joanne didn't need her dad's family, particularly since the child's paternal grandmother had never wanted to be in her life."

"I guess that makes sense."

"At least now, hopefully, Peggy and Joanne can gain something from Gloria Cline, even if it's just closure."

"And at least now they know the truth about our mom," Violet added.

"Exactly. So what time do you want me to come over tomorrow?" I smiled thinking about how much fun we'd all have.

"Is five okay?"

"Five is wonderful. I'm looking forward to it."

"Us, too."

After talking with Violet, I went to my file cabinet to check Save-A-Buck's previous delivery: three yellow, four white, and three spice cakes. I thought this time, they could use a couple of chocolate cakes, so I made this order for three yellow, two white, two chocolate, and three spice cakes.

I went to the kitchen, donned my apron, and got to work. I made the chocolate cakes first, and I increased the recipe enough to make two bitty cakes—one for tomorrow's sleepover and one to be put in the freezer. Of course, the cakes for Save-A-Buck would have to go into the freezer, too, until next week when it was time to frost them. I put the cakes in the oven, set two timers, and went back into the office to e-mail Bonnie, my friend in Tennessee. She and I had several days of catching up to do.

Unfortunately, as I was booting up the computer, the phone rang. It was Fred from Save-A-Buck. The surprise left me nearly speechless.

"Uh, what can I do for you, Fred?"

"My papaw's birthday is coming up. I was wondering if you could make him a cake with a picture of a snake on it."

"Yes, I could do that. Would you want the snake to look kind of scary or more along the lines of something funny?"

"I think a funny one would be good, don't you?"

"I think so, yes. What about if I make you a round cake with the border being a snake with the snake's head in the middle of the cake?"

"That'd be awesome. Could you write, 'Happy Birthday, Papaw' on it?"

"I can. When will you need the cake, Fred?"

"Um . . . next Sunday, if that's okay."

"That'll be fine."

We discussed flavors, and Fred chose a red velvet cake with vanilla buttercream icing. I decided phone interruptions weren't such a bad thing after all.

BEFORE GETTING READY for my date with Ben, I called Uncle Hal. Aunt Nancy answered the phone.

"Hello, dear. How are you?"

"I'm fine, Aunt Nancy. You?"

"I'm doing well, running your uncle all over town to this sale and that." She giggled.

"Is he there?"

"Yes, hold on a second."

Uncle Hal came on the line. "Hey, baby girl, what do you know?"

"First of all, tell me how Dad's doing. He calls and updates me about Mom, and even though he says he's fine, I'm not so sure."

"He is doing fine. Your daddy is a tough old goat."

"Does he need me to come up and help with Mom?"

"Honey, if he needed you to come up, he'd say so."

"No, he wouldn't. That's why I'm calling you—one of the reasons, anyway."

"All right. I'll keep an eye on him and if it appears he's wearing himself out, I'll give you a call," Uncle Hal said.

"Great. Thanks. The other thing I wanted to tell you is that Mom was never married to Vern March."

"No, I didn't think so." He kept his voice casual for Aunt Nancy, as if we were still talking about Dad.

"It was Gloria *Cline* he married when they were young."

"Okay. I'll keep you posted."

"Have you heard about your CT yet?"

"Yep, baby girl. That's looking peachy."

"Thank you, Uncle Hal—for everything. Oh, one more thing. What do you know about Walt Duncan's grandson Fred?"

"I believe he used to be a good kid before he was in that car wreck. I know Walt worries, but he doesn't say too awful much. Why?"

"It seems to me he has a Jekyll-and-Hyde thing going on.

Every time I saw him in Save-A-Buck last week, he acted like a total jerk. Today when I was getting groceries I saw him and asked him about his snake, and he was quite nice. In fact, he called later to order a cake for Mr. Duncan's birthday."

"You must be in demand if he's calling that far in advance."

"He said his papaw's birthday is next Sunday."

"Either that boy's memory is slipping—which is possible, given his condition—or mine is," Uncle Hal said. "I seem to recall Walt's birthday being in the spring."

I didn't have a response to that.

"It's probably all right," Uncle Hal continued, "but you be awful careful where that boy is concerned. He's . . . not stable."

"I'll keep that in mind."

After talking with Uncle Hal, I called Annabelle and updated her on Banjo's living arrangements. Apparently today was catch-up day!

"I hope they do keep him at Dr. Lancaster's office," she said. "That would be such excellent company for him."

"I agree. The receptionist has fallen for him already."

Annabelle laughed. "The little charmer. By the way, I got a call from the police department. The yellow stain on Mother's carpet was snake venom."

"How could that be?" I asked, feigning ignorance. "Do the police think there was a snake in the house?"

"They're not sure, but they do believe snake venom caused her death."

"How do you feel about that?" What was wrong with me? I had suddenly turned into Barbara Walters.

"Horrible. I hope she didn't suffer." Her voice cracked.

"I hope so, too."

"The officer I spoke with said he doesn't think she did."

"That . . . that's a comfort, then," I said gently.

"Yeah. I guess."

Our conversation had become so awkward I didn't want to prolong it. "I'm sorry, Annabelle, but I have to go. Please let me know if you need anything or if there's anything I can do."

"Just be careful, Daphne. Someone you know might be a killer."

I WAS PUTTING the finishing touches on my makeup when Ben arrived.

"I love your house," he said, stepping into the kitchen. "It smells like vanilla."

"That's one of the few fringe benefits I have in this business." I kissed his cheek. "Help yourself to anything in the fridge while I finish up. I'll be out in a second." I went back to the bathroom to finish putting on my face.

I heard Ben open the refrigerator door. "Anything interesting happen today?" he asked. He sounded as if his head was still buried inside the appliance.

"I had a lot of interesting things happen, actually. How about you?"

He closed the refrigerator door. "Nah, my day was fairly boring."

"I spoke with Annabelle Fontaine," I said as I returned from the bathroom.

Ben was drinking a bottle of water and leaning against the counter. "How is she?"

"She's coping. She did say the police had informed her of the cause of her mother's death." I held up a hand. "Don't worry—I acted completely oblivious about the snake venom."

He took a swig of his water. "Any leads they're discussing with her?"

"She didn't mention any leads or even any possible motive, for that matter. She did remind me that the killer could be someone we know."

"Statistically speaking, that's almost a certainty," Ben said gravely.

"Thank you for the reassurance."

Ben spread his hands. "I'm sorry, but it's true. In a town this size, what are the odds Mrs. Watson's killer was a drifter. And a drifter who went unnoticed by everybody else in town, no less?"

"Since you're starting to freak me out a bit, let's change the subject," I suggested. "You. Did you ever work for one of the larger newspapers?"

"Are we talking *The Washington Post* or *The New York Times*, or do you mean a smaller larger newspaper?"

"Either. You know what I mean. I feel you have too much ambition to work on a small-town newspaper. So why do you stay here? Are you writing the Great American Novel? Are you waiting for that one big local story to propel you into the national media?" I hoped he couldn't tell that I was fishing.

"After college, I had several good offers, but Dad's health wasn't so good. He had to quit work and go on disability. I stayed in the area to be near my family, to help them in any way I could. I'm an only child, you know." He took one last drink of water and recapped the bottle. "Dad's doing much better now. He's still on disability, but overall, he's fine."

"And yet you wanted to stay close?"

"Yeah, I did. I enjoy my work here. I have a position with at least some authority, and I have enough seniority to take off whenever I want. And, as I told you, I freelance some articles to larger papers and magazines, and I might very well write a book someday." He grinned. "Who knows? I may write a true-crime novel about the murder of Yodel Watson." He widened his eyes. "I could call it *The Hiss Fit*. Get it? A takeoff of 'misfit'?" He raised his hands and curved his fingers into claws. "Or how about *Venomous Vengeance*?"

"Stop it, okay? You're completely creeping me out."

He laughed. "Good. Let's go get some Chinese food. By the way, we're playing twenty questions about *your* life on the drive over."

"I don't think I've finished with my twenty questions about yours yet."

"Too bad, so sad. It's my turn."

We were laughing when we went out and got into Ben's Jeep. I wish I could tell you the mood for our date remained jovial the entire evening, but it didn't.

W HEN WE ARRIVED back at my house later, we got out of the Jeep and walked onto the porch, coming upon a shocking sight. Written in what looked like blood smeared across the flagstone were the words: *STOP INTERFERING*.

I gasped, and Ben immediately put his arms around me.

"We have to call the police," he said.

I nodded, then began looking around frantically. "Sparrow? Sparrow?"

"Who's Sparrow?"

"The cat. She's the cat. Somebody might've . . . Whoever did this—"

"It's okay." Ben turned me toward him and pulled me close. "It's all right. The cat's hiding. She's fine."

"But that looks like blood, and—"

"If she was a tame cat, I might be concerned. She won't even come to you at this point, Daph. You know she wouldn't let anyone else catch her."

I tried to get my breathing under control. "You're . . . you're probably . . . right. She's . . . okay."

Ben was peering over top of my head. "I don't think it's blood, either. I think it's paint. Anyway, let's get you inside and call the police."

He kept one arm around me as I handed him my key. He unlocked the door and preceded me inside.

"I'll check around and make sure everything is safe. You call 9-1-1."

"All right."

I made the call and was told that a unit would promptly be dispatched to my residence. I put the kettle on for some chamomile tea, hoping it would help calm me.

Ben came into the kitchen. "Everything's safe. How are you?"

"I think I'll be better after the police have come and gone. It always makes me uncomfortable to deal with the police."

"You talk as if you've dealt with them on a regular basis."

"Have you forgotten my past? Gun-crazy ex?"

"I'm sorry. For a moment, I did forget." He kissed the top of my head.

"You helped me forget for a moment, too."

"I'd like to help you forget for a lot longer than a moment." He leaned in and gave me a soft kiss on the lips.

The teakettle whistled.

And the police arrived.

I grabbed the kettle while Ben answered the door. The policemen turned down my offer of tea, so I poured a cup for Ben and myself. The officers confirmed that the message had been written with paint, not blood, and they asked me if I knew who might've left the message.

They already knew about my connection to Yodel Watson so I mentioned Fred and Mr. Dobbs. I refrained from implicating Joanne since her husband was on the force. As it was, the officers appeared doubtful that either Fred or Mr. Dobbs had left the message but said they'd check to see where the two men were this evening.

The police also told me they'd patrol the area more frequently for the next few days and asked me to call if I thought of anything else or needed any further assistance.

It wasn't until everyone had left and I was alone, in bed with the light on, staring up at the ceiling, that I gave more serious thought to Kellen Dobbs's attitude—and his venomous snakes.

IMAGINE MY SURPRISE when, before I'd even gotten up the next morning, China York was on my porch with a can of turpentine.

"Let me get dressed," I told her, "and I'll be right out."

"Take your time. I'll be working on this."

I quickly put on a tracksuit, pulled my hair into a ponytail, and hurried back outside. "I really appreciate your doing this, Ms. York, but . . . how did you know?"

"Heard it come over the police scanner last night. I listen to the scanner most nights. I like to know what's going on."

I took the extra rag Ms. York had brought and dipped it into the turpentine. She was scrubbing at one end of the painted message, so I knelt at the other end and set to work. We worked in silence until we were finished.

My legs were stiff and achy when I stood, but Ms. York seemed to have no discomfort whatsoever.

"How about I make us some coffee and heat up some crumb cake?"

Ms. York grinned. "Sounds like a winner to me."

We went inside. I washed up at the kitchen sink while Ms.

York cleaned herself up in the bathroom. By the time she joined me in the kitchen, coffee was pouring into the pot and the crumb cake was in the microwave.

She sat down at the table. "Who do you reckon you've ticked off, Daphne?"

"I doubt you have time to hear the entire list." I smiled wanly. "Mr. Dobbs seemed angry at me when I was in his store yesterday, but he pretty much always seems angry."

"He don't have a pleasant disposition, but I can't see him sneaking over here and writing on your porch at night. Generally, when Kel has something to say, he says it."

The microwave dinged and I took out our cake. I set it on the table between us, cut two squares, and put them on our dessert plates. "He didn't mince his words at the store yesterday, so I'll have to agree with you there."

The coffee was done. I poured two cups, put them on the table, and then set the cream and sugar out. I sat down.

"Can you think of anybody who *would* sneak over here and write on my porch?" I asked.

Ms. York spooned sugar into her coffee. "I can think of a few folks. Question is, who do you think did it?"

"I don't know of anyone—except maybe Fred—who'd skulk around my house and paint a message on my walk."

"Yeah, you do. Your subconscious knows. Your here and now just has to catch up."

"How do I do that?"

"It'll come to you."

"Can you make it come to me?"

She laughed gently. "No, child. Only you can do that."

CHAPTER

seventeen

I DECIDED TO decorate the bitty cake as a sleepover cake for Lucas, Leslie, and Violet. That meant another trip to Save-A-Buck. After cleaning the porch, I didn't have time to dawdle if I was going to get the cake finished and get over to Vi's house by 5:00 p.m. Unfortunately, Fred was bringing carts in off the parking lot and was in an uncharacteristically talkative mood.

"Hey, Ms. Martin. How are you? I heard there was some trouble over at your house last night."

"How—"

"Joanne Hayden was in here earlier."

"But Officer Hayden wasn't one of the officers who came to my house," I said, trying not to sound suspicious.

"Yeah, but he heard about it anyway. Look, I can come over

after work and help you get that paint cleaned up, if you want."

"I appreciate that, Fred, but Ms. York brought some turpentine over this morning, and we got it all off."

"Oh."

With a smile and a nod, I tried to walk on into the store.

"Hey," he said, "thanks again for doing Papaw's cake."

"You're welcome. Thank you for your business."

"No problem. People in a small town like this ought to take care of each other, don't you think?"

"Yes, it is good to support your town. I'd better get going. I have a cake to make for my niece and nephew." I hurried inside the store before he launched into more conversation.

I gathered the items I needed, noticed Juanita's line was short, and got in her checkout lane. I perused the tabloid covers while I waited and took a perverse delight in seeing some of the starlets caught without their makeup on. Some of those girls were downright plain without it.

Fred, of course, came over to bag for Juanita. She shot me a glance I couldn't read.

At last it was my turn. As Juanita scanned my items, she kept looking from Fred to me.

"How's everything going?" I asked.

"It's good," Juanita said. "Um . . . Mrs. Hayden was shopping earlier today and was talking about what happened to you last night. Please be careful."

"I will. Thank you."

"Yeah," Fred added, "it's dangerous out there. I don't mind coming by your house to check on you."

"Thanks, but the police are already doing that."

"Oh. Okay, then."

I paid for my groceries and left with a small, but polite, smile.

                              *   *   *

WHEN I GOT home, I had a message from Ben on my answering machine: "Hi, Daphne. I came by to work on that mess on your porch but saw that you've already taken care of it. Gee whiz . . . fast worker. Give me a call, all right? I'm at the office."

I would call Ben back, but it would have to wait until after I decorated the sleepover cake. Given all the drama of last night and this morning, I needed some normalcy to get my stress level under control. And for me, normalcy was decorating a cake.

I put a sheet of waxed paper on the island. Then I got the bitty cake and the mixing bowl full of buttercream icing I'd taken out of the fridge before going to the store. I crumb-coated the cake and left the icing to crust while I gathered the remaining ingredients.

I tinted a portion of my buttercream copper (for flesh tone) and a portion yellow for Violet's and the twins' hair. I'd melt some milk chocolate for my own hair. I also tinted some of the icing light blue for blankets and the cake's border.

By this time, the cake had crusted and I was able to ice it smooth. I had individual oblong, cream-filled sponge cakes to serve as beds. I carefully placed the sponge cakes vertically across the top of the cake. I took four jumbo marshmallows and flattened them into a pillow shape. With a small dollop of icing, I glued the pillows onto the sponge cakes and then piped a circle of flesh-toned icing onto each pillow. I took the blue icing and made several small rows of scallops on the sponge cake to make it look like a blanket was covering each "bed." I retrieved the bag with the flesh-toned icing and piped tiny feet sticking out from under the blankets at the ends of the beds.

I melted the milk chocolate in the microwave and used a

grass tip to make myself some long, straight hair. Before the chocolate got too cool to work with, I changed to a writing tip and piped closed eyes on our faces and Z's on the top of the cake.

I used another writing tip to give Violet curly yellow hair and to do the same for her towheaded twins. A light blue top and bottom shell border completed the cake. Leslie and Lucas would be delighted. In fact, I was pleased with it, too.

I put the rest of the sponge cakes, marshmallows, chocolate drops, and other snacks I'd bought into a lidded picnic basket. Then I curled up in my favorite chair in the living room and called Ben.

"What're you doing?" he asked.

"Resting."

"I imagine so. You did a good job on the porch, by the way."

"I can't take all the credit. China York got started on it before I was even dressed this morning. Plus, she worked rings around me. The woman is a dynamo," I admitted.

He chuckled. "Let me guess—she heard about it over her police scanner?"

"You got it."

"Ms. York is famous for her police scanner. She always knows what's going on."

"And thanks to Joanne Hayden, so does everybody else. Anyway, I'm grateful to Ms. York. It was sweet of her to help me out. She doesn't even know me."

"Yeah, she's a rather odd person, but she's a good one."

"Define 'odd,'" I said.

"Um . . . eccentric?"

"Does she fancy herself a bit of a mystic or philosopher or something?"

"I don't know. Enlighten me, grasshopper."

"Ha-ha. She told me that my subconscious knows who painted the message on my porch."

"I wish your subconscious would clue me in." Ben laughed.

"I wish it would clue *me* in. Any thoughts on how I could make that happen?"

Ben blew out a breath. "Writing always helps me. If I were in your position, I'd write down everyone in town who might want me to mind my own business—"

"That would be everybody I've met."

"Then put everybody you've met on the list and jot down why they'd want you to stay out of their affairs."

"I might give that a try," I said. "Tomorrow."

"Is that your coy way of letting me know you have plans tonight?"

"Maybe. I do have plans. Big plans. Major plans. Humongous plans."

"Humongous?"

"You bet. I'm going to a sleepover."

"That is humongous. May I join you?" he asked, his voice cheeky.

"I'm afraid not. The guy I'm sleeping over with might get jealous if I bring you along."

"Let me guess—Lucas."

"You certainly know how to spoil my fun, don't you?"

He laughed. "Sorry."

"You'd love it if you could come, though. Jason is out of town and I've made a sleepover cake and bought snacks and we're renting movies and—"

"Enough already. You're making *me* jealous."

"It's my turn to apologize," I said with a giggle. "I'm sorry."

"Have fun tonight . . . but be careful, too, okay?"

"You're the third person today to tell me to be careful. I'm beginning to wonder if I have a 'kick me' sign taped to my back. Or maybe it's a 'warn me' sign."

"Just be careful, okay?"

"I will." I smiled even though he couldn't see it.

I PULLED INTO Violet's driveway at four thirty. Hey, I couldn't wait—we hadn't had a sleepover in two years, and Armstrong sleepovers are about the only time I can truly let my hair down and act like a kid. Sure, I can be silly when the kids spend the night at my house, but there I have to be the adult. Violet gets to be the adult tonight.

I honked my horn as I approached the house. On cue, Leslie and Lucas sprinted out to help me carry in my things. They were both talking at once.

"Dad got to Chicago and called us late yesterday afternoon," Leslie said.

"Yeah, he's in stupid meetings all day today, but he's gonna try and find me a Bears' souvenir," Lucas chimed in.

"And me, too."

"You made us a cake. Cool!"

"And you brought snacks!" Leslie peeped into the picnic basket.

"Wait until we get inside," I said.

That comment sparked a stampede toward the front door. As soon as we walked into the house, I knew Violet was in the kitchen making dinner. The aromas of garlic and bread dough were enough to make my mouth water.

I put my overnight bag next to the couch and joined my sister in the kitchen. "What smells so good?"

"Homemade pizzas." She smiled. "You're not the only cook in the family, you know."

Lucas brought in the cake, put it on the table, and opened the lid. "Awesome! Leslie, check this out!"

"All right, you're not the *only* cook in the family—just the most popular," Violet said wryly.

"Wait'll you see the snacks Aunt Daphne brought," Leslie said as she strolled into the kitchen with the picnic basket. As soon as she saw the cake, she let out a piercing squeal. "I love it! Look at our little feet!"

Violet playfully muscled her way between the twins to look at the cake. She laughed. "That's adorable."

"Thank you. I thought since it's a special occasion, we should have a special cake."

"Can we cut the cake into four pieces and get ourselves?" Lucas asked.

"Yeah," Leslie agreed. "Please?" She looked at her mother, who nodded. The twins both bounced up and down excitedly.

"Was it hard being in school this week after last week's break?" I asked, trying to calm them down.

"Ish," Leslie said.

"She means a little," Lucas translated.

"Well, before you know it, you'll be getting out for Christmas break, and we'll be doing all kinds of fun stuff." I turned to Violet. "Maybe we can take them to that guitar museum."

"Yeah, and it's closer than we thought. I looked it up online. It isn't up near Roanoke after all; it's in Bristol."

"What's the guitar museum?" Leslie asked.

"Duh," Lucas said. "It's a museum for guitars."

Shooting her son a disapproving look, Violet said, "Actually, it's a building in the shape of a guitar. But, yes, I'm sure they have guitar memorabilia on display."

"Cool," Lucas said.

"Plus, we've got Christmas cakes and cookies and candies to make," I said.

"Yay!" Lucas and Leslie said in unison, and Leslie came over and hugged me so hard I was afraid she'd break one of my ribs.

"Oh, hey," Lucas said, "that creepy guy at Save-A-Buck is crushing on you way bad, Aunt Daphne."

"Who?" I asked.

"That Fred guy. Tell her, Mom."

Violet nodded as she put oven mitts on and took the pizzas out of the oven. "When we were there earlier, he was asking all these weird questions about you."

"Like what?" I got the pizza cutter out of the cutlery drawer.

"He asked me if your boyfriend minds all that baking you do." Violet frowned. "I simply said no because I knew he was fishing to see whether or not you have someone in your life."

"Do you?" Leslie prodded.

"Do I what?" I asked.

She rolled her eyes at me. "Do you have a boyfriend?"

"No . . . not really. I mean . . . no."

"Sounds like a yes to me," Lucas said. He wiggled his eyebrows at me.

"No," I said. "I've gone on a couple dates but—"

"With who?" Leslie asked.

"Wait, tell me what else Fred said." I didn't like being in the hot seat. "He called and ordered a cake for his grandfather's birthday, by the way."

"He mentioned that," Violet said. "He said you were making this 'totally cool snake cake for his papaw' in two weeks."

"Two weeks? He told me next Sunday."

"Do you think the cake is merely a ruse to get to know you?" Violet began cutting the pizzas into squares.

"I don't know. Uncle Hal knows Fred's grandfather, and he thought the guy's birthday was in the spring. But what can I do?"

"You can make it," Lucas said, snagging a square of pepperoni pizza. "And if he doesn't take it, we'll eat it."

"Yeah," Leslie said, "and next time, try to make sure your customers aren't mental."

I wondered if I should tell them I was designing cakes for a guinea pig's birthday party. I took a slice of the sausage pizza. Maybe I'd tell them later.

HOURS LATER, THE four of us were spread across the living room floor in sleeping bags, much like I'd had us positioned on the cake. Rather than being on the outsides, however, Lucas and Leslie were cocooned between their mother and me. The three of them were sleeping, but something woke me.

My ears strained at the silence. I knew I'd heard something, something so out of place it had snapped my mind out of a dreamless sleep. All I could hear now was the breathing—and occasional snoring—of my companions.

My eyes adjusted to the darkness and scanned the room. Nothing appeared to be out of the ordinary.

Just then I heard the crash of metal. It sounded like it came from Violet's kitchen. Heart pumping, I eased out of the sleeping bag and crawled into the hallway, staying low to avoid the windows.

Please, God, don't let me have brought some sort of calamity on Violet's house—or even worse, her family.

I thought about waking Violet and warning her, but I didn't want to make a commotion and risk waking the kids. They were probably safer where they were.

I flinched when I heard the sound again. I squared my shoulders and went into the kitchen. I took the meat cleaver from the knife block and tucked the cordless phone under my arm. Then I peered through the window of the back door. I couldn't see a thing, but I could still hear that racket. It—whatever *it* was—was still out there.

I held up the cleaver, unlocked the door, and flung it open. As I did so, someone grasped my cleaver-wielding wrist tightly from behind me. I struggled to get my wrist free.

"Are you out of your freaking mind? What are you doing?" Violet's whisper was soft but stern.

"There's something out there," I said. "It woke me up, and I—"

"It's the neighbor's dog. He's turned over our trash can again." She took the cleaver and put it back where it belonged.

"Are you sure?"

"Positive." She stuck her head out the door. "Come here, Bo."

A shaggy brown dog appeared in the doorway wagging its tail.

Violet bent down to pat his head. "You're a bad boy, you know. I should call animal control on you." Instead she opened the refrigerator and got him a hot dog. "Take this and go on home. And stay out of my trash."

Bo took his treat and wandered away.

Violet closed and locked the door. "I can't believe you nearly cleaved poor Bo. What's up with you?"

"The noise woke me up, and it scared me. I was checking it out, that's all."

"You're the one who's usually pragmatic about this sort of thing. I'm not used to seeing you standing by the door with a cleaver. Try again."

"I'm telling you the truth."

"Daphne." Vi was giving me her "I know better" look, and it reminded me how she's a really good mother. Tough, but not too tough.

"You know, you're a great mom, Vi. I'm proud of you," I told her.

"Thank you. But don't change the subject. Why'd you get so freaked out?"

I sighed and then broke down and told her about the writing on my porch.

"And you were planning on telling me this when?"

"Uh . . . probably never?" I gave her what I hoped was a cute, innocent look. It didn't work. I doubted it worked for Leslie and Lucas, either.

"I'm your sister. I should know these things. Do the police think you're in danger?"

"Shh," I whispered. "You'll wake the children."

"Hardly. A plane could land in the front yard, and those two would sleep through it." She pulled out a chair and nodded for me to sit. I did. She sat opposite me. "I'm serious. Why didn't you tell me?"

"I didn't want you to worry."

"Well *that's* what worries me."

I glanced up at the clock. "It's nearly four thirty in the morning, Vi. You should go back to sleep."

"No, I should make us some coffee so we can talk this out." She stood.

"Please . . . we'll talk about it tomorrow. I promise."

"I know you better than that, Daph." She put the coffee on and sat back down. "Are you scared? Do you think somebody's out to get you?"

"I don't know. I am a little scared, but I think that might be what the person was trying to do—scare me into minding my own business."

"Who do you think did it?"

"I have no idea . . . although China York says my subconscious knows."

"China York? What does she have to do with any of this?"

I explained about her police scanner and her coming to help me clean off the porch.

"So now we have to ask ourselves," Violet began, "was she sincerely wanting to help, or did she want to find out what you know—or rather, what you *think* you know?"

"Talk about acting out of character. Where's the Suzy Sunshine who always believes the best about people?"

"She had children. Somehow that tigress mentality makes you cast a suspicious eye on just about everybody." She got up and got us some coffee, fixed the way we both like it—heavy on the cream and sugar.

"It was nice of Ms. York to come and help you," Violet continued, "but how did she even know where you live?"

"Does the police scanner give out the address?"

"I guess so." She sat silent for a moment, obviously deep in thought. "Did Ms. York say why she thinks your subconscious knows who messed up your porch?"

"No. She told me some mumbo jumbo about allowing my subconscious to catch up with my here and now, but she said I'm the only one who knows how to make that happen." I rolled my eyes. "Like I know how to do that!"

"Sounds stupid to me. Wait here." Violet got up from the table and left the room, returning moments later with her laptop. "Let's see what we can find out about the workings of the subconscious."

While I drank my coffee, she logged on to her favorite search engine and typed in "unlock subconscious." Naturally, she got a lot of freaky hits. Shaking her head in frustration, she went to a respected medical journal's online site. Still, I had almost finished off my cup of coffee before she found anything worth noting.

"It says here that during sleep our subconscious goes through processes of both perception and ideation, and that at times, there is recollection. So . . . go to sleep?" She frowned at me. "I don't know. The best I can figure is that your subconscious picks up things you aren't consciously aware of until you need to be. Does that make sense?"

"No. Maybe. I don't know, Vi." I sighed. "While you're on there, would you do me a favor?"

"Sure. Want to check your e-mail?"

"No. I want you to see if you can buy snake venom online."

"Okay, that might be the strangest request I've ever received." She clicked keys. Then she clicked more keys. "Get this: some researchers think snake venom has medicinal value and could possibly slow cancer growth."

"How are they testing their theories?"

"I don't know. I'm looking to buy, not learn. Remember?"

"Of course. Buy, buy." I gestured her on.

She clicked some more. "Oh, my gosh! You're not going to believe this."

"Try me."

"You actually *can* buy snake venom." Now that her task was complete, her brain kicked in. "Wait, why did you want to know that?"

"I promised Ben I wouldn't tell anyone."

"Oh, okay." She quickly launched into a game we used to play when we were kids and promised Mom and Dad we wouldn't tell each other something. "You want to know if snake venom can be bought because you want to buy some?"

I shook my head.

"You wonder if someone else bought some?"

I nodded vigorously.

"Because someone has some?"

I leaned my head over to one side.

"Someone *had* some?"

I nodded.

"You know this because they *used* it in some way?"

I nodded and then fell onto the tabletop like I was sleeping.

"It was used to hurt someone? It was used to *kill* someone? It was used to kill Yodel Watson?"

I nodded.

She gaped at me. "Snake venom."

"Please don't tell anyone," I begged her.

"I won't. Okay, I'll probably tell Jason, but he won't tell anybody."

"I figured you'd tell Jason."

"But if it was snake venom, you have to look at the people in town who have easy access to it."

I nodded. "Kellen Dobbs."

Vi raised an eyebrow at me. "And Candy."

CHAPTER

eighteen

IT WAS midafternoon on Saturday, and I felt as if I could go to bed and sleep all the way through the night. I could only imagine how tired Violet must be; I didn't even have two rambunctious children to care for.

We had finally returned to our sleeping bags last night—or, rather, this morning   but I don't think either of us did more than doze. Leslie and Lucas were awake by seven, hungry and wanting me to watch all their favorite cartoons with them. Violet and I threw together a breakfast picnic so we wouldn't miss the shows. It was fun, but I was certain I'd sleep like the dead tonight.

I had taken a digital photograph of the sleepover cake and was now uploading it to my website. I'd just published the page when the doorbell rang. I wasn't expecting anybody.

My stomach knotted up as I backed my chair away from the desk. I'd locked the door behind me when I came home . . . hadn't I? And it wasn't like an attacker would ring the doorbell, in broad daylight, on a Saturday afternoon . . . would he?

I tiptoed down the hall. Whoever it was had come to the front door. Most of my visitors use the side door off the kitchen. I slipped into the living room and peered through the peephole. Peggy March stood on the stoop holding her brown leather purse with both hands.

I opened the door. "Hi, Peggy."

"Hello." She gave me a small smile. "I hope you don't mind my dropping by. I realize I should've called first, but—"

"That's okay. Please come in."

She stepped into the living room. "You have a lovely home."

"Thank you."

"And a precious cat. I saw her outside. What happened to her eye?"

"I don't know. She's a stray."

"Aw." Peggy sat down on the sofa. "I actually came by to thank you for telling me about Gloria Cline."

I dropped into my chair. "I can't believe Jonah didn't know who his mother was. What did his birth certificate say?"

"His birth certificate said his mother was Gloria March. See, even though her parents ran Vern off, they didn't officially annul the marriage until after she had the child."

"But didn't Jonah ever ask about his mom?"

Peggy lifted a shoulder. "He said every time he brought it up, his father would say they had each other and that's all that mattered. He'd say they didn't need Jonah's mother. Then Vern would be depressed for several days after they'd spoken about her. Finally, Jonah quit asking."

"That's a shame." I frowned. I didn't always get along with my own mother, but at least I knew she was there.

"Then when Vern and . . . and your mother . . . got together—" She bit her lower lip. "We all just assumed she was *the* Gloria."

"Makes sense, I guess."

"Oh, it did. Vern was happier than I'd ever seen him when he was with her. And he'd never dated much before."

"Whoa," I said with a humorless smile, "I didn't know Mom was such a femme fatale."

"I'm sorry. I don't think she was. I—" She sighed. "This isn't why I came. I don't want to make you feel bad. I came to thank you."

I waved away her apology. "It's okay."

"No, it isn't. I came to share my family's good news, not to bring bad news about yours."

"Then tell me your good news." I forced an excited smile.

"After speaking with you yesterday morning, I contacted an attorney. He's going to find out if Gloria left a will."

"She's dead, then? I'm sorry."

"Yes, he determined that while we were talking. He looked it up in an Internet database or something."

"What if she didn't leave a will?"

"He'll go back to the Clines' wills. They came to a tragic end—died when a plane they'd chartered crashed back in the spring of 1975. The lawyer told me that, too. In fact, I seem to remember hearing something about it on the news or reading about it in the newspaper. But it hardly meant anything to me at the time, and then Jonah's dad had his accident—"

"Do you think the Clines made a provision for Gloria's child in their wills?"

"Even if they didn't, Gloria would have inherited as a surviving child."

"And even if Gloria left no will," I said, "Jonah would have inherited as *her* surviving child."

"Correct. The attorney seems to think there might be something there for Joanne, provided not all of Gloria's estate was used for her medical care."

I smiled. "Well, I hope it wasn't. And even if it was, maybe Joanne can have some of her grandmother's mementos. It would be a way of getting to know her, at least a little."

Peggy smiled, too. "Yes, it would."

After she left, I got out my gum paste kit, turned on the classic TV channel, and watched *I Love Lucy* while making flowers. I hoped everything would work out for Peggy and Joanne, although I was beginning to doubt Joanne would ever learn to keep her mouth shut where I—or anyone else—was concerned. I did feel badly for her in a way. It was a shame about Jonah, his parents, and their screwed-up life. Besides, if Gloria Cline's parents had left them alone, Vern would have probably stayed happily married to her and kept away from my mother.

I wondered if Vern and Gloria had ever tried to reconcile, or if her parents and/or illness had prevented any such attempt from happening. I supposed I could ask Mrs. Dobbs, but she hardly knew me. I couldn't expect her to answer a bunch of questions about her sister.

Then I found myself wondering how Vern felt when the Clines' plane went down. I know he was sad for Gloria and her sister, but he had to have felt—on some level—a sense of relief that perhaps Jonah could finally reunite with his mother.

Curious to know more about Gloria Cline and how she

might've made a difference in so many lives—my own included—I decided to look for some answers at the mental institution.

Upon arrival at the institution—a building with a brick foundation and tan vinyl siding—I noted that Whispering Hills may not have been the wisest choice of name for a mental institution. Maybe the founder had intended to evoke memories of a cheerful Julie Andrews singing that the hills were alive with the sound of music, but I wasn't sure mental patients needed that kind of stimulus.

The door had a coded alarm system for staff and a doorbell for visitors. I rang the bell and a voice came over the intercom asking how she could help me.

"I'm just looking for some information," I said.

"Come in."

The lock tumblers clicked, and I opened the door. Immediately upon the door's closing, the tumblers turned and relocked the door. I bit my lip nervously and looked around for the reception area. It was straight ahead, but before I could reach the reception desk, an elderly woman in a wheelchair called to me.

"Miss? Miss? Come here!" she said.

"I-I'm sorry. I can't right now, I—"

"Oh, please," she said. "You're the most beautiful woman I've ever seen. Please help me."

I glanced over at the reception desk. The receptionist was talking on the phone. Surely I could spare this poor little old lady a moment. I walked toward her but was cautious about getting too close. After all, this was a mental institution.

"Can you get me out of here?" she asked. "I'll give you a dollar."

"I'd better not."

She flattened her lips. "I'll give you two dollars, but that's as high as I'm going. You should be ashamed, badgering an old woman for money."

"But I don't want any money," I began.

"Then you'll do it for free?" She looked up and down the hall. "Let's go while the coast is clear."

"I don't think we should."

"You young people are all alike," she said. "Selfish . . . and ugly."

"I need to talk with the receptionist now," I said. "Excuse me."

"Selfish!"

I turned, knowing I had a look of intense confusion on my face, and hurried to the reception area. The receptionist was still on the phone, so I took a seat by the desk to wait.

A middle-aged man with thinning brown hair wearing pajamas and a robe ambled into the reception area. "The dog barks at trains."

I nodded.

"The dog barks at trains," he repeated. "Now you say it."

I glanced at the receptionist, who was looking something up on the computer, phone still to her ear.

"The dog barks at trains," he said louder. "Say it."

"The dog barks at trains," I said quickly.

"What dog?" he asked.

The receptionist hung up the phone. "Henry, you need to go back to your room or to the recreation area. I need to speak with this lady."

"Yeah, okay," he said. "She likes dogs."

"All right, Henry," she said. "Thank you." When Henry had shuffled out of the room, she shook her head. "He's confused but otherwise harmless. The people you see walking around are fine. We have the dangerous ones locked up and under constant surveillance."

"Dangerous ones?" I echoed.

"Yeah, well, dangerous for us," she said. "The really criminally insane patients are elsewhere." She waved her hand. "But, anyway, what can I do for you? Are you looking to have someone committed?"

"No," I said. "It isn't that at all. I wanted to ask you about a former patient—Gloria Cline."

"Are you a relative?" she asked.

"No, but—"

"Then I can't divulge any information to you about Ms. Cline without the assent of her estate administrator."

"But Ms. Cline is dead," I said.

"Yes, but the estate still retains the right to her privacy," the receptionist said.

"I'm sorry. I should've known that." I sighed. "I just know her granddaughter, and I wondered if there might be some information I could pass along."

"Ms. Cline had a granddaughter? I've worked here a long time, and the only visitor I ever recall Ms. Cline having visit was her sister."

"I don't think Ms. Cline and her granddaughter knew about each other," I said. "Ms. Cline gave birth to a son when she was a teenager and was forced to give the child up. Joanne was born to that son."

The receptionist nodded. "I'd heard that was the reason Ms. Cline was here. Shame, too. I think she was as sound of mind as anyone." Her eyes widened. "I didn't just say that."

"No, of course not," I said, shaking my head. "I simply can't understand how Ms. Cline was kept here, though, if there was nothing wrong with her."

She leaned forward and whispered, "People with deep pockets can make lots of things happen."

"But—" I began.

She sat back. "I've said too much already. Please don't mention to anyone that you've spoken with me."

"I won't." I stood and ran my hands down the sides of my jeans. "Thank you for your time. Will you please buzz me out?"

"Sure."

As I was leaving, I heard the lady in the wheelchair call out. "Hey, come here! You're the prettiest woman I've ever seen!"

I turned to see who she was talking to. It was Henry.

I WAS ALREADY in bed and asleep when the phone rang. I don't know how many times it rang before I realized it wasn't part of a dream.

I rolled over and fumbled on the nightstand for the phone. "Hello?"

"Daphne, it's Candy. I'm sorry I woke you."

I struggled up onto my elbow and looked at the clock. It was ten thirty. "What's wrong?"

"This is the first chance I've had to call you back. But if you're sleeping—"

"No, it's all right. What did you need to talk about?"

"I'm sorry for the way Kel talked to you yesterday at the store."

"Candy, that's all right. It wasn't your fault."

"I know. But I feel I owe you an explanation at the very least."

"About why Mr. Dobbs was upset with me?"

"It's not only you. It's everybody . . . including me. On Wednesday, he was acting like himself and was positively upbeat about his birthday. When he came in on Thursday, he was . . . different. And he has been ever since."

I propped myself up against my headboard. "Birthdays are usually a time for reflection, especially if it's a significant year number or if there are . . . special circumstances or something. Maybe he is just taking stock of his life."

"You think he's finally gonna ask his wife for a divorce?"

I seriously didn't need to be hearing this.

"He's been unhappy for so long," Candy continued. "I don't know why he's been wishy-washy for all this time. He—"

"Give him a few days," I said, interrupting her. "It'll work out in the end."

"I hope you're right. I'll let you get back to sleep now. Thanks for talking with me."

"Anytime. Good night."

I hung up the phone and slid back down into bed. I wondered before I drifted off to sleep again what had truly happened to Kellen Dobbs to give him such a dramatic attitude adjustment.

ON MONDAY MORNING, I went to Johnson City. There's a neat little hobby shop there where you can get about anything you need to make whatever you want to make. Today I was looking for willow branches so I could weave a basket for Guinevere.

I found the willow branches, and then afterward I found Janey Dobbs. She was looking through bins of embroidery thread and referring to a list in her hand as she gathered skeins.

"Hi, Janey."

She turned. "Hello." She patted her hair, which, I have to admit, did look unkempt. "I didn't expect to run into anyone I know." Her face was wan and devoid of makeup.

I felt awkward, not knowing how to respond to her comment. I came up with "I'd better get going. It was good to see you."

"You too," she said. Then her face crumbled, she bowed her head, and she started crying.

And I'd thought things were awkward before. Part of me wanted to ease on out of the aisle and pretend I didn't notice the sobbing woman. It's not as if we were actually friends. I barely knew her.

But the compassionate part of me kicked in. "Is there anything I can do?"

Janey dug in her purse and brought out a tissue. She dabbed at her eyes and nose. "Could we get a cup of coffee? I'd rather like a good cup of coffee . . . and some company."

"Of course," I said. "I have what I need. I'll go ahead and check out."

"I'm nearly finished, too. How about I meet you at the café up the street?"

"That'll be fine. See you in a few."

I took a detour by the cake decorating aisle—I couldn't help myself—and I picked pick up a couple things, but I didn't linger as long as I would have ordinarily. I paid for my purchases and went out to the parking lot to put my bags in my car. I hadn't seen Janey come out of the store yet, so I walked up the street to the coffee shop.

I got a cappuccino and sat at a bistro table near the back of the shop. Janey came in about ten minutes later. She saw me and came over to the table to deposit her shopping bag.

"Thank you for doing this," she said. "Let me grab a coffee, and I'll be right back."

I smiled and took a sip of my cappuccino. I suppose I should've said "My pleasure" or some other such nicety, but it wasn't my pleasure. It was a terribly uncomfortable situation, especially in light of Candy's phone call Saturday night.

Janey returned to the table with her coffee. "I apologize for breaking down before. I've been under quite a lot of stress this week." She forced a smile. "But we aren't talking about that. We're having a nice coffee break." As if to underscore her point, she took a sip of her coffee. "Mmm, delicious. How's yours?"

"It's very good," I answered blandly.

"If only we had a piece of your cake to go with it, huh? I think I neglected to tell you what a marvelous cake that was."

"Thank you. I'm glad you enjoyed it."

"I . . . I did." Her eyes filled with tears again.

I bit the bullet. "If there's anything you'd like to talk about—"

She took another drink of coffee. "Have you ever been married, Daphne?"

I frowned. "Yes, I have."

"What happened . . . if you don't mind my asking?"

I did mind her asking. I certainly didn't feel comfortable enough with Janey Dobbs to share the details of my painful past with her. "We divorced." I said it as lightly as possible and then took a sip of my cappuccino.

"Do you miss him?"

I actually choked at that one. Janey got up and hurried to the counter to get me a glass of water. I drank some of the water and eventually got my coughing under control.

"Excuse me," I said hoarsely.

"It's okay. I'm sorry if I upset you." She opened her purse and produced another tissue. She handed it across the table to me.

I wiped my still-watering eyes and then took another drink of water. "So, have you got your Christmas tree up yet?" I asked, changing the subject.

"Not yet." She stared down at the table for a long moment. "I don't think this was such a good idea after all."

I didn't say anything. I merely switched back from the water to my cappuccino.

"It's hard not to have anyone to confide in," she said. "I'm a laughingstock. Everybody in town knows my business, or some concocted, perverted version of it."

My mind flashed back to the days after Todd shot at me. The press, the whispers, the conjecture, the humiliation. "I know the feeling."

Janey raised her eyes to meet mine. "You do?"

I nodded and took another sip from my cappuccino.

"How do you deal with it?"

I half smiled. "I eventually ran away and started a new life here."

"I wish I could run away, but I have nowhere to go." She paused. "Have you heard the rumors about my husband and his lovely assistant?"

I nodded again. I figured it was better to be honest and spare her the pain of having to tell me.

"I think it's true that they're having an affair," she said quietly. "But even worse than that, I think Kellen is trying to kill me." She looked back down at the table. "I believe he killed Yodel Watson, and now he's going to kill me."

I was too stunned to speak. I simply sat and stared wide-eyed at the top of her head until she looked back up.

"You probably think I watch too much television," Janey said, "but I'm not imagining things. I'm constantly afraid that each day will be my last."

"Have you gone to the police?"

She shook her head. "I have no proof. He hasn't come out and actually threatened me."

"And yet you're afraid. *And* you think he might've killed Yodel Watson. Janey, you've got to go to the police. I'll go with you. We'll—"

"I can't go to the police. Without evidence, they won't arrest Kellen, much less hold him. And if I was unsuccessful in my attempt to have him arrested, he'd hunt me down with a vengeance."

"You've moved out of the house, though, haven't you?"

"Not yet." She took a shaky breath. "Up until Thursday morning, I was doing my best to save my marriage."

"What happened Thursday morning?"

Janey took a drink of her coffee and appeared to be steeling her nerves. "It was before Kellen left for the store, of course. I was in the bedroom and I picked up the phone to make a call. Kellen was already on the line. He was talking with our insurance agent, asking all these questions about hypothetical circumstances of our deaths."

"Such as?"

"Such as if we were in an accident, would the death benefit be greater than if we died from natural causes."

"But he was talking in terms of both of you, right?"

"Naturally. He isn't stupid. He wouldn't come out and ask the insurance agent, 'How can I best profit from my wife's death?'"

"No. I don't suppose he would." I began fidgeting with my napkin. "You've got to get out of that house."

"I can't. If I leave Kellen, then it's desertion. I become the villain."

"It's better than being dead," I pointed out.

"If I leave, he'll take everything. I'll have nowhere to go, nothing." She sighed. "I can't do it."

"Okay, then, don't move out. Simply tell Mr. Dobbs you're taking a short vacation."

She considered my suggestion. "That might work."

"Sure, it would. Plus, you could go to the police with your suspicions and then hide until—"

"I've already told you, dear, I have no proof."

"What if the police do? What if all they need is a viable suspect?"

"But if it doesn't work—"

"They can help you, Janey. They'll know what to do."

"Maybe. I'll think it over." She folded her hands as if in prayer and put them to her lips. "Poor Yodel. I think he killed her with snake venom."

"What makes you think that?" I asked.

"He told me once that's how he'd kill someone, that here in Virginia it would be practically untraceable to determine snake venom as a cause of death in the absence of fang marks." She closed her eyes. "He said they might believe the victim had been poisoned, but they wouldn't suspect snake venom."

"But why would he kill Mrs. Watson?"

Janey opened her eyes. "Yodel knew. She caught Kellen and . . . that *woman* . . . in an embrace in the store. She told me about it. But Kellen doesn't know that."

"Still, she couldn't hurt him with that knowledge," I said.

"She could if she agreed to be a witness for me in divorce proceedings."

"But you said he didn't know she'd told you."

She huffed out a breath. "Don't you see? She didn't mind her own business. Kellen is unrelenting in protecting his privacy."

"She couldn't help what she saw."

"No . . . but he also knew about her book. She usually carried it with her and would take it out and write in it whenever the mood struck her. Kellen knew she wrote everything in that confounded journal of hers."

"If he knew that, why didn't he find the book and take it with him after the murder?"

"How do you know he didn't?"

I swallowed. "Annabelle has it . . . in Florida."

"He must not have been able to find it, then."

"Please go to the police," I said.

"I need to go." She stood up. "I'll think about going to the police. If I decide to go, will you accompany me? For moral support?"

"I'll be happy to."

She smiled. "Thank you." Her smile faded. "But whatever you do, don't let any of this slip to anyone. If Kellen knew I'd told you, your life would be in danger, too."

CHAPTER
nineteen

I CALLED BEN on my way home from Johnson City. "Would it be all right if I stop by your office?" I asked. "I need to talk to you about something."

"How about we meet for lunch? That way you don't have to deal with our nosy receptionist and we can have some privacy."

"Sure. Where would you like to meet?"

He named a sandwich shop where they have cozy niches for people to sit and chat while lunching. I told him I'd be there in half an hour.

When I walked into the sandwich shop, I didn't see Ben until he stood up and waved at me. He looked terrific—jeans, dress shirt, brown leather bomber jacket. His hair was a tad messy from running his hands through it in either concentration or frustration. It was all I could do to keep from running to him and launching myself into his arms. I did hug him, though. He seemed touched, and a bit amused, by the gesture.

"Rough day?" he asked.

I told him about my encounter with Janey Dobbs.

"That's . . . strange at best," he said. "Why would a man tell his wife exactly how he'd kill someone and then do it?"

"To scare her? To make her believe he knew how to commit a murder and get away with it?"

Ben opened his mouth to respond, but closed it when the waitress came to take our orders.

"I find it hard to believe Kel Dobbs would be that stupid," Ben said when the waitress left. "As one of the few people in the area with a license to own venomous snakes, he would surely find some other way to kill his victim. Anyway, he's already been questioned by the authorities about Yodel Watson's death."

"And?" I prompted.

"And he has a rock-solid alibi. Like I said, it would be idiotic for him to kill the woman using snake venom."

"But maybe he thought it would be undetectable—and it nearly was. Until the stain on Mrs. Watson's carpet was analyzed, the coroner knew she'd been poisoned but didn't realize the toxin was snake venom," I justified.

"True, but if I were a doctor, why would I kill someone using a scalpel?"

"Would an autopsy be able to differentiate between a scalpel wound and a wound made by some other kind of knife?"

"I think so," Ben said. "Look at Jack the Ripper. It was widely believed that he had a background in medicine."

"You're comparing apples to . . . to frankfurters." Now I was getting frustrated.

"How so? A killer is a killer. It's just that some are smart and some are dumb . . . and nearly all of them make mistakes."

"To my knowledge, Jack's wife never told anyone, 'Me hubby once expressed a desire to kill prostitutes with a medical kit, govna.'"

"I have a desire to kill that horrible cockney accent." He grinned. "Seriously, I respect your ideas and I sympathize with Mrs. Dobbs, but the police are no longer considering Kel a suspect."

"Because of his alibi."

The waitress arrived with our food—a club sandwich and fries for Ben and a chef salad for me. We thanked her hurriedly and she left just as quick.

"Let me guess." I speared a cucumber slice. "Candy is the alibi."

Ben nodded as he poured ketchup onto his plate.

"Then who do the police suspect?"

"Right now they're stumped."

I ate my cucumber. "I think he did it."

"What proof do you have?"

"The testimony of his wife and the snake venom, used because he thought it was practically undetectable, he had easy access to it, and figured the police—and our own local Clark Kent—would believe him too smart to use it." I jabbed my fork into my salad. "Come on. Don't you think he's the most likely suspect?"

"Probably." He dipped a fry into his ketchup. "But without proof, we're sunk."

I WAS SURE Kellen Dobbs was guilty of killing Mrs. Watson. I didn't know how to prove it, but I knew he was guilty. I stopped at the video store on my way home and rented an armful of mystery movies—everything from *Jagged Edge* to *The Hound of the Baskervilles*. Somehow I had to figure out how to help Janey Dobbs, trap Kel Dobbs in his own web, *and* get a ton of positive publicity for Daphne's Delectable Cakes.

Four hours later, I was no closer to a plan to get Mr. Dobbs arrested, but I felt confident I could do it with the help of Basil Rathbone, Glenn Close, and Robert Loggia. The trouble with that reasoning, though, is that they were on celluloid and I was here in real life. I was way over my head with this detective business.

There was one thing I had gained during those four hours of movie-watching, though. I had made almost enough flowers to complete Guinevere's cake, provided Belinda Fremont liked my designs, of course.

Still, as I stored the flowers and put away my gum paste kit, I couldn't shake the feeling that there was something more I could be doing. I had a nagging suspicion that Janey was right—if Mr. Dobbs thought I was interfering in his business, my life could be in danger, too. I couldn't let him go free and live here in fear for the rest of my life. I'd lived in fear before; it was no life.

My only idea was to call Candy. Luckily, she was home. Alone.

"Hi," I said. "Can you talk, or is this a bad time?"

"No, I can talk. What's going on?"

"I'd rather talk to you in person. Can we meet somewhere?"

"I reckon we can. You want me to come over to your house?"

"I hate for you to have to come all this way. I can come there, or we can meet somewhere in the middle."

"Oh, it ain't that far, and you sound kind of serious, hon. Why don't you let me come to you?"

"If you're sure—" I conceded.

"It's no problem. I'll there in a jiffy."

While I waited for Candy, I put *Rebecca* into the DVD player. I'd seen the movie before, but somehow a movie based on a book written by my namesake gave me a teensy sense of security. I know it's dumb, but I had to have something to cling to when I was getting ready to confront a killer's alibi. I decided to take on the guise of the perfect, cold, impenetrable Rebecca—not the unnamed, mousy heroine. Rebecca—with her expensive stationery with the fancy R—would be able to ferret out the truth.

Candy showed up, all smiles and concern. "Hi," she said. "You sounded upset over the phone. I hope everything's okay."

"Come on in. Can I get you something to drink?"

"No, honey, I'm fine." Her megawatt smile faded. "What's got you fretting?"

I bit my lip and decided bluntness was the way to go. "I understand the police found snake venom in Mrs. Watson's house."

Candy shook her head and flopped onto my sofa. "That Joanne Hayden. Ain't she got nothing better to do than run her mouth?"

"I'm not complaining—at least she's not running it about me this time," I said with a smile.

"Still . . ." She blew out a breath. "She and Yodel Watson must be kin somewhere down the line."

"So gossip is a genetic trait?"

"Must be."

I sat down next to Candy. "I'm worried about you."

"Why? You think Kel killed her?"

"Who else would have snake venom?"

"Anybody that wanted it, or anybody that wanted to set up Kel."

"Who'd want to do that?"

"I don't know, okay?" She was glaring at me now. "All I know is that one day the old woman was wagging her finger at us and not long after that she was dead. But Kel did *not* kill her."

"Are you sure?"

"As sure as I'm sitting here. Kel's wife had gone off to a spa retreat somewhere for a few days, and he spent that entire weekend with me." She stood. "Are you done?"

I got to my feet, too. "Candy, please don't be angry. I truly was worried about you. I didn't want you to be in danger."

"I appreciate your concern, but I'm not in danger, Daphne."

"Good. I'm glad. And I'm sorry someone made it look as if Mr. Dobbs was to blame."

"Me too." She marched to the door. "I'll tell you who else is gonna be sorry—Joanne Hayden. She's gonna be sorry she ever ran her mouth about this."

"Please, I don't want to be the cause of any trouble."

"You're not. She is." With that, she flounced out the door.

I sighed. I needed to learn to stop interfering in other people's affairs.

The irony of the message painted on my porch wasn't lost on me.

"I KNOW I took a risk by bringing only this one concept," I told Mrs. Fremont, "but I believe this exemplifies everything you're looking for."

"You say you got the idea from a Sylvia Weinstock book?" she asked, her eyes still on my designs.

"Yes. I modified it to incorporate not only lots of flowers but also gum paste fruit and vegetables to keep the cake closely tied to Guinevere's basket 'cake.'"

"Gum paste fruit and vegetables will be used on the cake

for the human guests, and actual fruit and vegetables will be in the basket cake, correct?"

"Yes. I know how important vitamin C is to a cavy's diet."

"Excellent! I'm impressed, Ms. Martin. You've done your homework, and I love your vision for both cakes."

"Thank you."

"Where will you be getting the basket? Will it be organic?"

"The basket will be organic, yes. I'll be weaving it from peeled willow branches."

Mrs. Fremont clapped her hands. "Fantastic. I appreciate all the thought and effort you're putting into this."

"Thank you for allowing me to be a part of your special occasion."

"The cavies are in their sitting room. Would you like to meet them?"

"I'd love to. Annabelle tells me they're all champions."

"They are. I'm quite proud of them."

"As you should be," I said.

As Mrs. Fremont led the way upstairs to the sitting room, I promised I'd be quiet and restrain myself this time.

The sitting room was an eclectic mix of Las Vegas fake fur, teen-girl bedroom, and penthouse posh. A white sectional sofa curved around the fireplace. Pink, blue, yellow, and green fake fur pillows adorned the sofa, giving it a whimsical touch. A fuzzy white rug covered the floor, littered with toys and treats.

Mrs. Fremont took a seat on the sofa and nodded for me to sit down as well.

"They hid when they heard us coming," she said, "but they'll join us in a moment."

She was right. We were soon surrounded by furry friends. She bent and picked up Guinevere.

"Here's our birthday girl." She handed her to me.

I set the guinea pig on my lap and stroked her silky hair. She began to make a purring sound.

"She likes you." Mrs. Fremont picked up a black-and-white guinea pig and settled him on her lap. "This is Lancelot."

"They're beautiful." I looked up at the photographs and ribbons displayed above the fireplace. "Annabelle was right—that's impressive."

"Thank you. Have you spoken with her recently?"

"Yes, I spoke with her on Friday."

"I need to give her a call. How's she doing?"

"As well as can be expected. The police confirmed that her mother was murdered."

"I'm sorry to hear that—though I'm not surprised. I cared for Mrs. Watson, but she could be a real piece of work." She smiled. "That woman would blackmail the devil if she had something on him." She placed Lancelot back on the floor.

"Annabelle is such a sweet person." I continued petting Guinevere. "I was dumbfounded by that when I first met her. Having already met her mother, I mean."

"She takes after her daddy. Everybody loved Arlo Watson. Nobody had much use for Yodel."

"At least she had Mrs. Dobbs."

Mrs. Fremont laughed. "You think Yodel Watson and Janey Dobbs were friends? How'd you arrive at that conclusion?"

"Mrs. Dobbs came to the house the day after Mrs. Watson died. She brought a casserole," I finished lamely.

"If Janey was at the house, she was there to make sure Yodel was dead." She took Guinevere from my lap, gave her a kiss, and returned her to the floor. "Annabelle once told me that Yodel had held the secret of Janey's sister over her head for years."

"You mean the secret of Gloria's baby?"

"I mean the so-called secret that the Clines bribed some-one at the mental institution to make sure Gloria remained there—and heavily sedated with narcotics."

I blinked. So *that's* what the receptionist at Whispering Hills had meant. "One teenage slipup led to Gloria being punished for the rest of her life?"

"It did indeed. And it left Janey the sole benefactor after her parents died."

My mouth fell open. "Gloria got nothing?"

"She'd been declared mentally incompetent, and Janey was given her sister's power of attorney," Mrs. Fremont explained.

"But what about Gloria's son?"

"From what I understand, there was no specific provision for him in the Cline's will. I suppose his father could've made some entreaties to the court, but he died before that could happen."

"You said the fact that Gloria was kept sedated was a 'so-called secret.' If everyone knew, then why was Yodel able to hold it over Janey's head?" I asked.

"To Janey, everything is a rumor until it's substantiated. Like the affair between her husband and his stock girl." She stood. "Well, then, let's go downstairs and make our final arrangements for the party." She then addressed the cavies. "Hilda will be up shortly to take you back to your rooms, darlings. I'll look in on you later."

BY THE TIME I'd left Mrs. Fremont's house, it was not only getting dark but had begun to rain. As my windshield wipers thumped out a rhythmic beat, I recalled what China York had said.

Your subconscious knows. Your here and now just has to catch up.

My subconscious was nagging at me, trying to tell me something. It was the same sort of feeling you get when you're watching a movie and someone looks familiar. It's hard to enjoy the movie because you're trying to recall where you've seen that person before.

But I wasn't watching a movie. I was driving home. Whatever my subconscious was trying to tell me was there on the fringes of realization, waiting in the wings. It was something about Vern March.

I know I'd been afraid Uncle Hal had caused Vern's accident, but why would he? Vern had left town; he wasn't seeing Mom anymore. Suddenly, the date of Vern's accident flashed into my mind: *Wednesday, May 7, 1975.*

I remembered Peggy March's telling me about the Clines dying in the plane crash in the spring of '75.

Janey would not have wanted Vern poking around after her parents' deaths. Was it a coincidence the accidents occurred so close together timewise? I recalled the day my car had a flat tire and Janey Dobbs happened to come along after visiting the guitar museum, which I now knew was two hours in the opposite direction. Had she been out seeing sites other than the guitar museum, or had she been following me?

I also recalled Candy's accusation that somebody had used snake venom as a murder weapon to frame Kellen Dobbs.

Kel's wife had gone off to a spa retreat somewhere for a few days, she'd said.

Kel had an alibi.

I tried to put all the little pieces of the puzzle together.

Then my painted porch message had warned: *Stop interfering.*

Thanks to my interference, Peggy March was now looking

into Gloria Cline's estate—an estate currently being overseen by Janey Dobbs.

My here and now had suddenly caught up with my subconscious. And both were saying "Uh-oh" because I'd just turned up into my driveway and Janey Dobbs's black Mercedes was blocking me in.

I reached into my purse and took out my cell phone. I flipped it open and turned it on, but it immediately died. I really should remember to charge that thing more often.

All I could do now was play it cool. Snoopy cool. Joe Cool. Stay Alive Until I Can Get Away cool.

I got out of my car; Janey was already out of hers. And the bumper of her Mercedes was nearly touching my back bumper.

"Hi, Janey! How are you?" I said as cheerfully as I could manage.

"I'm all right."

"Did you get out of your house yet?"

"For now," she replied with a shrug.

"Oh, that's good."

"Could we go inside? It's rather chilly out here."

She was chilly even though she was wearing a black leather coat and matching gloves? I don't think so.

"Actually, I'm on my way back out," I said. "I only stopped by here to get my design portfolio." I smiled broadly. "I have a potential new client."

"That's marvelous. Who is your client?"

I had to think quickly. "Juanita . . . from the Save-A-Buck."

"I'm surprised she can afford a decorator of your quality on her cashier's salary."

"Sometimes—especially when you're starting out like I

am—you do some work more as a goodwill gesture than anything. I'm sure you know that, though."

"Of course." She walked closer to my porch. "Don't you have a second to spare for me? You promised you'd go with me to the police . . . about Kellen."

"How about I run by the Save-A-Buck, tell Juanita I'm going to be late, and then meet you at the police station?" I gave a tight-lipped smile.

"Daphne, is something wrong?"

"No. Why?"

"You seem nervous."

"I . . . I am. I'm afraid Mr. Dobbs will come after you. Do you have family in the area? Or somewhere you could stay after we talk to the police?"

"No, but I'm not terribly worried about him anymore. I have everything I need to see Kellen get precisely what he deserves."

"You found more evidence?"

She rubbed her hands up and down her arms. "Could we please go inside and warm up a minute?"

"Let's go on to the station. I'll meet you there."

"But you said you had to get your portfolio."

"Since I'm going to have to reschedule, I don't need it."

"If you call Juanita now, you won't have to go to the Save-A-Buck, and we can drive to the police station together." Janey was using every trick in the book.

"I'd rather tell her in person. You never know how long you'll have to be on hold waiting for someone to answer the phone when you call Save-A-Buck."

"You can think on your feet; I'll give you that." Janey chuckled. "Let's go inside, Daphne."

"I'd rather not."

"When did you figure it out?" An arrogant smirk appeared on her face.

"What do you mean? I haven't figured anything out."

"Come now. We're through playing cat and mouse." She placed her hands in her pockets and noticed me staring. "No gun. I promise."

"Look," I said, "I don't *know* that you did anything to anyone. Let's both just forget about all this."

She seemed to deliberate on that. "No one would believe you anyway."

"Exactly."

"I do appreciate your friendship. I believe you realize I'm a victim here, nothing more." She took a step toward me. "Give me a hug to seal the deal."

I glanced back down at those hands in those pockets and took a step backward.

"I don't know what you're up to, Janey, but it's not going to work. I won't be your next victim."

She took her right hand out of her pocket. In it was a hypodermic needle filled with a golden fluid. "Yes, you will."

I nearly said "Puh-leez." I'd lived with an abusive husband—a man twice my size. I'd fought him every time he'd attacked me. I could defend myself from Janey Dobbs.

She came at me with the needle raised. As she drove her arm down toward me, I grasped her wrist in my right hand. I pivoted onto my left foot and turned her away from me. I placed my left forearm against her throat as we struggled for control of the needle. In the process, I was able to depress the needle's plunger and dispense the fluid onto my porch.

With her weapon now useless, I took my right leg and kicked the backs of Janey's knees, forcing her into a kneeling position. I pushed her over onto her stomach and immobilized her. Janey's cell phone dropped from her jacket pocket, and I used it to call 9-1-1.

Within fifteen minutes, it seemed every cop on the force—yes, Bill Hayden was among them—was on my porch. I had a cramp in my leg and was delighted the authorities were finally there to take Janey Dobbs away.

EPILOGUE

IT HAD only been a couple days since Janey was arrested, but already things were looking up.

The twins called to tell me they were coming over after school tomorrow to help me put up my Christmas tree. Thank goodness. With Guinevere's party approaching, I knew if I didn't get that tree up soon, it would be January before I got around to it. They said they'd help me do my Christmas shopping, too. I knew that meant mostly letting me know what *they* want, but that was all right. They're my favorite gift recipients anyhow.

Ben's exclusive on Janey Dobbs was on the front page of the newspaper this morning. He was proud as punch—as he should have been—and I was thrilled that although I was mentioned and Daphne's Delectable Cakes did get tons of publicity, the paper did *not* print a photograph of me making a sixty-eight-year-old woman kiss my porch. Trust me, it pays to be dating the guy with the exclusive.

On top of that, Candy and Mr. Dobbs came by earlier with a bag of cat food for Sparrow. They thanked me for bringing Janey to justice. Unfortunately, they'll have to come up with the money to open their own store. Mrs. Dobbs's assets have been frozen and Dobbs's Pet Store has been closed until further notice.

I don't know what effect the asset freeze will have on Peggy and Joanne March's lawsuit, but I suppose time will tell.

I made myself a cup of café au lait and wandered out onto the porch. I wasn't a bit surprised to see China York there scrubbing—again.

"I got the snake venom up last night," I told her.

"I know," she said with a smile. "I thought I'd go over it again, though, so your cat won't be licking at it. I'm using a citrus cleaner. Cats hate it."

I laughed. "I'll be right back with some coffee for you."

"Good. I was getting ready to knock on your door and ask for some."

When I came back, she set aside her pail and scrub brush and sat with me on the porch.

"You were right, you know," I began, nudging her shoulder with my own.

"'Bout what?"

"About my here and now catching up with my subconscious."

She sipped her coffee. "You don't get to be as old as I am without knowing a few things."

"If I hadn't figured that out—"

"But you did. And that's what matters."

I felt something furry on my arm and jumped a little. Sparrow had brushed against me and was walking away.

I smiled. Things were definitely looking up.

Want to learn how to bake
and decorate like Daphne?

Just turn the page
and step inside

Daphne's Kitchen

For additional recipes and useful tips,
check out Gayle Trent's website
http://www.gayletrent.com
and
check out Daphne's newsletter "Killer Cakes"
http://wwwgayletrent.com/blog

Pearls of Wisdom:
How to Decorate the Perfect Cake

 If you're decorating a cake that has been frozen, allow it to come to room temperature before icing to keep the icing from cracking.

 To smooth your buttercream frosting, dip your spatula in water and spread it in one direction over the iced cake.

 To save time, make buttercream flowers ahead of time and store them in the freezer.

 Store-bought fondant, including flavored fondant, has a shelf life of one year.

 In order to keep a ganache or filling from oozing out the side of the cake, pipe a buttercream border around the edge.

The Martin Family Turkey Dressing

Daphne's grandmother was famous for her delicious turkey dressing. Learning to replicate the dish at a young age, Daphne only shares the Martin family's secret recipe with her closest friends.

INGREDIENTS

   2 long loaves of bread
   2 medium onions (diced)
   Cooking oil
   Salt
   Pepper
   Turkey or chicken broth
   Rubbed Sage

DIRECTIONS

Preheat oven to 350°F. Toast the bread on both sides until lightly browned. Sauté the onions in enough oil to cover the bottom of the frying pan. Crumble the toast into a large bowl. Add salt and pepper to taste. Add the onions to the bread mixture and saturate it with broth. Mix well. Add rubbed sage to taste. Bake for approximately 20 minutes or until brown.

Original recipe by Marilyn Hicks.

Mocha Madeira Cake

Madeira cake originated in eighteenth/nineteenth-century England and was often served with a glass of sweet Madeira wine. Traditionally flavored with lemon (not with wine, as one might think!), the cakes are similar to a pound cake in texture and density. Madeira cakes have a firm consistency and tend to stay fresh longer than some other cakes, so they are an excellent choice for carved cakes or large tiered cakes. Today, Madeira cakes are often served with afternoon tea or liquor.

INGREDIENTS

1-1/3 cup self-rising flour

2/3 cup Dutch processed cocoa powder

1 cup butter, softened

¾ cup sugar, plus

3 large eggs

DIRECTIONS

Preheat oven to 350°F. Grease and flour a nine-by-five-inch loaf pan. In a small bowl, combine the flour and cocoa and mix with a wire whisk. Set the mixture aside. Cream the butter and sugar until smooth. Add the eggs one at a time and mix thoroughly. When smooth, add the flour mixture a little at a time as you mix. Pour batter into the prepared pan. Sprinkle a little sugar on top and bake for 1 hour. Cool in the pan on a wire rack.

Original recipe by Carroll Pellegrinelli
(Guide to Desserts and Baking, http://baking.about.com)

Cinnamon Rolls with Cream Cheese Frosting

Daphne and crew adore warm cinnamon rolls with their morning coffee. Though not a commonly homemade treat, Daphne's recipe is simple and easy to follow!

ROLL INGREDIENTS

¾ cup milk

¼ cup butter, softened

3-¼ cups all-purpose flour

2-¼ teaspoons instant yeast

¼ cup sugar

½ teaspoon salt

¼ cup water

1 egg

1 cup brown sugar, packed

1 tablespoon ground cinnamon

½ cup butter, softened

½ cup chopped pecans, lightly toasted

FROSTING INGREDIENTS

4 ounces cream cheese, softened

¼ cup butter, softened

1 cup powdered sugar

½ teaspoon vanilla

1-½ teaspoons milk

DIRECTIONS

In a medium pot, scald the milk by heating it until bubbles form around edges. Remove from heat and stir in 1/4 cup butter.

While the milk is cooling, combine flour, yeast, sugar, and salt in a large bowl and mix with a wire whisk. Add the water and egg to dry mixture and stir. Add the milk-butter combination, mixing well until the dough forms a ball.

On a floured surface knead the dough about five minutes or until smooth. Allow dough to rest on a damp cloth for ten minutes before rolling it out into a twelve-by-nine-inch rectangle.

Paint the rectangle with 1/2 cup softened butter, leaving a one-inch border around the edge of the dough. Sprinkle with brown sugar, cinnamon, and pecans.

Roll up the dough from the long end and use a serrated knife to cut it into twelve pieces. Place the pieces on a lightly greased cookie sheet, and cover with a damp dish towel. Allow the rolls to rise for 30 minutes. While rising, preheat oven to 375°F.

Place the rolls in oven and bake for 20 minutes or until the edges are lightly browned.

While rolls are baking, combine the frosting ingredients and mix until smooth.

Frost rolls five minutes after removing them from the oven.

Original recipe by Carroll Pellegrinelli
(Guide to Desserts and Baking, http://baking.about.com)

Lucas's Black Cat Cupcakes

Daphne loves making sweet treats for her sister Violet's children, Lucas and Leslie. So much so, that one year, Daphne gave Violet a hand and provided a special dessert for Lucas's school's Halloween party—Black Cat Cupcakes.

INGREDIENTS

Cupcakes (whatever flavor is preferred)

Chocolate icing

Chocolate-covered crème drops, cut in half vertically

Skittles, Reese's Pieces, M&M's, or some other small, round candy

Candy corn

Skinny pretzel rods

DIRECTIONS

Frost the cupcakes with chocolate icing. Put the chocolate-covered crème drop halves (white center facing the inside) side-by-side at the top of the cupcake for the cat's ears. Add round candy pieces for eyes, a candy corn pointing downward for the nose, and two pretzel sticks on each side of the nose (> <) for whiskers.

Daphne's Famous Swiss Dot Cake

Decorating an elegant and beautiful cake is no easy task. But Daphne makes it simple with her famous Swiss Dot Cake. Follow her instructions and have a gorgeous-looking cake in no time.

Prepare two square or one standard nine-by-thirteen-inch cake of your choice according to package or recipe directions. Let the cake cool completely. If using a nine-by-thirteen-inch cake, refrigerate cake for approximately 30 minutes and then cut it in half. Two layers will be needed for this cake.

Place one layer on a cake board and spread icing of your choice evenly on the top. Place the second layer on top of the first. Frost the entire cake smoothly using a long, angled cake spatula. If crumbs appear after one coat is applied, refrigerate the cake for 20 minutes and then apply a second coat.

Using a cake bag with icing tip number 4 or 5, apply medium to heavy pressure to pipe a series of medium-large dots for the top and bottom borders. When piping dots, hold the bag at a 90-degree angle to the cake. Squeeze, stop the pressure, and then pull the bag away. If peaks appear, slip the tip to the side when pulling away. Peaks can also be smoothed out later by gently pressing your finger dipped in cornstarch against the dot.

Pipe small dots on the sides and top of the cake using a number 4 or smaller tip. Use light pressure to achieve smaller dots.

Use a strand of pearls (from your hobby or craft store) to further adorn the cake. Estimate the length of each side of the cake and cut the pearls to size. Carefully place one strand against the outside of the top border, and repeat for the inside of the top border. Repeat on the bottom border, placing pearl strands above and below the border. Of course, the pearls are for decoration only, so please be sure to remove them before consumption!

For a finishing touch, pipe a large mound of icing in the center of the cake and insert a sprig of your favorite artificial flowers into the mound.

Discussion Questions

DAPHNE WANTS to know what you think about her and her story. So, pull up a chair, slice into a delicious cake, and enjoy!

1. What was your first impression of Daphne?

2. Did you find the town of Brea Ridge believable?

3. Have you ever lived or worked in an environment you felt was similar to Brea Ridge where everyone knows everyone, thinks they know everyone, or thinks they know everything about everyone?

4. Do you think Daphne's relationships with her family are realistic? Why or why not?

5. Were you surprised by the identity of Yodel's killer?

6. Do you have any sympathy for Janey Dobbs? Why or why not?

7. In what ways is the stray cat symbolic of Daphne's life?

8. Did you enjoy the book?

Acknowledgments

FIRST OF all, I give thanks to God for the many blessings He has showered on me. Thank you, Tim, Lianna, and Nicholas for your continued support, encouragement, help, advice, and joy.

I'd also like to offer my heartfelt appreciation to Robert Gottlieb, Kerry Vincent, Sheriff Fred Newman, Elaine Smythe, Lisa McCarty, Retta and Wayne Vaught, and Betty Trent.

About the Author

GAYLE TRENT is a full-time author. She lives in Bristol, Virginia, with her husband, daughter, and son.

Gayle previously worked in the accounting and legal fields, and her last such job was as secretary to a Deputy Commissioner in the Virginia Workers' Compensation Commission. Though she enjoyed the work, it was a long daily commute and she felt she wasn't spending enough time with her family. Now she writes while her children are at school; and thanks to a Crock-Pot and a bread machine, can often have dinner ready when everyone gets home.

"I think it's important to be here for my children . . . to take part in school functions and to be an active part of their lives," Gayle says. "I can certainly sympathize with moms who work outside the home—been there, done that—but I would encourage everyone to make time to visit their children's schools, to have lunch with them [at school] occasionally, to get a feel for who their friends are . . . little things like that."

Gayle loves to hear from readers who can contact her via her website, http://www.gayletrent.com.

Gallery Books proudly presents
a sneak peek at the next delicious
Daphne Martin Cake Mystery . . .

Killer Sweet Tooth

by

Gayle Trent

Coming soon from Gallery Books

IT ALL began with a little bite of innocent sweetness. It was mid-January, and Brea Ridge had been experiencing the type of "Desperado" days the Eagles would describe as "the sky won't snow and the sun won't shine."

Ben—my boyfriend . . . significant other . . . man I date?—was working late to make sure an article made it into the Saturday edition of the *Brea Ridge Chronicle*. He's not only the newspaper's editor-in-chief; he also writes articles and is a perfectionist who has trouble delegating. This isn't the first Friday night he's had to call and cancel a date at the last minute. We'd only been planning to go see a movie, but I was still disappointed. However, there were worse things than disappointment. My ex-husband's idea of a fun weekend evening had been to berate me and to prove how superior he was to me in both size and strength. Oh, yeah . . . good times.

Violet, my sister, was visiting her mother-in-law this evening with her hubby, Jason, and my precious tween twin nephew and niece, Lucas and Leslie. Try saying that three times fast. Anyway, Grammy Armstrong was celebrating her seventieth birthday. Violet's family, as well as the rest of the Armstrong clan, was gathering to wish Grammy Armstrong well. I'd made the cake for the occasion. It was a ten-inch round cake with a basket weave border and an assortment of flowers—roses, carnations, and daisies—in the center. I'd finished it off with a "Happy Birthday" pick in the center of the flowers.

I must selfishly admit I felt as if everyone had left me out in the cold tonight. Pardon the pun, but I was lonely. Lucky for me—or, at least, so I thought at the time—Myra was lonely, too. Myra is my favorite neighbor. She's a sassy, sixty-something (you'll never get her to admit to any specific age) widow who knows everything about everybody in Brea Ridge (or can find out). She has a heart of gold and is as entertaining as they come. So when I saw her pull into her driveway, I gave her a call. She agreed to come over for some freshly made cashew brittle and a game of Scrabble. Myra tends to make up words when playing Scrabble, but that merely adds to the challenge of the game.

At the sound of the doorbell, Sparrow, my one-eyed, formerly stray gray-and-white Persian cat raced down the hall toward my office. She has a little bed in there under the desk, and it's her favorite hiding place. She has begrudgingly made friends with me, but she isn't comfortable around other people yet. And don't worry about the one eye: the veterinarian said she was probably born that way. Plus, it's how she got her name. Lucas and Leslie named her in honor of Captain Jack Sparrow, Johnny Depp's character in *Pirates of the Caribbean*. They said having one eye made Sparrow look like a pirate.

I opened the door and Myra came in wearing jeans, an oversized blue sweater, and a pair of tan Ugg boots. She deposited the boots by the door and rubbed her hands together.

"I'm so glad you called," she said. "I've been bored out of my mind today. That's why I went out to the mall for a while."

"Did you buy anything good?"

"Not a thing. I just window-shopped until the stores started closing. That made me even more depressed."

"I know what you mean," I said. "Cake orders have been slow since New Year's."

"They'll pick back up. Valentine's Day will be here before you know it," Myra said as we walked into the kitchen. "You might even get to make a wedding cake."

"That would be wonderful," I said.

I'd only been back in Brea Ridge for four months—after more than a twenty-year absence—and opened a cake decorating business, which I run out of my home. I hadn't had the opportunity to make any wedding cakes yet, although I had been given the privilege of making a large, tiered cake for a guinea pig's birthday celebration. It was the closest thing to a wedding cake I'd prepared so far.

I had the Scrabble board set up on the island with the two stools set on opposite sides. The cashew brittle and chocolate-covered raisins were plated beside the board along with a large bowl of popcorn.

"What would you like to drink?" I asked.

"Something hot. That wind chilled me to the bone on my walk over," she said. "How about a decaf café au lait?"

I smiled. "Sounds good to me."

Myra sat down and began choosing her tiles. "Great. Nearly all vowels. How am I supposed to make a word out of this mess?"

"Just put those back and draw some new letters." I have a single-cup coffeemaker, so I began making Myra's café au lait as she continued her commentary.

"No, now, you know I don't cheat," she said. "I'll make do with the letters I have. Maybe some of this cashew brittle will help me think."

The next sound I heard was a howl of pain.

"Myra? What is it?"

"Owwww, my toot . . . my filling . . . fell out!" She rocked back and forth on the stool.

I turned the coffeemaker off. "Who's your dentist? I'll call him and ask if he can meet you in his office."

Don't think I was being sexist when I said "him." There are only two dentists in Brea Ridge, and they're both men.

"Bainworf."

I got "Bainsworth" out of the mumbled word and rushed into the living room to retrieve my phone book from the end table. I called the dentist's office and then dialed the emergency number left on the answering machine. Dr. Bainsworth picked up immediately.

"Hi, Dr. Bainsworth. I'm Daphne Martin. A patient of yours—Myra Jenkins—is here at my house. She bit into a piece of cashew brittle and lost a filling. She's in terrible pain."

"Ah, yes, I know Myra well." His voice was deep and rich and contained just a hint of amusement. "Tell her I'll meet her at my office in a half hour. In the meantime, do you have any clove oil?"

"I believe so."

"Then apply a little of the oil to the tooth with a cotton swab," he said. "It'll help dull the pain until you can get her here." He chuckled. "Good luck."

"Thank you." Apparently, he *did* know Myra well.

I returned to the kitchen. "Dr. Bainsworth will see you in his office in half an hour."

"Half an hour?" she asked. "I'll be dead by den, or at leash passed out from de pain."

I opened the cabinet where I keep my spices and retrieved the clove oil. "He told me to apply a little of this to your tooth. He said it will help with the pain."

"Eashy for him to shay." She continued moaning as I went to the bathroom for a cotton swab.

"Come on," I said when I had returned. "Dr. Bainsworth

says this will help. Move your hand away, open your mouth, and show me which tooth."

She opened her mouth. "It's 'is toot." She pointed to her second bicuspid on the left. "The one drobbing wit pain."

I dabbed a little clove oil on it. "There. Feel better?"

"No."

"Well, just give it a minute," I said. "Go ahead and slip your boots back on, and we'll go on to the dentist's office."

She got down from the stool, went into the living room, and put on her boots. It took a laborious effort, but she managed somehow.

I took my coat from the closet, grabbed my purse and car keys, and off we went.

Myra gasped and covered her mouth when the cold air hit her tooth.

"I'm sorry," I told her, "but the dentist is meeting us, and then you'll feel better in no time."

She nodded as I opened the passenger side door of my red MINI Cooper and helped her get in. I hurried around to the driver's side, started the engine, turned on the lights, and backed out of the driveway.

The traffic was surprisingly heavy for a winter Friday night in Brea Ridge. Here, we practically roll up the sidewalks at nine p.m. on weeknights and ten p.m. on weekends. But tonight at half past ten, we passed at least half a dozen cars on the way to Dr. Bainsworth's office.

When we got there, I was relieved to see the lights blazing in the back of the office. The doctor was already there and, presumably, had everything ready to fix Myra's tooth.

Myra pulled her sweater up over the lower portion of her face before stepping out into the cold. I walked ahead and held the heavy door open.

We stepped inside and looked around the quiet office. Empty offices always look creepy at night, don't you think? There was only one light on in the entryway, and in the waiting area the long, skinny windows allowed muted light from the street lamps to filter in, casting shadows throughout the room.

"Dr. Bainsworth? It's Daphne Martin and Myra Jenkins. Would you like us to come on back?"

He didn't answer, and I supposed maybe he couldn't hear us.

"Let's go look," I said to Myra.

She nodded slightly, and we walked back toward the examining rooms.

"Dr. Bainsworth?" I called again. "Are you there?"

I looked inside the first room. My eyes widened, and my hand flew to my throat. I turned to Myra in shocked silence.

"Wha?" She followed my gaze to where Dr. Bainsworth was lying facedown on the floor. A trickle of blood spilled from his head. "No!"

"It's okay," I said, putting my arms around her. "I'll call 9–1–1. I'm sure he'll be all right."

"My toot! Who'll fiss my toot!" she cried.

I heard a thud in the lobby as if someone had tripped over a piece of furniture. I froze, and Myra did too.

"Whoever did this to Dr. Bainsworth is still here," I whispered.

She nodded.

"We have to find something to defend ourselves with." I stepped into the examining room and grabbed a huge plastic toothbrush.

Myra armed herself with a model of a molar so big she could barely hold it. She raised it up to eye level so she'd be ready to strike someone with it if need be.

It was at that moment that we heard the sirens—which was odd because I hadn't called 9–1–1 yet.

I looked from my giant toothbrush to Myra's giant molar to the dentist bleeding on the floor. "This is not good."

I had no more gotten the words out of my mouth than two policemen, neither of whom I knew—which is also odd, given my past experiences here in Brea Ridge—came around the corner with their guns drawn. Had we wanted to, Myra and I could not have escaped. We'd brought a toothbrush and a molar to a gunfight.

I will say, however, that we had the element of surprise on our side. The officers were too stunned to speak. So I took the initiative.

"Hi," I said. I tried to smile but probably grimaced instead. "I know this looks crazy, but—"

"Be quiet and put down your weapons," the taller, older officer commanded.

I dropped the toothbrush and raised my hands.

Myra was a little slower. "Wea-ons?" She frowned at her molar. "Hiss is no wea-on—it's a 'lastic toot."

"Drop it," the officer said. "Now. And put your hands where I can see them."

She shrugged and dropped the tooth. It bounced across the floor and hit the officer's left shin before coming to rest at his feet.

"Hands," he said.

Myra rolled her eyes and held up her hands. I silently prayed she wouldn't get us both shot.

"My toot," she began. Then she looked at me. "Tell 'em."

"Um . . . yes, officers. Myra—this is Myra Jenkins, and I'm Daphne Martin—she hurt . . . well—" I cleared my throat. "Lost a filling, actually, out of one of her teeth. So, I called Doc—"

"Save it," he said harshly. "I need you both to step away from the body."

"Can you re-ive him?" Myra asked.

The officer looked from Myra to his partner to me. "What?" he asked.

"Re-ive! Wake him up . . . fiss my toot."

"Step away from the body now," he demanded again.

The other officer—shorter, trimmer, and cleaner shaven—stepped forward and lowered his gun. "This way, ladies. We'll go into the hallway until Officer Halligan can see to the victim."

"Ought to ee out cassing who did iss," Myra muttered as we followed the younger man to the end of the hall near the waiting room.

I could see the road beyond the picture window, and a light blue or silver car was speeding down the road. Could that speeder be Dr. Bainsworth's attacker?

"Did you see that car?" I asked. "It could be whoever did this. Shouldn't you call somebody?"

"We get our fair share of speeders on the weekends," the officer said. "Mostly kids in a hurry to get to Bristol or Johnson City or somewhere. Did you get a good view of the car? Make? Model?"

"No," I told him. "Do you think Dr. Bainsworth will be all right?" I hoped to show the nice officer that we were really more concerned about the dentist than about ourselves and our hurt teeth.

"Hard to say, ma'am," he said. "Did you see anyone else when you arrived?"

"No," I said. "Of course, we weren't looking though. We were just hurrying here to see the dentist about Myra's tooth. We did call him ahead of time. There should be a record of that."

Darn! Should I have said that? Will he think the call was a ruse to lure Dr. Bainsworth here so we could bash him over the head and take . . . take what? Toothpaste samples? I was panicking. It was obvious Myra *had* lost a filling and was in pain.

I noticed the officer held his gun at his side and hadn't holstered it yet. The other policeman came into the hallway. His gun had been put away—at least, for now—and he was removing a pair of latex gloves while talking into a microphone on his right shoulder.

"Yeah," he said. "Get Crime Scene out here right away." He turned to the three of us. "Let's all step into the waiting area. We need to secure this location and wait for the crime scene techs."

"Will Dr. Bainsworth be okay?" I asked.

"No. He's dead."

At that, Myra just flat out started to cry.

"It's gonna be okay," the younger cop—Officer Kendall— assured Myra as he eased us into the back of the patrol car. "I called the station and our department dentist is still there."

"You have a full-time dentist?" I asked incredulously. Given the small town's budget, I was more than a little surprised.

"Not usually. But we had a patient fall against his toilet and chip a tooth, so we called in the dentist we have under contract." He smiled at Myra. "So, you're in luck. Since we need to take you to the station for questioning and Crime Scene needs to go over Dr. Bainsworth's office, you get some free dental work on behalf of the Brea Ridge Police Department."

"Yay," Myra said sarcastically.

I glared at her.

"Wha?" she asked. "He's had his hans in a risoner's mouf and maybe a toilet."

"You're talking like Scooby-Doo," I said.

"You ought to know . . . Raphne."

I sighed and rested my head against the back of the seat. I shuddered to think what might be on it—blood, spit, snot, vomit—and decided I'd scrub my scalp raw in a scalding shower as soon as I got home. I thought about whether or not this was the worst night of my life. Sadly, this night didn't even make my top ten list.

I suppose number one on the list would have to be the night my ex-husband tried to shoot me. Fortunately, he'd missed . . . which is why he's now serving time for attempted murder in a Tennessee prison and why I moved back to my hometown in Virginia to start life anew at the tender age of forty.

If you're wondering why he shot at me, it was because the mileage on my car wasn't where it should have been at the end of the day. On my way home from work, I'd gone four-tenths of a mile out of my way to a bookstore—which turned out to be eight-tenths of a mile once I got back on track—so I knew I was busted before I'd even got home. But I was so tired of having my every move controlled, tired of having to ask permission to stop at the grocery store or to schedule a hair appointment, tired of turning over my paycheck to someone who wouldn't let me have a checking account or a credit card, tired of not being able to voice an opinion. I was just plain tired. So I did it. I knew there'd be a price to pay, but I was to the point of being willing to pay it. And the title of the book I'd bought that day? *Regaining Your Self-Respect: A Ten-Step Plan.*

So, you see, this night was cake compared to that one.

r t I almost laughed at the irony of my thoughts. That's my claim to fame here in Brea Ridge—Daphne's Delectable Cakes.

Well, that and seeing dead people. Not like the kid in that movie with Bruce Willis, but I certainly seem to have a tendency of stumbling across dead bodies.

Myra elbowed me in the side. "You awake?"

"Yes."

She nodded toward the windshield to show me that we'd arrived.

The officers parked the squad car and opened the doors to remove Myra and me. Officer Kendall, the nice one, said Dr. Huffington would fix Myra's tooth while they were interrogating me.

Officer Halligan punched in a code and we entered the jail. We were in the back part, so we walked past holding cells on the way in. It wasn't pleasant. In fact, it was downright creepy. It smelled like urine and sweat. Disheveled, drunken people—mainly men—yelled things—mainly obscenities—at us as we passed by their cells. I so did not want to wind up sleeping over at this establishment.

An oversized man barreled down the hall and exuberantly greeted Myra. "Hey, Ms. Jenkins! Remember me? Mark Huffington?"

Myra's eyes widened. "Utter?"

"Yeah!" He laughed. He looked at me. "Back in the day, Myra's son Carl Junior and the other kids called me Butter. You know, short for 'Butterfingers.' I couldn't hold on to a football or a basketball to save my life." He chuckled again, reminding me of a cross between John Candy and Christian Slater. "Better hope I'm not as clumsy with a drill, eh, Ms. Jenkins?"

She looked terrified as he led her away.

I didn't feel much better going into the interrogation room.

* * *

MYRA AND I had spent hours—which felt like days—at the police station. We'd been fingerprinted, they'd questioned me, then they'd waited for Dr. Huffington to fill Myra's tooth and for her novocaine to wear off so they could talk with her alone and understand what she was saying. After speaking to us separately, they then questioned us together. This after leaving us alone in the interrogation room for an hour or so to see if we would incriminate ourselves. We'd both seen enough crime shows to know better than to say anything at all to each other.

Naturally, our stories matched up. We were telling the truth. And we had both—separately and jointly—told the exact same story, down to when we'd picked up the dental props because we'd heard something in the office. They had then taken our formal, sworn statements. Finally, they'd agreed we could be released. Officer Kendall kindly offered us a ride to the dentist's office to pick up my car.

"It's been a long night," Officer Kendall said, as he ushered Myra and I into his patrol car. "I'm used to it. I work twelve-hour shifts from six p.m. to six a.m. every night. But I reckon you ladies are tuckered out."

"We're tuckered, all right," Myra said.

"I could probably take you home rather than to the dentist's office," he said. He turned to look at me. "It's late. Or early, rather. Is there somebody who can drive you over to pick up your car later this morning?"

"No," I said. "I mean, yeah, somebody could, but I want to get my car now."

"You're sure you can drive home?" he asked.

"I'm fine," I insisted.

"How about you, Ms. Jenkins? Would you like me to take you home?" he asked.

"Gosh, no," Myra said. "After being out all night, can you

imagine what god-awful things folks would say if I came rolling up in a police car? I'd rather take my chances with Daphne."

"Gee, thanks," I said. "You so give me the warm fuzzies."

Officer Kendall drove us back to—well, to the scene of the crime—where yellow police tape had been affixed across the front door.

I ran my hands over the knees of my jeans. "How did Dr. Bainsworth's assailant get in?"

"The crime scene techs said there was no sign of forced entry," Officer Kendall said. "They figure either Dr. Bainsworth allowed the person or persons in, that the murderer had a key, or that someone had neglected to lock all the office doors."

"Then you think it might've been an inside job," I said.

"It's too early to form a definitive conclusion at this time," he said.

"I wanna go home," Myra chimed in.

"All right. Let's go." I thanked Officer Kendall for the ride as he let us out of the patrol car.

We got into my car and I started the engine. It felt good to be behind the wheel—back in control of something. I noticed that Officer Kendall followed us for a while to make sure I was okay to drive.

After I had seen Myra safely home, I drove the short jaunt to my house and pulled into the driveway. The sun hadn't come up yet, but the sky showed that it was considering doing so. I was so weary it was all I could do to put one foot in front of the other as I walked to my front door. I still wanted that shower, but I didn't know if I could stay awake long enough to manage it. I fumbled as I tried to put my key into the lock.

"Well, hey, there, pretty mama," a warm, mellow voice drawled from behind me.

I slowly turned. It was Elvis. Elvis Presley. And he'd just

gotten out of a pink-and-white 1955 Cadillac Fleetwood with whitewall tires. This was the young, thin Elvis; he was wearing black leather pants, a matching jacket, and a white-and-black striped shirt.

I simply started laughing. Tears flowed down my face, and I couldn't stop laughing or catch my breath. The fact that I was so exhausted I was seeing Elvis and a pink Cadillac should have had me worried, but, oddly enough, I found it hilarious. I guessed it beat pink elephants.